"You do ~~st ... ~~ **to me, Marie. Not ever,"** said Elliott.

Her gaze didn't waver. And she didn't step back. "I have a tendency to go on sometimes..."

"And I enjoy listening to your voice." Some things didn't come with explanation. They just were.

"I'm glad you're going to be in Las Vegas," she said.

"Me, too."

Her mouth was lifted toward his. He needed to kiss her.

And he needed to let her go. To send her away from him.

Before he could do either, she raised up on tiptoe and touched her lips to his. "Thank you," she whispered, and slid past him to hurry down the hall and back out to her shop.

Dear Reader,

Welcome to the Historic Arapahoe! (If you've been here before, welcome back!) Though most of the residents here are elderly, they're still getting up at five-thirty in the morning to work, they're still going on romantic dates and protecting those around them. Including the three thirty-one-year-old friends who recently purchased the building so that the elderly, fixed-income residents wouldn't be forced into nursing homes or be put out on the street.

Who's really taking care of whom remains to be seen. Or maybe this is life, everyone doing what they can to take care of each other. Marie, one of the three owners, has been taking care of others most of her life. She owns the coffee shop on the first floor of the building and spends her days trying to make life a little easier, a little more pleasant, for everyone around her.

There's a stalker hanging around. And her father, a womanizer who broke up their family but also managed to be a good dad, is struggling. Marie tends to it all. And she's still lonely. Because, ultimately, she can't trust.

I think, in today's world, many of us struggle with trust issues. I also believe that happiness depends on our ability to trust, and that trust is still rewarded. I'm just not sure I can convince Marie of that fact...

I love to hear from readers! You can contact me at staff@tarataylorquinn.com; my website, tarataylorquinn.com; on Twitter, @tarataylorquinn; on Facebook; and on Pinterest, pinterest.com/tarataylorquinn.

All the best,

Tara Taylor

HEARTWARMING

Once Upon a Marriage

—

USA TODAY Bestselling Author

Tara Taylor Quinn

HARLEQUIN® HEARTWARMING™

Recycling programs
for this product may
not exist in your area.

ISBN-13: 978-0-373-36744-3

Once Upon a Marriage

Copyright © 2015 by Tara Taylor Quinn

Printed in U.S.A.

The author of more than seventy novels, **Tara Taylor Quinn** is a *USA TODAY* bestselling author with over seven million copies sold. She is known for delivering emotional and psychologically astute novels of suspense and romance. Tara is a past president of Romance Writers of America and served eight years on that board of directors. She has won the Reader's Choice Award and is a five-time finalist for the RWA RITA® Award, a finalist for the Reviewer's Choice Award and the Bookseller's Best Award. She has also appeared on national and local TV across the country, including *CBS Sunday Morning*, and is a frequent guest speaker. In her spare time Tara likes to travel and enjoys crafting and in-line skating. She is a supporter of the National Domestic Violence Hotline. If you or someone you know might be a victim of domestic violence in the United States, please contact 1-800-799-7233.

Books by Tara Taylor Quinn

Harlequin Heartwarming

The Historic Arapahoe

Once Upon a Friendship

Harlequin Superromance

Where Secrets are Safe

Wife by Design
Once a Family
Husband by Choice
Child by Chance
Mother by Fate
The Good Father

Shelter Valley Stories

Sophie's Secret
Full Contact
It's Never Too Late
Second Time's the Charm
The Moment of Truth

It Happened in Comfort Cove

A Son's Tale
A Daughter's Story
The Truth About Comfort Cove

MIRA Books

Where the Road Ends
Street Smart
Hidden
In Plain Sight

Visit the Author Profile page at Harlequin.com for more titles.

For Carol H. R.:

You face hardship in marriage with love and loyalty, and inspire the same.

I am grateful for your example.

CHAPTER ONE

ELLIOTT TANNER WAS in trouble. There was no denying it. Sitting in his parked SUV outside a downtown Denver nightclub, waiting for a very spoiled, overly made up daddy's girl to get bored and move on to her next hot spot, he tried to refrain from contemplating his utter stupidity.

Unfortunately the job he was on—babysitting said self-centered party girl—required no real effort, leaving him far too much possibility for losing the battle he was waging with a brain that just wouldn't let go.

"I can't believe I'm telling you this, Elliott." Marie's voice repeated itself in his brain—a replay of a conversation he'd had with the daughter of another client that afternoon. Difference being that Sailor Harcourt, tonight's job, knew her parent had hired him to keep an eye out for her safety. Barbara Bustamante, Marie's mother, adamantly refused to allow Elliott to let Marie, her daughter, know that

she'd hired Tanner Security Services to watch over Marie.

He'd been hanging out at Marie's coffee shop for over three months now. She'd gone through some tough times. Life changes. They'd talked. Become friends. But under false pretenses.

In fact, Marie thought Elliott was around to keep an eye on Liam Connelly—not only her best friend's new husband, but also their business partner. Elliott had capitalized on Connelly's circumstances, presenting himself as a bodyguard when the fraud scheme exposed at Liam's father's company was impacting Liam's safety. It was the perfect way to be close to the situation and protect Marie without her knowing that he was watching out for her.

Gabrielle, Liam and Marie. *Threefold*. The name of the business they'd formed to purchase the old apartment building that was not only home to Marie's coffee shop, but their home, as well. *Threefold* was also an apt description for the friendship forged in college that had made the three of them more like family to each other than their biological counterparts had been.

Cars passed. Groups of people moved down the sidewalk. A woman strolled alone in the balmy April weather. Not smart, no matter how nice this part of town was. Not after eleven on a Saturday night…

He'd taken on Liam as a paid client, albeit at a sub-rate fee, with the complete blessing of Barbara Bustamante, who had called him initially because Marie and her friend had just entered into the business deal with Liam, and Barbara had never trusted the Connelly heir. When threats and vandalism ensued just after the building purchase, Tanner had been present to ensure that no harm came to Liam—or to his two new business partners.

Keeping his gaze on the side door through which he'd instructed Miss Harcourt to travel to and from the club's interior, Tanner rubbed a hand across his face in the darkness and groaned. While his association with Liam was somewhat convoluted—the other man assuming that his estranged father had sent Tanner to him through the elder Connelly's own highly paid bodyguard—that particular subterfuge was only the beginning of Tanner's troubles.

"I can't believe I'm telling you this, Elliott."
Liam Connelly's father had not been charged in the Ponzi scheme that had robbed investors of millions, but his company, Connelly Investments, had been the conduit for

the scheme. Run by his corporate attorney and closest friend, George Costas, who'd been charged by a grand jury but who was still adamantly asserting his innocence to the point that the public wasn't sure who was misusing power and bullying by public persuasion and who was really the victim between the two men.

There'd been another couple of threatening letters left for Liam at Marie's coffee shop, which was on the bottom floor of the apartment building the three friends owned. With Liam and Gabrielle now married and occupying three-quarters of the third floor, Marie was alone in her large second-floor apartment, and Barbara Bustamante insisted that Elliott maintain his cover and remain right where he was—on at least one daily surveillance of the apartment building and coffee shop, investigating Liam and staying on top of the investigation involving Liam's father, while keeping tabs on Marie.

She was paying him well. He was holding the checks for now. Not comfortable with cashing them, the way he was feeling. Another reason why he was escorting the dilettante, Miss Harcourt, during her two-day visit to Denver. Her father, Rod, a man Tanner protected anytime he was in town, had specifically asked him to do so, believing her to be at risk simply for being born a Harcourt. Tanner needed to maintain his client base of paying jobs.

Tanner Security Services, a one-man fully licensed and accredited operation with a better than average reputation, wasn't usually in the habit of babysitting. Or working for free.

"I can't believe I'm telling you this, Elliott!"

Marie. Long blond hair came instantly to mind. Followed by those eyes. So filled with emotion. Always.

When he'd first met her, more than three months ago, the compassion he could read in those eyes—compassion for Liam, the man he'd been sent to investigate and protect her against—stabbed him in a way he'd never forget.

He'd wanted her to look at him that way.

And more, he'd wanted to make certain that no one, ever, caused her open heart to close up, to wall off in pain. He'd sworn to himself that he'd never let anyone hurt her.

Absurd.

He had no control over Marie's heart. Who she gave it to. Or what they did with it.

He was just an overly large guy her mother had hired to protect her.

The door he was watching opened. Hand going immediately to the ignition, Elliott straightened. Lord knew where Miss High and Mighty would insist he take her next— as if he were her driver. His job was to see that she arrived safely.

Two couples emerged. Neither of the women was Sailor Harcourt.

"I can't believe I'm telling you this, El- liott..."

She'd been leaning over the counter of her coffee shop, those big brown eyes warm and soft—and trained on him. It was as if the emotion that welled up inside her had over- flowed onto him, into him. He'd glanced down quickly, breaking contact. She was completely off-limits.

"Liam's a great guy. I trust him with my life. It's just...one of the reasons we were al- ways just friends was because Gabi and I know all the nitty-gritty about him. He's al- ways come to us to as his 'confessors,' he said. He likes women. A lot. He told us he'd be with one woman and get feelings for an- other. He was younger then and he's done nothing at all, that I know of, to warrant my fears, but until Gabi and he got together he hadn't seemed to change his inability to stay interested in one woman. And they've only

been married a month, and already he's out to dinner with this editor woman of his..."

She'd thought the fact that they were alone in the shop had been a stroke of luck. An opportunity to talk to someone impartial so that she didn't make a big deal out of nothing. She'd thought that he just happened to show up to her popular coffee shop during a brief late-afternoon lull. In actuality he'd been watching the place for half an hour. As he did at some point every single day.

Either by stopping in for coffee. Or simply observing.

"The worst part is, I know I'm being paranoid, but I just can't stop myself..."

When he'd noticed her alone in the shop— her morning-to-midday-shift full-time employees gone and her late-afternoon shifter unusually late for some reason—he was unable to stop himself from getting out of his vehicle parked across the street and going in.

"It's just, you know, I told you about my dad..."

That first month he'd been around, she'd made a derogatory comment about Liam's father, implying that scaggy dads were something the three friends had in common, which had given him an opening to ask about something that made him curious—Marie's father.

Barbara's ex-husband. When she'd sent over the paperwork required by Tanner Security Services, the woman indicated that she was divorced. She'd given him no idea why she was so mistrusting of Marie's wealthy college friend, but he'd figured it had something to do with personal experience.

What Marie had told him only solidified that supposition.

Marie's father had been unfaithful to Barbara. Marie had been seven the first time. Barbara had forgiven him twice. The third time, when Marie was twelve, she'd changed the locks and filed for divorce. According to Marie, the man had spent the next five years earning his way back into their hearts and home. He was devoted, dedicated and 100 percent faithful to them and their family. Barbara, who'd loved only him since they'd first met in high school, had finally taken him back. And during the summer after Marie's freshman year of college, when Marie and Gabrielle were at Marie's parents' home for a visit, they'd caught her father cheating again.

Barbara, who'd nearly had a breakdown, had been in counseling ever since.

The backlit LED on the dashboard clock was too bright, garish in the darkness, shedding light where he'd rather not have it shed.

Who cared if it was eleven-thirty? Sailor was known to party until dawn. Might as well be at the elite nightclub as anywhere else. Better there, really. Less hassle.

"I can't believe I'm telling you this, Elliott, but I fell for a lot of the same lines my father gave my mother the first time I fell in love." Marie's words from that afternoon came back to him. His gut clenched again as it had then. The closest he came to expressing intense emotion.

She'd said she'd fallen in love. That there had already been a first time for her (completely expected considering the fact that she'd passed her thirtieth birthday) and he'd tensed up like a kid. For a split second there he'd been overcome.

With jealousy.

MARIE MEASURED VINEGAR, poured it into the carafe. Added water. Poured the mixture into the water dispenser of the first of twelve professional-grade silver coffeemakers, flipped the button to make coffee and moved on to maker number two. One by one she filled carafes with the vinegar mixture, poured it into the dispensers and hit Brew.

Then, with all the blinds drawn so that she

wasn't on display like a fish in a bowl, she stood there and watched twelve pots drip.

Drip. Drip. Drip.

After midnight on a Saturday wasn't a good time to be calling anyone. So she was cleaning the water dispensers. It was a job that had to be done. At least once every three months.

Beat sitting upstairs alone in her apartment feeling sorry for herself.

She'd had a date. Of sorts. Dinner and the theater with Burton. A safe, completely boring man she'd met three years before during the intermission at *Phantom of the Opera*. Gabi had been going to go with her, but she'd had a custody emergency with a client. Unwilling to waste her ticket, or to miss one of her favorite shows of all time, she'd gone to the theater alone. Burton had been sitting a couple of rows back. He was a season ticket holder, as well. His companion had been his mother until she passed away.

Not wanting him to sit by himself, she'd invited him to join her.

Eventually they'd fallen into the habit of going to the theater together.

She was never going to fall in love with him. He was never going to expect her to marry him. The relationship suited her just fine.

Pot number one was full. Dumping it in the sink, Marie filled the carafe with clean water and dumped it back into the dispenser, hitting Brew again. And down the line she went. For all twelve coffeemakers.

And then another time.

Twelve-thirty. She had to be downstairs to open the shop at seven. Grace, the eighty-year-old spritely and self-sufficient resident who did most of her baking, would be there two hours before that. The stairs at the back of the shop beckoned. Or she could take the elevator next to them. Now that it was fixed, it required a code to travel upstairs from the coffee shop in order to prevent coffee shop patrons from having access to the private apartments on the remaining eight floors.

Her apartment did not beckon. After thirteen years of living with the same roommate, she found that adjusting to her best friend's marriage was proving to be even more difficult than she'd expected.

Hence the paranoia. She was letting things get to her that had no basis in fact simply because for the past thirteen years she'd run all of her thoughts by Gabi at night. She was becoming a ninny. Like worrying that Liam was heading toward a path of infidelity. And that Gabi could end up as heartbroken and destroyed as her mother had been.

Well, not exactly the same. Her best friend, a lawyer, had a stronger backbone than her mother had ever had. Gabi had been taking care of herself for most of her life and could give thugs on the street a run for their money.

Liam didn't stand a chance.

Nor did he need one. The two of them were besotted with each other. It didn't take a believer in true love to see that. The reason Liam had never settled on one woman was that he'd been in love with Gabi all along. That was the fact that was as clear as day.

Still, Marie would rather clean than face her own thoughts alone upstairs in the apartment she and Gabrielle used to share. She was going crazy with loneliness.

What she needed to do was talk to someone. Another voice to drown out the reverberating of her own mind.

And there was one person who owed her an abrupt awakening in the middle of the night. He owed her as many of them as she needed for as long as he lived.

He picked up on the first ring.

"Marie? Baby? You okay? What's wrong?"

"Nothing's wrong, Daddy. Are you alone?"

"Yes, of course I'm alone. You know the

only woman I've ever spent the night with is your mother."

"It's only a little past midnight. You don't necessarily have to be down for the night." She was being petty. She knew it. Hated it. And took a deep breath. "I'm sorry. And sorry for calling so late."

"Don't you ever apologize for calling me, baby. You know I'm here for you anytime you need me. Anytime."

Hard part of it was that she did know that. Her father was a great dad. Had always been a great dad. Even when he'd been sleeping with his assistant while Marie and her mother thought him hard at work on whatever architectural plans his firm had been implementing. Or getting a little afternoon delight from a less reputable source before arriving right on time to coach Marie's softball team to victory.

"I need to understand, Daddy. I need to know why. And how."

"Sure. Of course. What are we talking about?"

"The women. All the women."

Silence fell on the line. In all the years since her parents' divorce, she'd never asked that particular question.

Because she'd been too afraid of the answer? Because she didn't want to see her mother in a new and less favorable light?

"I don't know that I can answer that."

"Can't or won't?" Now that she'd asked, she couldn't let it go. "It's making me crazy, Daddy. I... Did you love her?"

"No!"

Okay, then. Though she was actually shocked by his vehemence. Frowning, she slid down to a seat in a shadowed corner of the deserted shop. The one thing she'd thought a given through her rocky years growing up had been her father's love for her and her mother. Both of them.

She'd bet her life that her mother believed he'd loved her. Still did. Though he knew better than to ask for a third chance. For Barbara's sake.

"Does Mom know that now? Maybe if she knew you've never really loved her you'd set her free."

Because one thing was for sure. Barbara Bustamante was still helplessly in love with her cheating ex-husband.

"Wait. What? You were asking if I love your mom?" It sounded as though there was a bit of her shock running over into his voice.

"Yes. Of course." If she'd been referring to anyone else, she'd have had to use the plural. And then some.

"Then, yes! Unequivocally. I thought you knew that. All my life I have only ever loved one woman. Your mother."

Her heart sank. Liam loved Gabrielle that way, too.

"So why?"

Gabi said Liam and his editor had just had dinner once, to go over strategy for the series of articles he was writing on his father's life and the ongoing investigation. They'd needed to speak out of the office, and Liam was careful not to bring any aspect of his father's life to the historic Arapahoe—their apartment building—not only for Marie's shop and their home, but also to preserve the homes of the elderly residents who'd been there most of their lives and who had been soon to be put out on the street.

But Marie's father's first affair had started out with just one working dinner with his assistant. And then another had been necessary. After which he'd taken her home because her car was in the shop.

Or at least that was the story she'd been told.

"Why, Daddy? If you loved Mom, why were you unfaithful to her?"

"I wish I could tell you that."

She could feel her father's sigh all the way from Arizona.

"I wish I had the answer for myself."

"Try. This is important."

"You in love, baby?" Was that a note of hope in his voice.

"No, Daddy, absolutely not. I'm just..." She was not going to tell her father about her fears where Gabi was concerned. Still couldn't believe she'd actually told Elliott.

She knew they were unfounded. Knew that she had severe trust issues. Unfortunately that knowledge didn't erase a lifetime of example. Or the worry that stemmed from having been hurt by that example.

And not just from her father.

He was just the only unfaithful male she had access to at the moment.

The thought did occur to her that she was obsessing over Liam's ability to be faithful as way of avoiding an even harder truth.

Gabrielle was married, and Marie was alone. All alone. And didn't see any hope for a remedy to the situation.

She was going to end up like Grace—able to change the insides of a toilet when she was eighty because she'd been alone for so long.

Worse than Grace. At least the older woman had known true love. He'd just died too young.

"Hurting your mother was the last thing I ever wanted to do..." Her father sounded old. Tired. And sadder than she was.

"Then why did you?" She'd been there. Still felt the pain. She knew who'd wronged them.

"I...guess I thought I could get away with it. I never thought she'd find out."

The answer made her angry. And frightened her at the same time.

"What were you thinking when you were with them, Daddy? Did you ever even think about Mom and me waiting for you at home?"

"What I thought was that I was desperate to save my marriage."

She scoffed. And then choked. Such a ludicrous remark didn't deserve comment.

"Your mom and I had reached a state of comfortable, secure, forever love. I wanted that kind of love. Had always wanted it. But something inside me was missing. I was getting irritable with you. With your mom. Starting to feel trapped. While at the same time craving every minute I spent with you both and missing you every minute I was away."

She listened. Needing something from him. Just not sure what he could give her that could help.

"I guess I thought that I could fill the hole

inside with the excitement of meaningless afternoon liaisons, and then come home to the
perfect life."

"How'd that work out for you?"

"You want the truth?"

"Yes." She'd asked. And she braced herself.

"For the first several years, it worked out
just fine. Better than I'd imagined."

She'd asked. Struggled to breathe. "Y...
Y..." Her throat was dry. "Years?" Marie
glanced at her newly cleaned pots, wishing
for a sip of water. Standing, she steadied herself with a hand on the small brown wood
pedestal table and then pushed off toward the
counter.

"You asked."

All those years, when he was swearing his
fidelity, begging to be let back into the family, he'd been...

"What made it not work anymore?" She
was an observer of a tragic accident now.
Watching with horror, but needing to see.

"I got caught."

Thank goodness she was close enough to
the counter. It caught her as she swayed back-
ward. She leaned there. Letting it take her
weight. "You mean you were unfaithful for
years *before* Mom knew?"

"From before you were born."

She wanted to die. To cry. To pull the covers over her head and stay unaware forever.

But she couldn't.

If Liam Connelly turned out to be anything like what she feared he was… He'd once told her and Gabi that he'd never been in a relationship for more than a few months before he started to feel attraction to other women…

Other women like his editor? Was it too late already? Her parents had only been married a year before she came along.

But Liam adored Gabi. And…

Some men were just seemingly born to cheat.

Or her perceptions were too skewed to see reality.

Whatever. One thing was for sure. She was going to stand up. Be strong.

She was going to be ready if Gabi needed her.

CHAPTER TWO

AT 1:22 A.M., Miss Sailor Harcourt, twenty-five-year-old heiress to a $2.3 billion fortune, texted him.

Sorry I'm keeping you so late.

His job didn't entail a response to Sailor's comment. He was being paid to keep her safe. Not happy.

When he heard his phone buzz again, every nerve in his body went on alert.

Something was going on. Sailor, who obviously found him a nuisance, usually ignored him.

The man I'm with doesn't know I have a bodyguard. He doesn't know I'm related to Rod Harcourt or that I'm rich enough to need protection.

He didn't need a blow-by-blow of her evening. He'd prefer if she'd get her butt outside,

into his car and let him take her home. He had
to be back to get her in a matter of hours to
take her to the airport.

He's asked me out to breakfast. I've agreed
to go.

The third text had him out of his car, gaze
glued to the door of the club. And then, ready
to move, he texted her back.

You ride with me.

No.

This isn't my deal. You made the deal with
your father. You go out only if I drive you. I'm
just doing my job.

His fingers might be overly large, but they
could text as fast as any kid's. Came from a
lot of hours on surveillance, sitting in his car
with only his phone for company.
His phone buzzed again.

I know. I'm an adult. My father can't make me
get in a car with anyone. Or prevent me from
doing so, either.

He can take away your allowance.

This wasn't Elliott's first time chaperoning the spoiled heiress.

I'm twenty-five. I have access to my trust. And I'm a working girl now.

Daddy had hired her to manage the production of a fashion magazine he'd inherited in a buyout the previous fall. According to him she'd found her niche, but Elliott figured there were probably highly experienced professionals doing a lot of the work.

How many drinks have you had?

He didn't expect an accurate account. But he needed to know how bad the situation was going to be.

None.

It was going to be bad.

I'm a working stiff who needs to get paid for this job. Please come out and get in the car.

Even drunk she'd know he meant business.

He felt for the revolver he was wearing under his black sweater. And another text came through.

I understand what you think you're dealing with here. I admit on other occasions I've given you reason to treat me like a recalcitrant child. But I'm different now, Elliott. I've found my own purpose in life, separate and apart from my father. I've also, just tonight, met a man who has somehow enticed me to spend the entire night sitting in a corner talking. We didn't drink. Didn't dance. Just talked. And now he's invited me out for breakfast. I intend to go with him.

Even someone who texted as a primary means of communication shouldn't be able to string that many letters together, that quickly, on a QWERTY keyboard, without a single mistake. Most particularly if they'd been drinking.

Could she be telling the truth? She'd met someone without trying to impress him with Daddy's money? And hadn't had a thing to drink?

Before he formulated a response, she'd sent him another text.

You can follow if you'd like. I'm an adult. Legally, you can't force me into that car with you.

She was right. He had several certifications and licenses, but not one of them allowed him to get away with kidnapping.

So he'd follow. Glue himself to them. And make certain that he didn't let the two of them get out of his sight.

But first…

I'll make a deal with you. He typed fast. Not wanting her to think he'd given in. You sit tight long enough for me to check his credentials and then I'll concede to following you on your breakfast date.

He expected argument. Was prepared to enter the club, show his identification and get his charge out of there.

Deal. His name is Terrence Metcalf. He says he's a yacht designer, Sailor replied.

And Elliott didn't like it one bit.

FIVE MINUTES LATER, after Elliott had sent the okay, Ms. Sailor Harcourt burst out the front door of the well-known, upscale club she'd been in since 10:00 p.m., her bare arm entwined with the suited arm of a man Elliott had never heard of before that night. Not in the dossier he'd been handed by the woman's wealthy father—a respected client who'd been on Elliott's roster for four years—nor in any research he'd done on his own in preparation for Miss Harcourt's impending visit to Denver.

But he'd run the man on his member-only people-finder database. And had seen plenty. From charity contributor, to the Better Business Bureau. The man was clean. And who he said he was.

His vehicle was running and he was standing outside it, just in case Ms. Harcourt sent him any kind of signal that she'd changed her mind. His eye was on the man still attached to Sailor's arm. He was of average height. Slender. Clean-cut. The spitting image of the man Elliott had just pulled up on his tablet. Elliott could take him with two fingers. Not that he wanted to hurt anyone. Ever.

When Ms. Harcourt didn't even so much as glance his way, Elliott slid quietly behind the wheel of his car. His clothes were dark. His hair was dark. As long as he stayed behind the wheel, he'd blend in. Remain anonymous. And see Ms. Harcourt safely to her plane a few hours hence.

But he wouldn't hesitate to put someone's lights out if he had to do so to keep his charge safe.

MARIE WATCHED FOR Elliott all day Sunday. Though things had calmed down a lot since George Costas, Liam's father's attorney, had been formally indicted for fraud, Liam was still paying Elliott to keep an eye on things around the apartment building. He'd also permanently hired the security team Elliott had brought in to man the private residence entrance in the back of the building.

"You can leave that. I'll get it," she said to Sam, a twenty-four-year-old single father who was in his third year of a business degree program and also one of her full-time employees. He worked weekends to make up for the two days of classes he took during the week, and did the rest of his studies online or in the evening, while his mother watched his two-year-old son. "You said your mom had to leave for the funeral at three."

"I'm off at two," he said, continuing to restock under the cupboard supplies from the back room. A chore he did every afternoon that he worked. "I'll make it in time."

Sam lived with his mother in an apartment a few streets over. "Go now," she said, motioning him toward the door. "I've got this."

They'd had their Sunday morning rush. It was past noon and the only people in the shop—three tables' worth—were sitting with computers. She'd finished the weekly orders. Grace had handled the baking. The walk-in was filled with the veggies she'd need to make sandwiches in the morning.

"If you're sure," Sam said, untying his Arapahoe apron with a frown. "I just don't want to leave you in the lurch."

Sam was a nice guy. The woman who'd left him and their newborn to go to New York to be a dancer was a fool. Smiling, she shooed him out.

She wanted him gone in case Elliott came in. She had to set the bodyguard straight. To apologize for unloading on him the day before. What had she been hoping? That he'd betray his client and give her a rundown on everything he knew about Liam? Like she didn't already know far more than Elliott would ever know about the man who'd been one of her two best friends for more than a decade—since she and Gabi had lived next door to him their freshman year in college.

Liam wouldn't purposely or knowingly hurt Gabi. Or her, either.

The door rattled and she looked up to see... not Elliott. A young woman, dressed in leggings and a spandex top with expensive-looking running shoes, wanted a cappuccino with peppermint spice. Drink made and money collected, Marie watched the woman out the door and couldn't help glancing up and down the sidewalk. No Elliott.

She didn't see him every day. Or ever know what time he'd show up if he did. He had other clients and was a private investigator as well as a bodyguard—a private security expert, he'd once told her. And it wasn't as if he was working for her. Liam was the one getting threats.

Liam's dad, Walter Connelly, had had a bodyguard on staff for years. When you worked in high finance, you made a few enemies.

And when your company stole millions of dollars from investors, even if you didn't know it was happening, people still blamed you. Still, there hadn't really been much danger around the Arapahoe. Early on, Liam's car had been vandalized—but not when he was home. He and Gabi had been in-line skating late one night and Liam's car had been the only one left in the park's lot.

After that they'd received a total of three anonymous notes: one left at the coffee shop shortly after the car incident and two others slid under the door since the first of March—when Liam's first installment of a series he was writing about his father's life was pub-

lished. Both of those notes had arrived during
the night when the shop was closed, proclaim-
ing that Liam would get what was coming to
him. All three notes had been addressed to
Liam. Not Gabi or Marie.

When Liam's car had been painted with
graffiti just after news of the Ponzi scheme
at Connelly had hit, Elliott came to them as
a recommendation from Walter's bodyguard.
Elliott had been to school for both guarding
bodies and investigating. Was certified and
licensed in both fields.

From the beginning Marie had felt safe
with him.

A mild feat considering her ready propen-
sity for mistrusting the male species.

But she didn't really know that much about
him. He couldn't talk about his work—clients' business was private, and there was a
code of ethics he was sworn to follow or risk
losing not only his good reputation but his license to practice. He had an aunt and cousin
in California somewhere. His parents had
been killed in a small plane crash when he
was a toddler.

She knew nothing more.

Except that she'd told him about her paranoia, how fearful she was that Liam was
ready to cheat on Gabi.

Made herself sound like a crazy woman. When, in fact, she knew her fears were completely groundless. She was just obsessing because she had too much time to think. Too much time alone. But she'd adjust.

She'd known she and Gabi weren't going to live together forever. She'd just never seen herself living alone. But it wasn't as if she didn't have enough to do. Or enough friends.

And she still saw Gabi and Liam all the time. Pretty much every day…

Another customer came in. And then two more. A group of law students were studying in the corner, making use of the free Wi-Fi Liam had just had installed for the entire building. Elliott was nowhere to be seen.

At three, Eva, her new evening part-timer came in, and the two of them spent the next two hours serving a steady flow of sandwich eaters and coffee drinkers. Elliott Tanner wasn't among them.

At six the back door of the shop opened—someone coming in from upstairs. Expecting to see Liam or Gabi—or both, as was the case more often than not these days—she was surprised when Dale Gruber, an eighty-two-year-old retired railroad worker, came toward her with a worried look on his face.

"What's wrong, Dale?" she asked, moving

from behind the counter down the hall before Dale made it halfway into the shop. "Is
it Susan?" she asked after the man's wife of
more than sixty years.

"Yep," Dale said, heading into the shop,
still frowning. The man didn't move as
quickly as he once did, but he kept a pretty
good clip. "It's Susan, all right," he said,
standing in front of the nearly empty bak-
ery case.

"Did she fall? Did you call 911?" Marie
wasn't sure the man, who was normally sharp
as could be, was all there—perhaps demented
with panic? She grabbed her cell phone out
of her apron pocket. "Can she talk?"

"What's that? Call who?" Dale's false teeth,
a little too big for his mouth, hissed a bit as he
talked. But she had his full attention.

"Is Susan hurt?"

"What? No! But you can bet your dinner
that I'm going to be if I don't find something
pretty quick that can pass as a cake and a
present and not look like I just come down
here and got it last minute," he said, staring
at the case again. "I darn forgot her birthday,"
he said, looking perplexed as he glanced at
Marie again. "Sixty years of knowing when
my wife was born, and I forgot today was

the day. Eighty-one she is today. And a fine-looking woman still."

With a little adrenaline remaining, Marie went into high gear. She pulled a chocolate cake out of the walk-in, making a mental note to replace it before morning so Grace wouldn't have to, sent Eva down the block to the drugstore for candles and one of the puzzle books that Susan and Dale liked to work on together and then, with a brain flash, hurried back to her office, opened the safe and pulled out the two theater tickets for next month's Broadway performance. Grabbing an envelope and a piece of paper, she hurried back in to Dale, who was pulling money out of his pocket so it was ready to give to Eva when she returned.

"Here," she said, pulling a chair out from one of the small round tables toward the back as she set down paper, pen, envelope and tickets. "Write something. And wrap the tickets in this," she said. Dropping the envelope beside the pile.

"Tickets?" His teeth clacked as he spoke.

"To the theater. Susan would love to go to the theater, wouldn't she?"

Dale's grin made her day. Her week. "That she would," he said, smiling at her. "You have theater tickets to sell me?"

She'd been planning to give them to him. But one look at his face and she changed her mind.

"What do I owe you?" he asked, pulling a roll of bills out of his pocket. Mostly ones.

"Twenty dollars," Marie said, trying to remember if the seventy-five-dollar ticket price was on the actual tickets.

"Twenty dollars." He began counting bills, handed them to her and pulled the chair out to sit down. "I'll hire a car," he said. "She can wear that pretty rose-colored dress and her sparkly earrings and I'll even get a shave and a haircut…"

He bent to his writing.

The door rattled again. Eva returning, Marie hoped.

She looked up, a smile on her face. And blinked.

It wasn't Eva.

It was *him*.

CHAPTER THREE

ELLIOTT HADN'T PLANNED to see Marie on Sunday. Or anytime he could avoid seeing her in the near future. After a long night watching Sailor and Terrence Metcalf, the yacht designer, seemingly fall in love at first sight, finding himself relating, he'd been forced to admit to himself that the things he was feeling for Marie Bustamante weren't just passing infatuation.

He'd found it so easy to identify with the poor guy, who'd looked at Ms. Harcourt as though she was the sun, moon and stars all rolled into one.

And so, with a few hours' sleep in his own one-bedroom apartment after seeing Miss Harcourt to the airport that morning for her flight back to New York, he'd called Barbara Bustamante. His plan was twofold. To fire himself. And to acquire her permission to tell her daughter who he was.

Asking Marie out, which was his ultimate goal, would follow the meeting of those goals.

He'd failed on both counts. Mrs. Bustamante categorically refused to allow him to tell Marie—ever—that she'd hired him to watch her. Her paranoia had already rubbed off far too much on her daughter. She didn't want Marie to know that her own mother didn't trust her to make wise decisions where men were concerned. Specifically where her new business partner, but longtime friend, Liam Connelly, was concerned.

And second, she warned him not to quit. Not while things were still so raw with Connelly Investments. Not while he was still watching Liam. He had the perfect in. She'd financed the plan he'd put in place. It would be highly unprofessional for him to just walk out. She could file a complaint against him.

He'd been tempted to tell her that it would be highly unprofessional for him to have a thing for his client's daughter, but refrained.

Because she was right. He'd signed on to do a job that was not yet complete. No one else was going to be able to step into his shoes and have Liam believe that his father's bodyguard had sent him. Elliott's ability to do that had been a fluke of timing. A godsend. And had worked so well in part because Liam hadn't been speaking with his father at the time. And also because everyone had assumed he'd been hired in secret and hadn't asked too many questions.

Later, when Walter Connelly had denied having any part in Elliott's presence in their lives, Liam had taken the words with a grain of salt. His father might not be an embezzler, but he'd been found out to be an inveterate liar.

If not for the plea agreement he'd been offered in exchange for full cooperation in the ongoing investigation of the Ponzi scheme being run through his company, Walter would be facing his own trial on lesser charges. And Liam was now in position to know everything that went on in his father's company, and in much of his personal business, as well.

If anyone else stepped in to watch over the Arapahoe and her owners and occupants now, a big question would be raised as to why. As to who'd sent the new bodyguard. Liam would ask questions Elliott couldn't afford to have him ask. Barbara's role in all of this could very well end up being exposed.

The Professional Private Investigators Association of Colorado would have cause to take action against him for a code of ethics violation. He could lose everything.

Falling for Marie could be a code of ethics violation, too. If he acted on his feelings.

So the only solution here was to stay away from her.

Or come clean with Barbara and risk Marie's safety.

He'd decided to give things another month. If no other threats had come forth, if Liam Connelly's life had no longer appeared to be in danger, he'd pull the plug. Get the heck out of their lives.

Barbara wasn't ever going to let him tell Marie the truth about their association and he couldn't enter into a relationship with Marie without doing so.

Not that he was even certain she'd have had him. All of which was a moot now.

"I just spoke with Liam," he said as Marie joined him at the door of her shop. With a quick look around, he knew they couldn't talk out there. "He and Gabi are on their way down. I need to speak with the three of you in private. Can we go back to your office?"

He didn't see anyone behind the counter. Marie wasn't supposed to work alone. Not since Liam's father's company had been under investigation right after the three of them went into business together and Liam moved in.

Coincidence?

Probably.

But he'd agreed with Barbara on her initial assessment of the situation three months before. The coincidence was too suspicious.

He just no longer suspected Liam Connelly of any subterfuge or wrongdoing. The man had been framed.

"Eva's..." The front door of the shop opened behind him and he swung to see Marie's newest employee, a somewhat ditzy college sophomore, come in.

"Back," Marie finished. "You go ahead to the office," she said to Elliott. "I've got something to finish up here and then I'll join you."

Elliott thought the better idea was to wait for her out front. So he stood as inconspicuously as a six-foot-seven-inch, broad-shouldered man could stand, and waited while she helped an old man put some things in an envelope, watched Eva put candles on one of Marie's amazing double-fudge cakes and then watched the front while the two women escorted the man down the back hall and to the elevator.

Liam and Gabi got off the old car as Dale, Marie called him, got on. Trading places with Eva, Elliott made his way back to Marie's office.

"What's up?" Liam, who was standing behind his wife's chair, arms crossed, faced Elliott as he shut the door. The Connellys, in dark dress pants and shirts, looked as though they'd just stepped out of a boardroom—on a Sunday evening. Marie, in the armed office chair behind her desk, on the other hand, was far too attractive in her stained blue-and-yellow Arapahoe Coffee Shop apron with tendrils of long blond hair falling out of the pony tail she always wore.

"I'm upping your security alert level." He got right to the point. This was business. And he had no business finding any pleasure while he was there. "It's just a precaution," he added, raising a hand when all three mouths facing him opened at once. "But to be on the safe side, we're back to no one in the coffee shop alone, even during the day, and you call me every time you have to go out." The latter was directed at Liam.

"I'm available to see Gabrielle to work every morning and home again in the evening if you so desire." The protocol Liam had insisted upon when he first took Elliott on.

Gabrielle looked at Marie. "Did you get another letter? We should have been here. I'm so sorry…"

Marie shook her head. "No," she said, glancing toward Elliott with concern written all over her face. And then, with her expression softening, turned back to Gabrielle. "And you have no reason to be sorry. It isn't every day that Liam's father invites you two to accompany him, and brunch at the governor's mansion is an honor. A sign of his growing acceptance and respect."

Elliott had known Walter was in town for the weekend to take care of some business. He hadn't been told exactly what the business was.

"I'm assuming your father's on his way back to Florida?" he asked Liam, just to make certain that there hadn't been a change of plans.

"Yes. Tamara's got a softball game tomorrow night. They're in the play-offs."

Tamara Bolin, the fourteen-year-old half sister Liam had just found out about during the initial investigation of his father's company. She lived with her mother, Missy, in a beach cottage Walter Connelly had purchased for them years before. Walter and Missy were married now and Walter, having given Liam a lot more control in the business he'd almost lost, was spending a good bit of his time in Florida. Working from his home office. With trips up to Denver to meet face-to-face with the powerful and moneyed clientele he'd taken on over the years.

Most of whom were still with them.

"So what's going on?" Gabrielle sat forward, her expression stoic but focused. She reminded Elliott most of himself.

A woman who kept her heart under lock and key.

Except when it came to Marie and Liam.

He envied her them. Or would, if he allowed himself foolish luxuries.

"I've noticed a car parked down the street on several occasions lately. The driver is always inside, slumped down wearing a baseball cap. Today, when I approached, he—or she—pretended not to see me motion him to roll down the window and drove off. I ran the plate on the car. It was stolen."

Marie sat up straight on the edge of her seat. "Someone in a stolen car's been watching us?"

"I'm not saying that." He enunciated this carefully. "And no, I'm not saying the car is stolen. The plate was stolen. It came back as belonging to an '82 Ford Granada belonging to a woman who died six months ago. The Granada has been parked in an alley behind a garage at her grandson's house while they waited for the estate to settle. No one noticed the plate missing."

"You're sure they were watching this place?" Liam asked. Elliott had labeled him the Pollyanna of the group.

"No, I'm not." He had to be honest. "But with everything else that's gone on, we'd be remiss not to treat it like it was."

Marie looked at Gabrielle and the two women exchanged glances with Liam, who slid his hands into his pockets.

"Fine," Gabrielle said. Marie nodded.

"I'd appreciate it if you'd see my wife to work every morning," Liam said. "I can have the company car pick me up."

"Not a good idea," Elliott said. "A stretch limo parked out back would be salt in a wound around here."

"I agree with him, Liam," Gabrielle said. "I can get myself to work. You're the target. Elliott should go with you."

Pulling his hands out of his pockets, Liam faced Elliott. "You go with her." He nodded toward his wife. "I'll work from home for the next couple of days. Let's reassess later in the week."

One by one, Elliott looked at his three charges. One by one they nodded.

And he turned, wanting only to get out of there.

MARIE SAW ELLIOTT ready to leave, and her heart dropped.

What was the matter with her? It had no

business dropping because the giant her friend had hired was going home.

Without giving her a chance to set things straight between them.

No wonder he was so eager to leave. He probably thought she'd been hitting him up for information on his client. Trying to coax him into breaking his code of ethics, or client/investigator privilege or something.

The elevator door opened before Elliott made it out to the hallway.

"Oh! Good! You're all here!" Eighty-one-year-old that day Susan Gruber, slender and statuesque in a flowered housedress and black shoes with inch-thick soles, blocked Elliott's departure. Dale, right behind her, stood there grinning.

"I just had to thank you," she said. "Dale told me you all helped him plan my little party and gift, and I just don't know when he's made me so happy." She told them, in second-to-second detail, how he came in the door with the cake and presented her with the envelope. She talked about the last time she went to the theater—thirty years before—and remembered exactly what she saw.

Marie, who ordinarily would have wanted to take the couple out to the coffee shop and sit with them through every detail, watched Elliott. Afraid he was going to slip out.

Instead, it was Liam and Gabi who did so. They had another couple upstairs in their huge, luxuriously remodeled apartment, someone Gabi had met at the governor's mansion that day who could help her get more funding for indigent legal services, and the four of them had just been sitting down to a glass of wine when Elliott contacted them.

And by the time Susan and Dale left, she could see from the hallway that the coffee shop had closed and Eva was gone, too. Expecting Elliott to head straight out, she stopped just as they reached the shop.

"Can I make you a cup of coffee? Dark roast with a shot of espresso, black?" She knew what he liked. Just as she knew a good many of her clients' preferences.

Expecting him to refuse, she was ready to talk him into at least taking it to go—which would give her time to apologize for her behavior the day before. She was shocked when he said instead, "Have you got a piece of that double-fudge cake to go with it?"

Which reminded her she had to bake another cake for the next day. Grace baked cakes twice a week. Tuesdays and Saturdays. She'd used up Monday's double-fudge allotment with Dale.

"One piece," she said, hoping that Eva

hadn't sold Sunday's last piece of cake during the time she was in the back office.

Her chances of getting him to stay while another cake baked were pretty slim.

As she walked with him into the shop, moved the remaining piece of cake from the serving dish to a plate and started his coffee, Marie considered the ironies of life. Her life with men usually consisted of her thinking of ways to get rid of them.

Not to get them to stay.

Standing at the high-top table closest to the coffee counter, Elliott didn't wait for his coffee before starting in on the cake. Marie grabbed a bottle of water for herself and took his drink over to him as she slid up onto one of the two stools at the tall round table. Even then, she was shorter than him by a good six inches.

Standing, it was more like a foot and a half. Which could be why she felt so safe with him.

Elliott was like a big umbrella, sheltering her from the storm that was threatening their lives.

"I'm sorry," she blurted as she opened her water.

"For what? This is great." He didn't even look up from the cake he was devouring.

"For yesterday. Saying those things about

Liam. I'm not as crazy as I sounded, and I know Liam would rather die than hurt Gabi."

But then, her father had felt the same way about her mother. The reminder from the previous night's conversation with her father popped unwanted into her head.

He nodded. Which meant what? That he forgave her? That she had sounded crazy? That Liam wouldn't hurt Gabi?

Or just that the cake was good?

"It's just…it's not just what my father did that makes me paranoid," she heard herself saying. Justifying. As if the only thing that mattered was that he understand her.

Or maybe it was just that sometime over the past three months, she'd fallen into the habit of confiding in him.

Because he was safe. He was licensed to keep people safe.

Chewing, he glanced at her. Took a sip of his coffee.

Elliott was a man of few words. She knew that about him.

Luckily she'd always had an overabundance of them. "I dated a guy almost my entire freshman year of college," she said. If he knew the whole truth, he'd understand. "Mark Yarnell. He was from Arizona, too. I thought we'd see each other over the summer, said something to him about it, and that's when I found out that he had a fiancée back home in Phoenix. He wasn't in love with her and had thought that maybe he'd break up with her and ask me to marry him. But she was a member of his church and he said it was the right thing to do to marry her."

"Were you in love with him?"

"I don't know. I know I liked him more than any other guy I'd ever dated." She'd gone to church with him, too.

"Then there was Jimmy Jones," she said, taking a sip from her water bottle and glancing up at him at the same time. His body blocked the overhead light, putting a shadow on the table. Shoulders that big, all in black the way they always were, should be somewhat intimidating. But they weren't.

Nor was the serious look in those dark eyes. The cake was gone. His coffee almost was, too.

"Jimmy Jones?" He asked, his brow raised.

"Gabi and I met him at a rodeo our junior year. He played us against each other. Telling her she was the one he really liked and telling me the same thing. Luckily for us we tell each other everything."

"And I'm guessing he lived to regret what he'd done," Elliott said, a grin teasing the corners of his mouth.

"Let's just say he'll probably always cringe a bit when a loudspeaker comes on before a show."

"You got someone to put a message out over the loudspeaker at a rodeo?"

"We did better than that. The reason we were at the rodeo was that the father of a friend of ours owned a team. Jimmy rode for an opposing team. We recorded him talking to me on the phone. And then making similar promises and proclamations to Gabi. We both got him to play it up big. And then we turned the tape over to our friend. It was her father's idea to play it in public."

"What did he do?"

"I have no idea. We opted not to be present." Because they weren't mean-spirited. But had been young enough to think they could make a difference. Teach him a lesson. Prevent other women from being hurt...

"And then there was the medical resident my senior year," she said. "I was probably in love with him. Until I caught him with a girl I worked with at the coffee shop. She'd asked me to take her shift at the shop, and I'd agreed because he was going to be studying. When I got off early I made him his favorite coffee and stopped by to surprise him. I was the one who got the surprise."

There. He knew her history. The facts. She wasn't crazy. She had good reason not to trust men.

Elliott didn't seem moved by anything she'd said—other than the stuff about Jimmy Jones. But then he hadn't seemed all that put off by her words the day before, either.

So why was she feeling so defensive?

"A study was done recently at Rutgers University," she blurted when she'd just told herself not to say any more. "And other places, too. By renowned psychiatrists and relationship specialists. At least one said that seventy percent of married men cheat on their wives, and some even go so far as to state that a relationship that lasts a lifetime is a rarity these days."

His eyes narrowed. "You looked up statistics?"

"No." She wanted to smile, but couldn't quite. "My mother did. Many times over the years. She was looking for validation, needed to know that she wasn't the only woman who'd been duped. And also wanting to know that a lot of women took their husbands back after an affair. Depended on where she was in her life, but she'd always quote the statistics to me when she wanted me to accept whatever she was feeling."

"But you said the Rutgers study was recent."

"My father was trying to talk her into another chance. He tried to get me involved, to get my approval, and that's when she called me with the seventy-percent study. She got that one from some website about cheating husbands."

"You were siding with your father?"

"No! He'd just told her he talked to me. I'd already chosen not to get involved."

"Would you have supported them trying again?" It wasn't a bodyguard question. But then, their conversations over the past weeks hadn't contained much about Liam or the issues that had brought Elliott to them.

"In my head, yes. It's their life, you know? But in my heart?" She shook her head. "I think they truly love each other. But my father's a cheater. And Mom's a woman who gives her all and needs all in."

He studied her for a moment. Nodded. Looked as though he had more to say.

And then turned away. "How much longer until you're ready to go up?" he asked, pushing a couple of chairs back in under tables. Something that was part of closing procedures. Something Eva should have done.

The girl wasn't the best worker she'd ever

had. But she was all heart. And great with customers. Marie liked the way the place felt when Eva was around.

"I can go now," she said, guessing that he wasn't going to leave her down there alone, and sensing that he wanted out. "I finished my ordering earlier today."

He knew her routine. Sunday night was order night.

He didn't have to know that she'd just decided to get up at three in the morning to get the cake baked before Grace came to work.

Elliott rinsed his cup and put it in the commercial-size dishwasher. Eva hadn't started it, so she did. And then led him down the hall to the elevator, noticing how he turned off lights as they went. Leaving on the ones she always left on.

One thing was for sure, investigative bodyguards were observant.

She'd have said so. Said thank you. Good night. Anything. If his phone hadn't just rung. Motioning for her to get on the opened elevator, he took the call. She stepped on and tried not to take it personally when Elliott didn't return her wave as the doors closed in front of her.

CHAPTER FOUR

HE'D KNOWN WHEN he made his mind up to give the Connelly situation a month to calm down that there was reason to believe the danger wasn't over. He'd already seen the old blue car lurking across the street on two separate occasions. Perhaps that car had been part of the reason he'd allowed himself to be talked into staying on the case.

He wasn't going to leave Marie or her friends in any kind of danger.

He wasn't worried about himself actually acting out of turn, as much as he hated the subterfuge. Elliott was nothing if not in complete control of himself at all times. And it wasn't as if he'd already fallen for Marie Bustamante. He just found her...interesting.

To the point of taking a vision of her, taking the memory of her words, with him everywhere he went. And he went a lot over the next few days. Escorting Gabrielle to and from work. Picking up a British client who was in Denver for a brief lunch stop on

Tuesday, standing guard just feet behind him during the two-hour lunch and then delivering him back to the airport in time to get Gabrielle. The rest of the hours, in between watching the Arapahoe Coffee Shop and conferring with the private security at the residence entrance of the Arapahoe, he canvassed the area, looking for anyone who'd seen the old blue car with the stolen license plate. The Denver police had made a cursory round, but a stolen license plate was hardly worthy of their stretched-thin time.

On Wednesday he knocked on doors and talked to residents in the neighborhood where the plate had been stolen.

No one had seen anything in either area. And because he had nothing else to go on, he ended up at the coffee shop that afternoon after dropping Gabrielle off at the resident entrance in the back.

Eva was there, behind the counter. There was no sign of Marie. He ordered a dark roast minus the espresso. Had a seat in the corner. And sipped.

He really needed to speak with Marie. It was important to check in with his charges on a regular basis. You never knew when they might have seen something, witnessed something, that was harmless in and of itself, but that could spell potential danger to one who was trained to see such things.

While he'd seen her at a distance every day, they hadn't spoken since Sunday. Barbara Bustamante was paying him to do better than that.

Twenty minutes passed with no sign of Marie. She took time off. But not often. And not usually with only one person behind the counter. Most specifically not with just Eva downstairs—though the girl was handling the small rush of late-afternoon customers with aplomb.

And shouldn't have been alone in the shop. That was the rule he'd thought he'd established.

He waited until everyone had been served and then approached the counter. He'd just asked where Marie was when he saw her outside, walking toward the shop in the company of a man not much taller than she was. His brown hair was cropped, his pants a little short to be stylish and he was wearing a sweater vest instead of a suit jacket.

Nothing stood out as a threat. Elliott recognized him anyway. Burton Augustine. Her longtime theater date. She should have told him that she had matinee tickets. He'd let them know they were under higher security protocol. She knew what that meant. All three of the Arapahoe owners knew what that meant. It hadn't been that long ago that they'd all lived under the protocol full-time.

Waiting while she bade the other man goodbye at the door, Elliott approached her before she had her purse off her shoulder.

"We need to talk." His voice was always an octave below base. Came with his size. But even he heard the extra note of...displeasure in his quietly spoken words.

And wondered at it. She'd gone out, escorted, in the light of day. Yes, he should have known. If something had happened to her...

But, really, the infraction wasn't so great as to raise his ire...

At a fast walk, Marie led him down the hall to her office, dropped her purse on her desk and shut the door behind him.

"What's up?" Her cheeks, her lips, were pinched.

And he felt like a heel for upsetting her.

"You should have let me know you had tickets to the matinee." He'd toned down the potentially threatening tone. Had a lot of practice doing so. His voice, as low as it was, had a tendency to scare people.

Something he'd learned while he was still in high school and had been called to the principal's office for allegedly trying to intimidate a teacher—after which he'd learned to keep his mouth shut as often as possible.

"I didn't have tickets to the matinee," she said, frowning. Grabbing her purse, she moved it to the drawer at the bottom of her desk where she normally kept it, locking it in. She looped her apron over her head, giving it a yank when it got stuck on her ponytail. Dropped the desk keys into the pocket. She sat. And then stood. "Burton and I went for a short drive and shared an avocado sandwich."

Freshly made that morning, he translated. By Marie. For sale at her shop with the rest of the organic lunch options on her limited menu.

"And before you say anything else, Eva wasn't supposed to be alone. Sam was here. He just left because his mother called saying his son had a fever. They called me and I came straight back."

She'd seen Burton for lunch. A change in their routine. Could indicate a change in the relationship from casual to more serious.

The tightening in Elliott's stomach was as unexpected as it was uncomfortable. Emotion swirled within him. Negative emotion. Not warning signals. Not a sense of imminent danger.

He sat. And so did Marie.

"I'd appreciate it if you'd stick to the high-security protocol for at least a few more days," he said.

She nodded. Looking straight at him, but for once the warm look in those big brown eyes was absent. Her gaze was almost vacant.

As if she was looking past him.

He'd grown accustomed to the compassionate openness she'd shown him since the first night they met.

"Have I done something to displease you?" he asked. Hoping that his tone of voice hadn't put her off. He'd had no business being...

Jealous.

"No, of course not." she said, appearing to focus on him now. "If anything I was beginning to think I'd scared you away," she said with that unique openness of hers.

Such an incongruent woman, she was. Open and sharing and giving everything of herself. And trusting no man with her heart. No wonder her mother worried about her.

She was the type of woman people took advantage of.

"I don't scare," he said. "But just for full disclosure, what do you think you'd done that I'd find distasteful?"

He'd eased down in his seat and rested an

ankle over his knee. And she still had to look
up to meet him eye-to-eye.

"All that nonsense about thinking Liam
would be unfaithful to Gabi. And giving you
my disastrous love life history…"

He'd already known about the ex-boy-
friends. Marie's past relationships had fed
Barbara's own fears about her bighearted
daughter following in her footsteps. Her "disastrous" love life, as she'd just described,
was a big part of the reason Barbara had felt
compelled to hire a private investigator bodyguard when Marie called to say that she was
investing her savings to go into business with
Liam Connelly and, with Gabrielle, purchase
the historic Arapahoe.

"How could I possibly think less of you for
caring about your friends? Or for the fact that
the men in your life have treated you shab-
bily? If anything, I was impressed by the way
you handled the Jimmy Jones situation."

Barbara hadn't told him about that one.
Maybe, with the whole thing happening
so quickly, Marie had opted not to tell her
mother about the debacle. A shame, really. It
would have done Barbara good to know that
her daughter had been able to see through
the man and then take care of herself quite
effectively.

He'd have lingered awhile, curious about what else she might have to say, but Eva buzzed her, letting her know they had a line out front.

Reminding her that they were on high-security protocol, Elliott watched her all the way to the front of the store and then let himself out the back.

SHE DIDN'T HAVE to make a trip to the members-only bulk store that exact night. Marie bought enough in advance to always have extra supplies on hand. But she'd opened her last case of organic chips and the store had a coupon special on them. She also wanted a new air purifier for the apartment and those were on sale, too. Ben Schumann, the seventy-seven-year-old who, with his wife, Matilda, lived on the second floor with her, had been smoking in the hallway again and the stench was beginning to permeate her apartment and was driving her crazy.

Probably because she had enough quiet time to notice it there, all alone as she was.

She didn't, technically, have to call Elliott to let him know she was going out, either. But he'd asked. Insisted. And she didn't want to be more of a pain in his backside than she'd already been.

When his agreement to accompany her lit a burst of excitement inside her, she knew she had to start getting out more. To get a life.

Living alone, being alone every evening, just didn't agree with her. Maybe she should find someplace to volunteer in the evenings. And start looking for a new roommate.

The fact that the weight had started to slowly lift from her heart as she walked down the huge aisles of floor-to-ceiling warehoused bulk sale items with Elliott walking quietly beside her, his hands in the pockets of his black chino pants, reiterated her earlier thought. She needed a roommate. To get out more.

She…

"Sorry about that." His deep voice sounded beside her as he pushed the oversize cart that was getting heavy beneath the load she was piling in it. Cases of organically grown beans for salads. Toilet paper for downstairs and up. Paper towels. Trash bags for home and the shop.

"Sorry about what?" With a frown she glanced over at him.

"The stares. They can be off-putting the first few times."

He didn't quite smile. But she liked the way

his eyes had softened. She was also confused. "What stares?"

With a movement of his shoulder he directed her gaze to the right. A teenager was looking at them. He turned away as soon as he saw them noticing him.

And she glanced at Elliott. "Maybe he likes your sweater."

"Maybe." He didn't say anything else, and Marie turned down the aisle of professional-grade vacuum cleaners, smoke detectors and air purifiers. She read the specifics of the three models offered. Couldn't decide between more BTUs or square footage estimates. Asking Elliott, as she'd have asked Gabrielle anytime in the past that she'd been purchasing a home appliance, she was relieved by his input and made what she was confident was the best choice.

"Is this for the shop?" he asked as he lifted it into the cart for her.

"Nope. It's for home." She told him about Ben, smoking in the hallway.

"It's against Arapahoe rules to smoke in any public places," Elliott said.

"I know."

"Did you serve him a notice?"

"No."

"But you asked him to stop?"

"No."

He didn't say any more. Didn't question her. But she felt as if he had.

"Ben's got cancer. He's dying. His wife, Matilda, doesn't want him to smoke, afraid that he's shortening what time he has left. The man's been a smoker since he was a kid working in his dad's auto shop. It's one of the few pleasures he has left. If he can have a few happy moments each day, sneaking his smokes out in the hall, and keep Matilda happy, too, thinking that he quit, then I'm sure not going to stand in his way."

Not waiting for Elliott's response, she moved on to the next aisle. And noticed, as they rounded the corner, the shocked look on the face of the middle-aged woman who'd been standing in front of a display of pots and pans. She looked from Elliott to her and back to Elliott again. Eventually she turned back to the cookware, leaving Marie with a huge dose of defensiveness where Elliott was concerned.

He didn't say anything, so neither did she. And on they shopped. Not saying much. It was just past dinnertime and employees were out with little metal carts, serving samples of many of the food items the warehouse had for sale that week. As always, she passed them by. Elliott didn't skip a single one of them—earning him another stare or two.

She earned herself one—from him—when she made a stop at the candy aisle and added a ten-pound bag of little individually wrapped chocolate bars to the cart.

"You serve all homemade food."

"I know."

"Surely you don't go through that amount of candy at home." She noticed him look at her figure.

"It's not for me," she said. "You've met Janice Maynard and her mother, Clara." Janice, a seventy-three-year-old spinster, who lived with her ninety-five-year-old mother, had been in the shop one of the days reporters had swarmed the place after news of Connelly Investments' fraudulent activities hit the internet. Janice had been upset by the cacophony and Elliott had personally escorted the two women to the private elevator and up to their apartment.

"Janice and her mother are almost as small as you are."

Maybe. Though Marie had never thought of herself as small. Gabrielle was small. Neither of them was overweight. They both had good figures. But Marie took two sizes bigger on top, which made it difficult to share clothes.

"Janice's mother has a penchant for snatching candy out of bowls or off from tables and hiding it in the seat of her walker," Marie said. "I make it a habit to always have some on hand for her to snatch. It's harmless."

It was only as they were waiting in line to pay that Marie realized how much of a kook she must look to him. And wondered why the idea bothered her so much.

She'd never really cared before what other people thought of her. She liked herself, and that was what mattered. Or so her mother had always said.

But as a little girl gave a bit of a yelp when they approached her in the parking lot on the way to the car, hiding behind her mother's leg as she watched them walk past, Marie couldn't help being bothered. "That's why you were apologizing, earlier. You get this a lot, don't you? People staring at you?"

His shrug made her curious. More than curious. She wanted to know what it hid. Wanted to know everything he didn't say to her.

"I'm larger than what most people are used to," he said with no inflection as he began to load her purchases into the back of his SUV.

"I'm not only tall. I'm broad. I have to special-order my pants and shoes."

The words were personal. She wanted more. "What size shoe do you wear?"

"Sixteen and a half."

Marie glanced at his feet. They were huge. She'd never really noticed before. Because they fit his body.

And she'd made him feel uncomfortable. Which wasn't her way at all.

"Burton's in love," she blurted as soon as they were buckled into the SUV for the drive home. She hadn't meant to tell him. It wasn't as if Burton's love life had anything to do with him.

But the news had depressed the heck out of her.

And she'd had to say something to get rid of the awkwardness that had arisen between her and Elliott.

He looked over at her before he'd even started the vehicle. Tall, bright security lights popped on around them as dusk was turning to darkness.

"That's why he asked me to lunch today," she babbled, to fill the silence. "He wanted to tell me that he won't be able to accompany me to the theater anymore. He and Rebecca are getting season tickets together."

There. She'd told someone. She hadn't even been able to keep a boring mama's boy faithful to her.

Not that she'd tried. She'd told Burton, quite emphatically, that she was not and was never going to be interested in a romantic relationship with him.

"I'm happy for him," she blurted next. Why didn't he turn on the car? Get them home where she could take a hot bath and forget life's little embarrassments?

Or cry in a glass of wine?

"The timing kind of sucks, though," she added when he just sat there.

"Why's that?"

He'd been listening to her. "You know, with Gabi and Liam all newlywed-like. At least I could count on Burton for a night out when I needed it."

She couldn't believe how selfish that sounded. Out loud. What about what Burton needed?

"I really am happy for him," she said, feeling better for no reason whatsoever. As evidenced by the smile she sent Elliott's way. She'd just needed to talk the whole thing through. Would have done so with Gabi by now if her friend were around more.

"I think you really mean that."

"Of course I do. He's a nice man. A good man. He deserves to be happy."

He'd probably be faithful, too.

Marie kept that last thought to herself.

CHAPTER FIVE

LIAM, WHO'D GRADUATED with a degree in finance and business administration, but a minor in journalism so he could pursue his first love—writing—had a full day at the Connelly Building on Thursday. Jeb Williams, his father's bodyguard and also a financier on the top floor, had Liam's back while he was in the building, but Elliott insisted on seeing the man to and from the downtown high-rise. Gabrielle first, then Liam. Reverse on the return. With time in between to watch the neighborhood around the Arapahoe. To talk to people. Get a report from the security guard checking residents in at the back door. Something was amiss. He just didn't know what.

So there'd been a blue car with a stolen plate that had left when he approached. Didn't mean it had anything to do with Liam Connelly. Or was any threat to Marie.

His gut was telling him not to walk away from this one. Not to let go.

Because there was something he hadn't seen yet? Something he'd missed?

Or because he needed to believe there was still danger so he'd be forced to stay on this job?

Liam waited inside the employees' private parking garage entrance to the Connelly Building until Elliott pulled up in the SUV. Finally. He'd been telling his client to take his safety more seriously since news of his father's duplicity—and the company's criminal activities—first broke.

"Williams is going to be calling you," the expensively suited man said as he settled casually into the seat. Before Elliott could ask why, his cell rang and Williams's name popped up.

"You got Connelly there with you?" The man, whom Elliott had first visited during his initial investigation of Liam on behalf of Barbara Bustamante, didn't introduce himself.

"Yes."

"Has he told you about the reporters?"

"No." He didn't look at his charge.

Pulling out of the darkened garage into bright sunshine, Elliott turned left, making another quick left to head toward the building that housed the public law offices where Gabrielle worked.

"He sent me an email while I was out. While he assured me he was going to be lunching in, after which I kept the business lunch I'd scheduled, he instead skipped out to a corner deli apparently to meet with his editor to go over last-minute edits to the May installment of the series he's writing on his father's life..."

The words earned Liam Connelly a sharp look from Elliott, but the financier didn't seem to notice.

Elliott knew better. Liam Connelly was a smart man. He knew he'd made a mistake. He'd emailed Williams.

And warned Elliott.

Liam was an honest man. He also was his own man. He did what he thought was right. To the point of stupidity, in Elliott's opinion. Not that he blamed the guy. Liam's adamant independence was a product of growing up under the abusively domineering hand of a father who'd been determined to control him at all costs.

"Let me talk to him," Elliott said now, breaking into whatever Williams had been about to tell him. "I'll get back with you."

He didn't work for Jeb Williams. Didn't really even know the guy. Other than to know that his initial association with Williams had inadvertently allowed him to walk into the perfect cover for the job he'd been on. And while Liam Connelly was paying him—a nonnegotiable term on Liam's part, one that Elliott had fought—even Liam was unaware that he'd come to them initially through Barbara Bustamante. And was still on her payroll, as well.

"I screwed up," Liam said as soon as Elliott slid his smartphone back into its holster.

"How bad is it?"

"That jerk reporter, Tarnished Truth…"

Elliott recognized the name. The sleazy reporter who sold his work to sensationalistic independent internet news sources had gone after Liam and Gabrielle back in February, lying in wait and then infusing slimy innuendo into the stories he reported.

"He must have followed me," Liam said. "I can't believe it was the coincidence he claimed that he happened to be there. He said that he thought he owed it to me, because of his unbecoming behavior earlier in the year, to let me know that there's been some talk at a bar he hangs out at—some reporter hangout, according to him. Word is I've now taken over my father's business."

"You've taken on a more active role," Elliott said.

"He claims that the rumor is that this whole scheme was prearranged, like Agent Menard and the FBI originally thought. That my father and I had some big plan to frame George so I could take over if the Ponzi scheme ever came to light."

"They have reams of proof that George Costas was behind the fraudulent investments." Elliott tackled the obvious while his mind worked furiously on the real piece of news.

The press—at least certain members of it—were still out to hang Liam. Probably because he was young, good-looking and recently married, making him of keener interest to their readers. He was good for drama to those who cared more about such things than about newsworthy facts. And a source of jealousy to a lot of people.

"You and I know all about the evidence against George. Doesn't mean the press knows."

"My understanding was that Costas could be close to a plea deal." He'd heard that straight from Liam.

"That's what Gwen Menard told me when I spoke with her last week." The FBI agent who'd originally questioned Liam.

Talk of a plea deal was worth nothing until it actually happened. Could change in the space of a heartbeat—or a conversation. And until it was done, Liam and his father were going to be under attack.

Even after it was done the suspicious-minded would probably still doubt them. Still wonder. Still tell the stories conjured up by their conspiracy-theory mind-sets.

"I'm assuming you set him straight," Elliott said, making the last turn that would allow him to pull up at the curb right outside Gabrielle's building.

"Of course I did. And he thanked me for allowing him to know the truth firsthand."

"He's up to no good," Elliott said aloud.

"That's a strong possibility."

He couldn't stop a reporter from reporting—even when the news was false. The guy would just claim that he believed his story to be the truth. Liam could always sue for defamation of character, but not until after the damage was done.

"So I'll call and get some extra security for the front of the coffee shop just in case. And we stay on high alert," Elliott said, sliding the vehicle into the curb as Gabrielle, in a navy pantsuit and with briefcase in hand, came outside.

"I was afraid you'd say that," Liam grumbled. But he didn't argue.

MARIE WAS ALREADY UPSTAIRS, having left Eva and Nancy—another college student, a weekend employee who'd asked to pick up some extra hours—to close up the shop for the night, when Gabrielle got home. Gabi called her to invite her to share Chinese takeout in their apartment.

Chinese takeout that had already been ordered and that would be delivered momentarily. Which meant one thing to Marie. Trouble was brewing.

She hoped to God it wasn't between Liam and Gabi.

Anything but that.

Putting the tuna she'd been mixing in a container and shoving it in the mostly empty fridge, she changed into a clean pair of jeans, a black tailored blouse and sandals before heading out. In the olden days, during most of the past thirteen years that Gabi had been living with her, Marie would have shown up to the table for Chinese takeout in the sweats she'd had on. But in the olden days, they'd never gone to Liam's world. He'd always come to theirs.

As soon as she stepped into the apartment, she was glad she'd changed. Elliott Tanner was there, his big body looming over the small cardboard cartons from his seat at the table. Liam was in the kitchen getting drinks. But it was clear from the table setting that she'd been left to sit next to the bodyguard.

She wanted to be upset about that.

Or at least unmoved.

It would be their first dinner together.

She pulled out her seat with such force it almost toppled. "How'd you know I'd be free for dinner?" was the first question she asked.

And then, with a glance at Elliott, she answered her own questions. "Because you have my schedule."

He nodded. Offered her the honey walnut shrimp. "Gabrielle says this is for you."

They had more for her, too, she found out as they started to eat. With apology written all over his face, Liam confessed his actions of early in the day.

Marie cared about the reporters. Didn't want their residents or her customers harassed. She cared that Liam and Gabi could be dragged through the mud again socially.

But what worried her most was that Liam had been caught out at an undisclosed lunch meeting with editor woman.

TARNISHED TRUTH'S THEORY made it onto two internet news sources Friday morning. Elliott had had to search three levels deep, but he'd found the proclamation that Liam and his father had concocted the entire rift in their relationship in an attempt to distance Liam— not to protect him. Liam was completely innocent, as Walter had publically confessed when he'd admitted to his own duplicity in hiding the Ponzi scheme he'd discovered in his company. He'd intended to protect his son from any kind of accountability so that he could take over his father's business, keep it in the family, in the event that Walter ended up serving any kind of prison term for obstruction of justice. But Liam had not been in collusion with him.

Walter's plea deal, which included no prison time, had already been accepted and recorded. Either Tarnished hadn't done his homework, or he simply hadn't cared, as the ultimate sentence couldn't have been known at the time that Walter and Liam would have made the plan.

Didn't really matter at that point. With the news out there, Elliott was bound right where he was. Working for Liam and using the job as a cover for watching over Marie Bustamante. He'd been bound anyway.

He'd known that. Until the Connelly case was settled, tensions around the family were going to be running high with a lot of angry people trying to recover from financial ruin.

They'd get their money back. Walter was seeing to that—paying them out of arms of his company that were legitimate and fluid. But for some the return would be too late in terms of lost credit and homes.

Which inevitably led to some broken relationships, substance abuse, lost jobs, lost hope...

All things that made people desperate.

And that was where he came in. Protecting his clients from desperate people.

He'd been sitting outside Marie's coffee shop just after nine on Friday, having dropped off Liam and Gabrielle at their respective places of work, watching for any replay of the reporter fiasco they'd had two months before the Connelly investment news first hit the airwaves, when his phone rang. A past client of his—an esteemed doctor who'd been threatened by the family of a man who'd died under his care.

He answered on the first ring.

And by the time a second could have pealed, he had hung up again. To quickly dial the security guard positioned by Marie's front door, warning him that he was going to be gone for a bit.

There was an alleged gunman at the doctor's son's elementary school. The place was on lockdown. He wanted Elliott there, to do anything he could to assist in saving the lives of the endangered children. The sum he'd offered was astronomical.

But having his services hired allowed Elliott to be at the scene.

He'd worry about money later.

MARIE WAS IN her office with Grace, her eighty-year-old baker, having lunch, when Edith Larkin, a seventy-year-old widow who lived on the fifth floor, came off the elevator. "Do you have your television on?" she asked, clearly agitated as she wiped her hands on the apron she seemed to wear from morning until night.

The small flat-screen in the corner was off. Grace, who was closest, grabbed the remote and turned it on.

Certain that she was going to see something to do with Gabi and Liam—or at the very least Liam—Marie braced herself. She'd had the news on in the shop all morning, just in case, so she could warn her friends, but all morning there hadn't even been a Connelly mention.

Leave it to fate to blast news during the

half hour she took to enjoy a broccoli and cucumber sandwich.

"There," Edith proclaimed as soon as Grace had turned to the local channel. "Isn't that our head security guy?" the woman asked, pointing to the screen.

Heart pounding, Marie had already noticed Elliott on the screen. But was confused by all the flashing lights coming from the cars and trucks and ambulances surrounding the scene. Where was he?

"...don't know any more yet, but stay tuned. We're on the scene and..." The female announcer's voice-over could be heard loud and clear.

"Where are they?" Marie asked. "What's going on?"

"There's a gunman at Heathrow Elementary," Edith told her. "Why is our security man there?"

Marie had no idea.

Jumping up from her seat, she moved closer to the screen, scared to death.

CHAPTER SIX

THE FBI HAD been called to the school and was in charge. Police were working the scene with them. Because of the credentials he showed and the fact that his client's child was inside the building, Elliott was permitted to remain at the scene.

And do little else. So far no shots had been fired. No injuries reported. Because he had to be of use, Elliott made himself a media guard, keeping reporters at bay so that those who were trying to save lives could do their jobs unimpeded. He didn't have the authority to move everyone back. Or to stand guard over them, but he did it and they responded.

He spoke to no one. Didn't want to be the source of any false alarm or false hope, either. He knew as little as they did.

And kept his eye out for anyone suspicious. He was licensed to shoot if he was being threatened with a gun. He'd put himself in the perpetrator's way, if need be, to be able to save innocent people from being hurt. He'd get the first shot off. And make certain that he hit his mark.

Voices were white noise around him. Clouds blocked blinding sun, making it easier for him to see. Uniformed officers had surrounded the perimeter of the building on foot—and in a larger ring farther out in vehicles, too. He'd heard a description of the alleged gunman. Male. Late teens or adult. In a hooded sweatshirt, a balaclava and baggy jeans. It was sixty-three degrees outside.

Even warmer in the building.

Nervous tension, worry, buzzed through the air—electrifying every breath taken. Elliott was aware and yet distant. In a world of his own. Standing tall above the crowd. A world where silence was preeminent, and crystal clear vision the only focus. A world he'd discovered young, having reached six feet in height by junior high.

A world that gave him the ability to be so good at his job.

Cars were lining up in the distance—back two blocks—behind the crime scene tape the police were hanging. Parents had been sent to a nearby church to wait for their children. Not all of them had followed orders. He didn't blame them.

No one was leaving the building. No buses

were transporting kids to safety. A couple of vans with station call letters emblazoned on their sides were inching their way forward. They wouldn't be allowed through the tape. Only those first responders who'd arrived before the FBI were permitted access to the first block cordoned off area. The area where Elliott now stood.

Every once in a while he caught the sound of a police radio. From a car, or a belt, he didn't know. The houses across the street from the school were silent and still. They'd already been evacuated—through their back doors.

Elliott didn't think twice when he saw, over the heads of the reporters he was guarding, the blur of gray and denim, running away in the distance. He ran.

The blur of color had a good head start on him, but with his long legs, Elliott was able to cover twice the distance with half the stride and was closing in when officers exited cars en masse and cornered his suspect.

A kid. Maybe fifteen. With a loaded hunting pistol. On his knees on the ground, with his gun in front of him, the boy put his hands behind his back. And sobbed.

He didn't hurt anyone. He hadn't been able to hurt anyone. And he wanted his mom.

As much as Elliott abhorred the terror the

boy had caused—as much as he knew that in spite of the fact that the teenager hadn't been able to follow through on his plan, his intent to kill had to be punished to the fullest extent—Elliott felt sorry for the troubled kid, too.

And wondered when he'd started to get soft.

SHAKING, MARIE CALLED Liam and then Gabi. Neither of them had heard from Elliott since he dropped them off. Neither of them knew anything about the drama being played out at one of the city's wealthier elementary schools.

Both said they'd see what they could find out. But it wasn't as if anyone was going to call Elliott's cell phone, distract him from whatever job he was doing and possibly put lives at risk.

They weren't his only clients, after all.

Nor did they actually need him for anything at the moment.

Marie went back out front, made the wrong coffee and had to start over. Her thoughts were entirely on the children who might be at risk. And Elliott. She rang up two orders and gave away three free coffees—all the while trying to keep an eye on the shop's mounted flat-screen.

The news was on, but only with occasional updates to the breaking story across town.

They were out of cucumber sandwiches. She'd already added an additional five to the daily numbers from a month before. Would add another five starting tomorrow.

"You okay?" Eva asked during a brief lull.

"Fine."

"Grace said to tell you she's heading upstairs," the other woman said. "She was trying to get your attention from the kitchen door…"

Marie nodded. Running a register report while she had the chance, she dropped a taped stack of twenties in the floor safe. Grace wouldn't nap until she knew that Elliott was okay. She was upstairs watching television, Marie was sure of that.

And probably fielding questions from any of the other residents who might have seen the news. The old woman had somehow become the building's unofficial superintendent long before Marie and Gabi moved in.

"It's terrible, isn't it?" The woman, a latte customer Marie had never seen before that day, stood on the other side of the counter. She, like Marie, was looking at the screen. She was also holding an empty cup.

"Yeah," Marie said, nodding toward the cup. "You want another?"

"Yes, please." The woman handed Marie the cup. "My neighbor's daughter's friend goes to that school," the woman continued while Marie filled and added and mixed, almost unaware of what she was doing. "I sure hope the kids are all okay." Worry lines marked her face.

Marie nodded again. There'd been no further updates. No live coverage. Just a recap of what they'd already seen and heard. One of which included Elliott.

She put a lid on the latte. Passed it back to the woman. Gave her the credit card receipt when the register spit it out. She had to get out of there. Get...

The knot in her stomach tightened to painful intensity when she turned to see Edith Larkin coming into the shop through the back hallway. She was looking straight at Marie.

God, don't let it be Elliott.

Were they watching another station upstairs? One with more coverage?

"Gordon is sitting at my kitchen table," the woman said. "I was at Grace's, watching the news, and went downstairs to get us some tea—Grace is out, bless her—and Gordon is just sitting there. He won't leave."

The man was ninety. A widower. And half senile. They'd inherited him when they bought the Arapahoe three months before. But Marie and Gabi, as residents, had known the man for ten years. And while he, technically, should probably have been placed in assisted care years before, the residents collectively cared for him.

All except Edith. Whose apartment he seemed to help himself to most often.

"I'll get him," Marie said to the other woman. "You go on up to Grace's if you'd like…"

"No…no, I'll just come with you." Edith, her cheeks more pinched than usual, shuffled her feet. She waited while Marie told Eva where she was going and then, without a word, rode up to the fifth floor with her.

Marie, thankful that Gordon was only sitting at Edith's table and not relieving himself in her bathroom as he'd done a time or two in the past, wondered why, if the fidgety woman was so bothered by Gordon, she didn't simply keep her door locked. As had been suggested every single time she had to deal with Gordon's uninvited presence in her home.

She wondered, too, why Gordon always chose Edith's place to get lost to.

And knew that there were just some things that weren't meant for her to understand.

Like why a gunman would choose to wreak terror on innocent children.

And why Elliott's presence at the scene was stopping her in her tracks.

"It's over!" Grace said, meeting them at the door of the elevator on the fifth floor. Her voice might have lost some of its even tenor over the eighty years of her life, but it still rang with purpose.

"Gordon's back home?" Edith asked, sounding more surprised than pleased.

"Yes, I came looking for you when you didn't come back up immediately, and I found him in your kitchen. He's taking a nap now. In his own bed. And if you don't want him in your house, then lock your doors, woman." She glared at Edith. "You don't need to go bothering the kids over Gordon. I told you that already. They've got enough to do with their jobs and running this place. They saved our lives, and we don't need to thank them by filling theirs with nonsense we can handle ourselves."

With that Grace turned to Marie. "The gunman is in custody."

Sweet relief made her weak. "Was anyone hurt?"

"No. The kiddos are terrified, of course, and their parents, too, but everyone is safe."

Uniformed personnel had been all over the scene she'd been watching on television. They'd done their job well.

"And no shots were fired?"

"Nope."

It was over. She could relax.

Feeling as though she needed a good cry, Marie excused herself back to work.

"DID YOU TALK to Marie?" Gabrielle fired the question at Elliott before she'd closed the passenger door of his SUV behind herself. His gut clenched.

"No. What's up?" He'd been by the Arapahoe twice that afternoon. Once after he'd dropped his client's very scared son off at his father's office. And again after his trip down to the local precinct to fill out paperwork regarding his part in the day's arrest. Neither time had he gone inside the shop. He'd seen Marie, though, through the window. And when he'd canvassed the neighborhood, everything had seemed fine. Normal.

Had another threatening letter appeared?

"She saw you on the news this morning. At that school. She was pretty upset."

Oh. It wasn't another threat. He put the car in gear. "Everyone was pretty terrified," he agreed. "Thank God it all worked out."

Watching in his rearview mirror, he slid out into traffic. Liam couldn't always be relied upon to wait inside. Which meant Elliott couldn't be late.

"I heard they caught the guy," Gabrielle said, her gaze turned in his direction. "They said he was just a kid."

"Yeah, that's what I heard, too." Elliott couldn't say any more than that. Not about the underage alleged perpetrator. Nor about why he'd been there.

"You were there because of a client?" Gabrielle asked next.

"Yes."

He caught her nod in his peripheral vision. He liked Gabrielle, respected her, but her penchant for not being chatty didn't mesh well with his habitual reticence, leaving them in silence.

"Marie was really upset."

With a quick glance her way at the words, Elliott pulled into the employee parking garage behind the Connelly Building.

"Everyone was." He was saved from further awkwardness as he spotted Liam just coming out of the secured door and pulled up to pick up his second charge.

"You talk to Marie?" Liam asked before the back door of the SUV was closed behind him.

What was it with these two? They and Marie were close. Elliott knew that loud and clear. A guy could easily feel like the odd man out around the owners of the Arapahoe. If he'd been anything other than a hired professional there to keep them safe. But still… he hadn't called either of them after the morning's events, either.

"I already asked." Gabrielle forestalled Elliott's response.

"And?"

Catching a glimpse of Liam's raised eyebrow in the rearview mirror, Elliott said, "No, I haven't spoken with her. But I've checked on the Arapahoe twice."

"Have you talked to her?" Liam asked Gabrielle.

"I've been in back-to-back meetings all afternoon. But I spoke to her briefly after it was all over."

Liam leaned forward and massaged his wife's shoulder. Gabrielle covered his hand with hers. The two exchanged a smile Elliott half caught in his peripheral vision. And he stepped on the gas.

"I WAS THINKING," Liam said as Elliott turned the corner that would take them to the private entrance behind the Arapahoe. "I want to take my wife out for dinner—Connelly-style—

and since you deem it wise that I not be out without your protection, we'll need you to accompany us. That is, if you're free tonight."

"I'll make myself free." He was a freelancer, which made him more affordable to those who only needed bodyguards on occasion. And able to work at a moment's notice.

That evening he'd been planning to work out. And then veg out with the new political thriller he was reading.

He stopped by the back door. Nodded to the security guard, who stood and exited the small booth Liam had paid to have built the previous month.

"Liam…" Gabrielle wasn't exiting the car. "We're having dinner with Marie tonight. Remember? We…"

Her voice broke off and at her continued silence, Elliott looked at his client in the backseat via the rearview mirror.

"It'll be almost like a double date," Liam said, grinning. But Elliott wasn't fooled by the man's little-boy charm. His guise of innocence. Liam Connelly might be fun-loving, but he was extremely smart and always aware of everyone around him and of everything he did.

Elliott was being set up.

"I cannot participate in a double date," he

said, never more serious in his life. "It would be a conflict of interest when I'm working."

"So I'll fire you." Liam was no longer smiling.

Elliott had put up a bit of a battle to get the younger Connelly to accept his help to begin with. Liam had finally capitulated— and only, Elliott suspected, because he believed Elliott had been sent via his father's bodyguard, Jeb Williams. Liam, who was only paying a cut rate for Elliott's services, knew that Elliott was being paid elsewhere to watch over him. He'd had to disclose that information. He hadn't been obligated to say who was paying his salary. Liam believed that his father was Elliott's real employer.

It worked in Elliott's favor to have Liam believe that.

And to have Liam believe that his father— Elliott's supposed employer—would be very displeased with Elliott if Liam fired him.

The man was impressive. But not good.

"So, what do you say? Dinner at seven?" Liam asked.

Barbara would insist that he go.

"I don't know, Liam," Gabrielle, who only spoke when she had something important to say, butted in.

Elliott liked her more than ever.

"Don't you think we should ask Marie first?" she asked.

Liam shrugged his expensively suited shoulder, opening the back door of the SUV. "It's dinner," he said, obviously done now. "The three of us are going to dinner with bodyguard protection at the table with us. If Elliott and Marie make it more than that, that's up to them."

With a look of apology to Elliott, Gabrielle joined her husband outside the vehicle.

And Elliott wished life were even half as simple as Liam Connelly wanted to believe it could be.

CHAPTER SEVEN

"ELLIOTT REALLY SAID he wanted to go to dinner with me?" Marie asked as Gabi, who'd come down to help her choose what to wear, twisted Marie's blond hair up into a black-and-white-flowered clip and then curled the ends that floated down around her shoulders. In a black-and-white tweed and Lycra shift that hugged every curve, ending several inches above her knees, she felt as if she were getting ready for the prom.

Except that she was a heck of a lot more nervous. She'd liked her prom date well enough, but wouldn't have gone out with him if it hadn't been for the prom. She hadn't been the least bit interested in dating anyone seriously back then.

Not that she was interested now. She just... really liked Elliott.

"Liam didn't give him a chance to say what he wanted," Gabi said now. "He just told Elliott we were going and invited him to share our table with us if he was going to insist on protecting us. But Elliott's a grown man. He could have refused."

"Not with his code of ethics, he couldn't," she said. "Walter Connelly wants him watching Liam, more now than ever, I'm sure, since Liam's taking a much more active role in the company."

"True."

She could always count on Gabi to call it like it was. Which was one of the reasons Marie loved her best friend so much. One of the reasons why Gabi *was* her best friend...

"You like him, though, don't you?" Gabi's question came just as she finished with Marie's hair and set her free to fasten a black-and-white pearl-and-onyx-flowered earring in her bottom piercing. And pearl studs in the second one back.

Marie didn't know how to answer the question. *Liking* was not how she'd describe her feelings for the bodyguard. Not in the like-like sense Gabi seemed to mean. Yet she couldn't deny, especially after the day she'd spent worrying about him, that she cared more than just friends.

Still...

"That's why Liam set this up," Gabi said. "The way you reacted today, being so beside yourself upset when you thought Elliott was in danger... Liam thinks you have a thing for Elliott. I just need you to know what he's doing so that you don't think I'm part of something behind your back."

Marie got hot from the inside out. Flushing from her head to her toes. And then cooled just as quickly. "Does Elliott know that?" she asked, afraid to look at Gabi. To see the truth in her friend's eyes.

She didn't look at herself in the big bathroom mirror they were both standing in front of, either. She looked at Gabi's short dark hair. At the diamond stud she was wearing in her right ear.

"I don't know." Gabi's finger gently pushed a tendril of Marie's hair back behind her ear as her words washed softly over her. "Nothing was said. Not in the car. I just wanted you to know..."

Marie nodded. Had no answer for the question lying there between them. Was she falling for Elliott Tanner?

"He could have suggested that we eat at home and have a meal catered in," Gabi offered after Marie just stood there, looking at herself in the mirror.

Having the meal catered, at home, where they were safely guarded, sounded like something Elliott would certainly have preferred. "He didn't suggest any alternatives?"

"No."

Marie's grin started with butterflies in her belly and blossomed. Until the butterfly crashed. "Do you think Elliott knows that I've...that I would go out with him if he asked? If he didn't think asking would be a conflict of interest? If Liam said something..."

"He didn't," Gabi quickly inserted. "At least, Liam didn't say anything about you liking Elliott. But we both asked if he'd spoken to you," she added. "When he picked us up from work. Just because you'd been so worried. But you always worry. He knows that..."

Elliott knew that she always worried about Liam and Gabi. Not about him.

"Don't be mad at Liam," Gabi said. Marie looked at her, saw the very real, very tender, concern in Gabi's eyes and marveled again that her friend was so in love with the man who'd been best friend to both of them for more than a decade. She'd feared that Gabi, who deserved home and family and security more than anyone else she knew, would never give herself a chance to have it all.

Marie was going to do some serious damage to Liam Connelly, business partner and best friend or not, if he ever did anything to take that soft look out of Gabi's eyes…

"He's only trying to help," Gabi continued. "You're lonely with me moving out so suddenly. We all know that. And you know Liam. He sees a problem and thinks he has to fix it."

"I'm not mad at him," she said now, not hiding the hint of peevishness in her tone. Wouldn't have done any good anyway. This was Gabi. Gabi knew Marie better than Marie knew herself.

"You like Elliott, don't you?"

Turning so she was facing Gabi, whose tall slender body looked model perfect in the short black dress she was wearing, Marie said, "I don't know."

It was the truth.

"I've…never…"

"Tell me what you feel when you're with him."

"That's the problem. I don't feel just one thing. It's like…he walks into the shop and I feel *him*. Like he draws me. And it's exciting. And dangerous. And yet the most compelling thing about him is that he makes me feel…safe."

Afraid, when she saw Gabi's frown, Marie said, "What? Why are you looking at me like that?"

"I don't want you to get hurt."

"You think he's going to hurt me?"

"I'm more afraid that you're going to hurt yourself."

"How would I do that?" Marie was a pro at keeping herself, her heart, at arm's length. She'd been protecting herself from getting hurt by the opposite sex since junior high. Or at least it seemed that long ago.

"Because it sounds like you're finally falling in love, and I'm afraid you won't just go with it. Won't just let it happen."

She was falling in love?

She and Elliott were friends. And they were that much only because they'd spent a lot of hours chatting in the coffee shop over the past few months he'd been watching over Liam and the building.

They were friends because of proximity. Nothing else.

She didn't want to fall in love.

Ever.

She'd promised herself she'd never be that vulnerable to any man.

But Gabi knew her...

"Don't look so scared, Marie. See, that's what I'm talking about. You get in your own way and..."

"I'm...not convinced I'm falling in love."

She blurted the thought in her head. "Love is a roller coaster. It's angst and exhilaration. I feel neither of those things."

"Just promise me that if Elliott gives you any indication that he's interested in you, really interested, you won't run in the other direction? You'll give him a chance?"

Marie nodded. Because at the moment, the way she felt, there didn't seem much point in not doing so. Gabi knew she wanted to go out with Elliott.

"What if he doesn't feel anything for me?"

"The way he hangs around you so much when it's Liam he's working for? And Walter? Besides, Liam says he can tell by the way Elliott watches you when you don't know he's looking that he has a thing for you. Bad, Liam said. He's got it bad."

Gabi fidgeted with Marie's hair and then turned to readdress her own lipstick.

"And it's not like he's working for me," Marie reemphasized. "He's working for Liam. And if Liam's good with him going out with me, then he wouldn't be breaking a code of ethics or having some conflict of interest."

"Exactly."

"Unless I distract him, he misses seeing something and Liam gets hurt."

"Elliott is too much a professional to miss

any danger to anyone within a five-mile radius," Gabi said dryly. Exaggerating, of course, but not as much as one might think.

"He's always so careful about not doing anything that could jeopardize his license or his reputation with his clients," Marie said, thinking out loud about previous conversations with the bodyguard to expel some jitters. "I think it's because his career is everything to him."

Which might not bode well for a long-term relationship. A sense of crushing disappointment assailed her. But it was quickly followed by a resurgence of her good mood. If he wasn't an option for forever, it made him even more perfect for her.

Because she wasn't, either. Marie didn't believe in happily ever after.

As she applied her lipstick, something she'd been doing several times a day for years, Marie steadied herself.

"I trust him with my life," she said to Gabi, completely serious, as she straightened. For Marie, it was not only a first. It was a miracle.

"You and all of his clients." Gabi's quip lightened the moment.

And Marie smiled. Grabbed her black silk clutch with pearls. Slipped into three-inch heels. Nervous. Excited. And...

"You really think I'm falling in love?" She glanced back at Gabi as they left the apartment. Liam was standing by the elevator, holding the door.

"Just go with it," Gabi whispered as they got on behind him.

Marie nodded one more time.

FEELING LIKE A fraud in his dark suit, white shirt and black tie, Elliott headed out the door in his shined dress shoes, far more eager for the evening than he should have been. Adjusting the holster of his gun beneath the suit coat, he reminded himself that he was on the job.

Working.

He'd just gotten off the phone with Barbara Bustamante. He'd told her that he'd be sitting at the table as a guest, the fourth in a two-couple foursome, with her daughter and the newly married Liam and Gabrielle Connelly for dinner that night.

She'd been glad to hear that he'd have an opportunity for an entire evening of eavesdropping, an entire evening to watch how Liam treated the two women.

He'd warned that it was going to look as if he was Marie's date.

She'd warned him to watch himself.

At which he'd suggested she find herself another bodyguard.

She'd reminded him that no other guard, hired at this late stage of the game, would likely be able to convince Liam that he was there via his father, thus allowing him to protect Marie without her knowing that she was under protection.

And then she'd apologized for her earlier implication.

But her point had been taken.

In between the time he'd dropped off Liam and Gabrielle after work and now, Elliott had familiarized himself with every aspect of the floor plan of their evening's destination. Assuring himself that he was only working, that he would keep his feelings firmly in check all night, running restaurant security measures through his mind, considering options in the event someone attempted to approach Liam Connelly during dinner, he turned the last corner to approach the back lot of the Arapahoe for the second time that night—this time to pick up his charges for their evening out.

And just missed being hit by the police car that pulled onto the lot ahead of him.

What the...

Barely getting the SUV out of the way and

stopped, he was outside, running toward the guard gate where the police car had stopped.

Two uniformed officers were on the black-top, looking in the door of the small guard house.

"I'm telling you I'm fine," the man Elliott had waved goodbye to an hour and a half before was saying.

"An ambulance is already on its way," the female officer said.

"What's going on?" Elliott spoke calmly. Not the least bit out of breath for having run toward them. And hands in the air to show he wasn't armed as the larger of the two officers, a man about Elliott's age, reached for his gun. "Sorry, Officer," he said. Cursing his unprofessionalism. "I'm Elliott Tanner, an armed and licensed bodyguard. If you'll allow me to reach for my credentials?"

With his gun trained on Elliott, the man nodded. And looked over the card Elliott showed him. After which Elliott and the two officers turned immediately toward the guard sitting on a stool at the small counter in the booth, facing them.

In his forties, the man had obviously been in a fight. His cheek was swollen. His lip split.

"He came out of nowhere," the man said.

"I heard a sound out by the cars and went to check it out. The guy came at me and got a couple of punches in before I knew what hit me. I fought back. Busted his nose. I heard it crack and felt it, too. He took off, but I wasn't going to leave my post. For all I knew there were more, waiting for me to go so they could get inside. I came over here and called you." He nodded toward the police.

"What car was he by?" Elliott asked the question. But he knew.

"Mr. Connelly's, sir. He came out from between his car and that old white Buick parked beside it."

Grace's Park Avenue.

Before they could say anything more, another siren closed in on them and an ambulance pulled on the lot. The back door to the building flung open and Liam Connelly, visibly pushing two beautiful, poshly turned out women back into the building behind him, came outside.

Elliott had to get all three of them out of there. Let the officers sort it all out. And then he'd figure out what to do.

Handing the female officer his card while her partner tended to the security guard, Elliott waylaid Liam before he could make it around the ambulance and to the booth.

"Let's get the ladies and go," he said, his hand on Liam's arm.

It spoke to Liam's intelligence that he didn't argue.

IT WASN'T A DATE. Liam and Elliott rode up front, the doing of both men as far as Marie could tell. She wasn't all that sorry to be huddled with Gabi in the backseat.

"So you think that guy was after Liam?" she asked, shivering in spite of the balmy weather outside and climate control in the car.

"No." Elliott's tone bore no hesitation. "If anything he was after his car."

"To sabotage it?" Marie asked. She was thinking about bombs.

"The back tire was slashed," Elliott said. He'd gone back and spoken with the police for a few seconds after he got Liam and Gabi and Marie settled in his car.

Always the professional.

Liam swore. "My tires are slashed?"

"Only one of them. Probably would have been all four if the guard hadn't heard something."

"Thank God it was your car and not you." Sitting directly behind Liam, Gabrielle leaned forward and ran her hand along the side of his neck, a tender move that belied her somewhat harsh tone.

It wasn't Liam who'd raised Gabi's ire. Marie knew that much for sure. Pity the guy who was behind these threats against Liam. An attorney who didn't take no for an answer, Gabi would see the sod prosecuted to the fullest extent of the law once he was caught.

"You think it's the same guy who spray-painted his car in the park?" Marie was looking at Elliott in the rearview mirror. Could see the serious expression on his face as he focused on the road. Dusk was quickly falling.

"Could be. The police haven't been able to link either the car or the letters to each other, let alone to an actual person," he said.

"But then with budget cuts it's not like they can afford to put this at the top of their lists," Gabi said. "Not when it's just car vandals and anonymous notes without a threat to life."

"Striking a guard will up the offense," Elliott said, to which Gabi nodded.

"So you think a detective will give this more time now?" Marie asked. She wasn't sure she liked that idea, either.

It made the whole thing seem so much more ominous.

"I think they'll be looking harder for a connection between the incidents and, yes, probably assigning more hours to the task."

"So you think there's more than one person behind all of it?" she asked. Because chattering was what she always did when she was upset. Or in a good mood. Or bored. Or interested in something. Or...

"I hope to God not," Liam said. "But you can't blame people for being angry. George robbed them of their life savings, some of them. And though they're going to get it back, some of them have already been foreclosed on. We can't give them back their credit."

In the olden days, Marie would have touched him, squeezed his hand or patted his shoulder for saying such a thing. Before he was Gabi's property. Now she just smiled inside, loving that he was one of them.

"I'd like to believe there's only one guy working alone," Elliott said as he stopped at a red light. Her gaze met his in the falling darkness as he glanced back in his rearview mirror. "Anonymous notes and car vandalism, he's showing a pattern of staying in the shadows." He didn't sound worried. But he clearly wasn't happy about the evening's turn of events.

She nodded. The light changed and he

moved on. Gabi squeezed her hand and she held on.

The streets and sidewalks were buzzing. Friday night on the town.

With someone out there wanting to hurt Liam. Possibly watching them.

Shivering again, Marie looked at the immense spread of Elliott's shoulders. And was glad she was with him.

CHAPTER EIGHT

ELLIOTT WASN'T NEARLY as much fun to be with when he was working. Or maybe it was just the night. Marie ordered her favorite—filet mignon. She drank part of a glass of wine. Loved the windowed table in the eighteenth-floor restaurant.

She was with the people she cared most about in the world.

And none of them seemed to be having the time of their lives.

She told Gabi and Liam about Gordon. About Edith and Grace. And Grace telling Edith not to "bother the kids."

"Sounds to me like there's something a little more between Edith and Gordon," Elliott said, cutting his steak, but looking around him as he did so.

"Edith and Gordon?" Marie and Gabi said in unison.

"He's ninety, she's seventy," Liam told the other man.

"And?" Elliott's attention was on the conversation, and yet it felt as though he wasn't really with them. He hadn't made direct eye contact with her once that night. Not even when, at the hotel while they waited together for the elevator to take them to the restaurant and Liam had walked Gabi over to look at the menu, she'd told him that she was really glad that no one had been hurt at the school earlier that day.

The elevator door had opened and it wasn't until later that she'd realized he'd never responded.

"You think Edith has a thing for him and he doesn't return her feelings? That's why she's always so irritated with him but doesn't lock her door?" Marie asked now, trying not to be hurt by Elliott's distance.

He was working, she continued to remind herself.

And she, for one, was glad that he was.

"I think it sounds as though there's something else going on there." Elliott's deep voice spread softly around them. "I can't say what that something is."

"Ask Grace," Liam said, handing Gabi the bread basket before she'd even asked for it. "She'll know."

And so it went. They talked about the Arapahoe. About business at the shop. Even a little bit about Threefold's finances. The trio had had to have a name for the LLC that bought the Arapahoe and Marie's choice of Threefold had won the vote. The LLC currently held title to the building and all leases therein—including the one for Marie's coffee shop. They had two non-senior citizen renters, both of whom paid on time, and a list of repairs that were waiting their turn. New wiring was going to be starting the following month. Enough to get the entire building up to code. It was only during that business discussion that Elliott had seemed to fully participate in their evening at all. But Marie wasn't fooled. He'd asked seemingly pertinent questions—many of which were similar to ones he'd asked before—so she knew he hadn't really been engaging with them.

When everything with Liam's father had first gone down, Elliott asked to see the Threefold paperwork. Liam and Gabi had been racing the clock to prove to the FBI that Liam was not involved in his father's company's illegal dealings. Marie had gone over Threefold's files with Elliott.

Their waitress stopped to offer more wine. Everyone declined. And before they were through their main course, they'd exhausted historic Arapahoe conversation and moved on to the weather.

No one mentioned the stalker out to get Liam. Or Elliott's episode with danger that morning. No one mentioned anything that would bring tension to the table.

But it was there anyway.

ELLIOTT MEANT TO push the button for the second floor. Drop Marie first. And then ride up one floor to see Liam and Gabrielle safely inside their more luxurious apartment.

Habit had his finger on floor three as soon as he was in the elevator. His work for Barbara Bustamante Connelly didn't require him to visit Miss Bustamante's apartment often. Generally he was on the third floor with Liam.

He was overeager to get home. Made a tactical error. Not one that put anyone but him in any danger.

It was late. He'd seen the worry in Marie's eyes that evening. Remembered how concerned her friends had been over her worry about him earlier in the day. Thinking he should have called her. As if there was something between them.

It had felt good. For a second there. Having a woman worry about him.

Too good.

He shouldn't be alone with her.

But alone he was as soon as he did a well-being check of Liam and Gabi's home and reentered the ancient elevator with Marie. It took thirty seconds for the door to close, the elevator to bump its way down a floor and reopen her doors. Seemed like five minutes to Elliott.

"Did I do something to offend you?" she asked as he held out a hand for her key and unlocked her door—as he'd done with Liam moments before.

"Of course not," he said, all business as he strode through the flowery-smelling apartment and tried not to notice all the colorful, homey, soft touch arrangements everywhere. From the painted glass in one room, to the colorfully flowered ceramic décor in another, he focused on safety concerns.

"You didn't have to check my place," Marie said. "I'm not, nor have I ever been, in any danger. Liam's the target, not me. Besides, in case you didn't notice, I have one entrance and two dead bolts. Courtesy of my mother. You think my worrying is bad, you should meet her."

She'd tossed her clutch on a light-colored leather sectional filled with pillows.

He shouldn't meet her mother. Ever. Didn't need to. He knew her too well via phone. And mail. Her paychecks came right on time. Every time.

He also didn't need the reminder that he was working.

His mind had been fully aware of that fact every single second that evening.

"Everything's fine here," he said, hoping he could get her sweet scent out of his senses as quickly as he was going to make it out her door. He made a straight shot.

Had his hand on the doorknob.

"You're sure I didn't do something to make you mad?"

She looked like a siren standing there. And with that blond hair, she was an angel.

One who had been visibly upset to her friends when she'd thought him in danger earlier that day.

The feeling was sweeter than he'd imagined. Something he wanted. And wasn't going to have with her.

But those big brown eyes…they needed something from him.

Her mother was paying him to make certain that she didn't get hurt.

Only in that moment did Elliott realize that she'd hired him to do the impossible. He could protect Marie's physical body from harm, maybe even protect her finances from ruin, but no one could guarantee that another's heart would not be hurt.

"I'm certain I am not upset with you." He did the best he could to dispel the shadows in her eyes. And turned to let himself out.

"Then why haven't you looked me in the eye all night?"

"A man attempted to harm my client tonight, if not directly then indirectly with his car. For all we know he might have intended to do more than just slash the tires. He'd have had access to the underside of the car. He could have cut any number of things, or planted any number of things, that could have put Liam at risk." He spoke harshly. Not because of her. But because of what it was costing him to keep his back to her.

"I've seen you right after Liam was in trouble before." She spoke directly behind him. He'd felt every move she made as she approached. Her breath was like a breeze against the back of his neck.

And couldn't possibly have touched him. He was almost a foot taller than she was.

She wasn't going to let him go.

Against every instinct he had, Elliott turned enough to meet that wide-open gaze and say, "I am not angry with you. If anything, I like you too much." And then he was out of there.

Kicking himself all the way down the stairs that he'd taken at a run.

I like you too much? Why on earth had he said that?

Marie Bustamante demanded honesty. Needed honesty.

He'd given it to her.

But he was deceiving her, too.

Because he had to.

"HE SAID HE likes me too much." Marie took cookies from the cooling rack, making room for Grace to put the muffins. Two cookies per bag. Fold. Attach gold Arapahoe Coffee Shop seal. "What does that mean?"

"Could mean any number of things." The old woman, tall and mostly straight backed even as she bent over her tins, frowned.

Marie waited. Needing to hear what all of those "any number of things" were. Needed to get her head back on right. To have shoulders as strong and able as Grace's.

Five-thirty on a Saturday morning after a restless and mostly sleepless Friday night, and Marie wasn't feeling strong or able about much of anything.

"Did you think to ask him?" Efficient as always, Grace emptied the last tin, carried it to the utility sink and washed it clean.

She'd thought to ask Grace. Not the man in question. Not her best friend. Or her mother. Definitely not her mother.

No, she'd gone straight for the grandmotherly type. Like she'd needed a giant hug.

And if that didn't tell Marie she was in trouble, she'd be just plain lying to herself.

ELLIOTT SHOWED UP at the coffee shop before eight o'clock Saturday morning. It was a further testament to Marie's flustered state that when he walked in the door she dropped the carton of cream she'd pulled out of the small refrigerator under her counter on her way to completing one of her more famous frothy coffee drinks.

Grace had gone upstairs, Nancy was busy taking orders and Eva was just getting her apron on, so Marie cleaned up the mess herself. She would have anyway. She was a stickler for cleaning up her own messes.

He'd be fourth in line. Nancy could wait on him. Eva would be on the counter by then, making the drinks. And she'd have the flush out of her face enough to smile and say hello.

Maybe even go out front and talk with

him for a few. Like old times. A week ago. A month ago. When he'd been a person she was compelled to spend time with, enjoyed talking to, a person who was easy for her to talk to, not like now, when first and foremost he was...a man.

"Marie." She was bent over, staring at the floor, corralling cream into the paper towel, when she heard Elliott's voice above her head. Glancing up, she saw his face, almost right on top of hers.

Only Elliott would have been able to lean over quite that far. For him it wasn't even a stretch.

Absurd thought. She smiled. "Yeah?"

"We need to talk. Liam and Gabrielle are waiting upstairs as soon as you're free to get away."

They were in the middle of their Saturday morning rush. "Is it an emergency?"

"No."

"Can you give me an hour or so?" She mopped cream, glancing up at him.

"Of course."

"Thanks." Marie didn't look at him again. Didn't need another rush of the wonderful feeling that swept over her when his eyes connected with hers. Didn't need any more complications, period. She threw away the paper towel. Cleaned the area with disinfectant to make certain there'd be no residual sour smell greeting them in the near future. And stood, with her back to the room, to survey the list of tickets waiting to be filled.

Making coffee was something she was good at. Something she enjoyed. It wasn't about measured grounds, water and pushing a button for her. Every cup started with freshly ground beans, in varying amounts, with fresh accents, added individually...

Coffee was art to her. And the fact that her coffee made her a decent living was testimony to the fact that she knew what she was doing. She had no idea how full the shop was. What tables were occupied. What seats were available. The shop's bell rang, indicating another customer had entered. Or exited. She had no idea if there were any tables that needed to be cleaned. She'd been avoiding more eye contact with Elliott.

He'd been number four in line. His dark roast with a shot of espresso had come through. Long enough ago that he should be upstairs.

She turned.

Surveyed the room.

He was at the small round table to the right of counter. With easy access to the door. And a view of both the room and the street outside.

And she was glad.

CHAPTER NINE

MARIE COULDN'T GET away long enough for a meet up in Liam's apartment. Watching her blond ponytail swing with the fluid swiftness of her movements, positioning herself in between her employees, moving around them, handing them what they needed before they had a chance to ask for it, Elliott tried not to be impressed.

But he was.

She didn't miss a beat. Didn't lose her smile—even when someone brought a half gone cup of coffee and demanded a remake. She provided it cheerfully. Along with a coupon for a free coffee at a later visit.

There were no vacant seats in the shop. And the door just kept opening. New customers ordering. Those without seats taking their coffee to go. Elliott watched it all. And he watched the people outside the shop, as well.

His perp was male. He knew that much now. Which allowed him to eliminate a lot of suspects. Unless there was more than one perp. Or the perp had a female accomplice.

Where there should have been peace and quiet, steady focus, there was frustration, and it was eating at him. It wasn't really his job to catch the bad guys. Just to protect his clients from them. Or ferret them out and turn over his information to the proper authorities. He'd never felt so helpless in his life.

And he had to speak with his clients. He'd already been on the phone with Barbara Bustamante that morning. Liam, Gabrielle and Marie were next.

She was coming toward him, wiping her hand on the blue-and-yellow apron.

"Sorry," she said. "Busier than usual this morning."

He smiled. He couldn't help it. "That's good," he said. For her. For her business. Her future. Not for the man who was being paid to keep her out of danger.

"Gabi just texted. She and Liam are on their way down. Is it okay with you if we just do this here?"

"In your office." He stood. But left his coffee and grabbed a newspaper to put next to it. He was coming back to the table.

LIAM AND GABI, both in jeans, sat together in one chair. Gabi perched on Liam's thigh.

Marie took the chair behind her desk—trying not to be jealous. To feel lonely.

She loved them. Both of them. And wanted them to be happy. She was happy for them.

And Elliott, closing the door, stood by it. He was the only one of them not wearing jeans. His usual dark attire looked more sinister than usual.

Or maybe it was the grim expression on his face.

Her assessment from the night before, that he might be ticked off at her, faded as fear escalated.

"The police caught the guy who slashed your tire." Elliott came right to the point, focusing on Liam.

"Oh, good!" Marie couldn't help herself. Relief was sweet.

Until she saw Gabi shake her head.

"It's not good, is it?" Gabi asked. Always the one to see the worst. But her gaze was steady on the bodyguard. "We wouldn't be here if this was all over."

"The guy they have in custody slashed the tire, but not because he has anything against Liam. He didn't even know whose car it was." Elliott included all three of them in his conversation now.

And Marie was still not seeing the bad

news. "Then it was just a random act," she blurted. She wanted this over. Wanted everyone safe.

And Elliott gone?

No, she didn't want that.

But maybe…if he wasn't working for Liam…

He'd said he liked her too much…

He liked her…

And Lord knew, she liked *him*…

Elliott was shaking his head.

"Liam's vehicle was the target," Elliott told them. "The guy had been hired to disable it. Permanently. He only slashed a tire as he ran, after his attempt to do worse damage was interrupted. He wanted to get paid."

"Who hired him?" Liam's voice was sharp. Marie recognized the tightness of his chin. Liam Connelly might have grown up the pampered son of a very rich man, but he did not sit back and let others do his dirty work for him.

At least not easily.

She and Gabi exchanged a glance. A silent promise to work together to watch over Liam and make certain that he didn't do something stupid. Like get himself killed.

A promise to keep an eye on him and remind him of everything he already knew. To help him stay calm while he let the police—and Elliott—take care of this situation.

And then Marie processed what Elliott was telling them. Someone really was out to get Liam.

"So this guy…he's going to lead you to whoever hired him, right?" she asked. And wished she was more surprised when Elliott shook his head.

"He was just some guy who approached him on the street. Outside the car shop where he worked. The perp's story is that this guy comes up to him as he's leaving work, tells him he was told in a bar the perp frequents that the perp needed some extra money, would definitely know how to 'fix' a car and knew how to look the other way when he needed to."

"He's committed crimes before," Gabi said. "He has a record?"

"For penny-ante stuff. Steeling bikes, pickpocketing, that kind of thing. His older brother's upstate for armed robbery with attempt to harm."

"Great," Gabi said just as Liam asked, "So we have a description of the guy who hired him?"

Again Elliott shook his head. "Not much of one. The guy was wearing a trench coat that hung loose and he stayed in the shadows. Besides which, it was dark. He thinks he's white. No facial hair that he could tell. He's not sure about the length or color of his hair because he had a hoodie on under the coat. Average height. Not sure about his weight. The one thing he noticed was that the guy wore what the perp called a flashy ring. He figured if the guy could afford jewelry like that, he'd pay him as agreed. And that's all he really cared about. Our slasher has a bookie after him."

"Did he say why he wanted the car disabled?" Gabi asked.

"No. Just told him the make and model and where to find it."

"So he didn't have Liam's license plate number?" Marie asked, remembering the first time Liam's car had been vandalized right after news of the Ponzi scheme had broken. That first time had brought Elliott to them. But the other time, his car had been the only one in a deserted public park lot.

"Yes, he did," Elliott said, glancing down and then back at Liam and Gabi, almost as though he'd been reluctant to give the information.

Because it meant that… "This is more than just pranks," Gabi said.

"He's seriously out to get me," Liam said.

"But he just doesn't want me hurt, he wants to play with me first. To make me suffer."

"No," Marie blurted. "That's ridiculous. He's angry, but not dangerous, right?" She looked to Elliott.

He towered over them as he shook his dark head. "Liam's right." His words hit Marie hard. "The pattern shows a desire to stay low-key and anonymous—playing a game, like Liam said—but it's escalating. You don't go looking for a thug to hire, or hire one, if you're not serious about doing harm."

"And Liam's the target." Marie forced the words through the sudden dryness in her throat.

"That's correct."

"I'm moving into a hotel." Liam stood, setting Gabi on her feet beside him. Marie could see the fear in her friend's eyes when Gabi looked over at her.

"Wait." Elliott held up his hand. His body in front of the door was enough to prevent any of them from leaving. "I don't think anyone should go anywhere," he said. "We have full security set up here. We're contained. The police are putting extra surveillance on this place. Staying put is the quickest and best way to draw this guy out."

"I am not putting my wife or Marie in danger," Liam said. "Or any of our residents, either. I'm leaving."

"But..." Gabi looked to Marie, as though she could somehow make things better.

"You're not going anywhere, Liam." Marie said the only thing she knew. "This is your home. We're a team. Family..." She stood now, too, in spite of wobbly knees.

"Your leaving will only put everyone more at risk." Elliott's deep tone stilled the room. No one moved. Or said a word.

"Whoever is after you knows by now that you're married, regardless of how quickly and quietly you two got it done. He obviously knows you're in business with Marie and Gabrielle, as well. The purchaser of the Arapahoe is public record, as is the incorporation of Threefold's LLC. If you disappear and he can't find you, or if you move someplace where it's not as easy to access you, chances are good he'll go after you in a way that he knows will hurt you. Through your wife and best friend. He seems to be getting something out of stalking you. You take that away and he might try to hurt you worse, by going after your loved ones instead. He knows where they are."

"Here," Marie said. "If he can't get Liam, he'll get us."

Liam's lips were tight. Gabi's eyebrows drawn together. Marie's stomach was one big knot.

"What do you propose?" Gabi was the first to speak. She slid her fingers in between Liam's. And Marie was glad. They'd stay together, like always.

She looked over to the large man dwarfing the door of her office. And now they had Elliott.

They were going to be fine.

ELLIOTT CLEARED HIS SCHEDULE. Until Liam's attacker could be found, he was going to be at the Arapahoe full-time. Liam had insisted on his presence. Barbara Bustamante also offered to pay him to stay on the premises. He couldn't take her money for that.

"But you're undercover as Liam's bodyguard at my behest," she'd said early Saturday morning when he first called her to tell her what he was going to recommend to the newly married financier.

"And he's not going to believe my cover if I don't charge him extra for the time," he'd said to her. "Besides, he can afford me."

He'd looked into Barbara's finances. She wasn't destitute, but she wasn't wealthy enough to afford, for too many more months, the fees he normally charged for the work she'd hired him to do.

For once the woman had relented. Elliott had packed a bag.

Which was now settled in the spare bedroom in Liam Connelly's apartment. There'd be a twenty-four-hour security guard at the front of the building as well as the back until the perp was caught. Police would be doing extra patrols.

And Walter Connelly had called insisting that his son fly to Florida for the duration.

Liam had told his father what he could do with that suggestion. Elliott could only hear Liam's part of the conversation, but was a bit surprised when it ended as soon as it did. In congenial tones. Walter Connelly's topple off his high horse must have softened him up.

"So, what now?" Liam asked as Elliott came out of the room he'd been allotted in the back of the condo. He and Gabrielle were standing in the kitchen, salad fixings on the counter.

"Now we go on as we have been," Elliott said. "I'll accompany you wherever you need to go, take you and Gabrielle to work and generally just be around."

"What about Marie?" Gabrielle looked up from the lettuce she'd been breaking into a bowl.

"As long as Liam is around, neither I nor the police believe Marie is in any danger. She's in business with Liam, not married to him."

Liam's jaw tightened, and Elliott surmised the man was upset at the reference to the danger his wife could be in.

He felt for the guy.

"But I'll be watching the shop, as usual," he added. "As I said downstairs, I'm going to set up shop at the table by the front window, and pretty much, when I'm not escorting one or the other of you, that's where I'll be."

Slowly churning inside, an hour at a time, as he watched the beautiful barista go about her daily business. If earlier today had been any indication.

He'd be uncomfortable. His charges would be safe.

And life would go on.

It always did.

BY SUNDAY AFTERNOON, Marie felt like a nervous twit, flitting around her shop washing counters and floors and then rewashing them as her afternoon help served the customers that came through. She could be upstairs. Or out shopping.

She could be watching a movie or reading a book or in-line skating.

She didn't want to leave the shop. Because Elliott was there. Finally forcing herself back to her office so she wouldn't look overeager—after all, the man was paid to be observant, and there was clearly little for her to do out front—she focused on the week's stock orders. Normally a Sunday night job. She finished them. Finished filing her bank receipts, going over the books and writing checks to her employees.

Then she called upstairs. Liam was working on the next installment on his Walter Connelly series for June Fryberg, his editor. Gabi had been working, too, but was ready for a break. Marie asked her if she'd help her with inventory.

Until Gabi's marriage, the biweekly chore had always been shared by the roommates.

When she opened her office door to her friend ten minutes later, Gabi stood there with a bowl of popcorn. "Want some?" she asked, holding out the stainless steel bowl she'd inherited when she'd married Liam.

Prior to that their popcorn bowls had been plastic.

Where some women craved chocolate, Marie was a sucker for popcorn. And hated that her friend thought she needed to be spoiled. As if something were wrong with her life. Or that, if something didn't change, people were going to start thinking she was... pathetic.

Not that anyone gave any indication that they thought that. Maybe it was just Marie who was feeling it...

"So..." Marie ventured an hour later when the two were finishing up the last of the counting—paper products that lined the entire back wall of the storeroom. The popcorn was nearly gone. "You and Liam okay?"

The question could have been in reference to the news they'd had the day before, to the new roommate they had. Or it could have been more.

"Yep."

Gabi's upbeat tone made Marie happier, too.

"Is it weird, being so newly married and now having a...roommate?"

From up on a ladder, leaning over the top of a tall shelving unit, Gabi chuckled. "You want to know what Elliott's like to live with, don't you? I could always send him down to you."

She wouldn't, of course. But Marie warmed inside, just thinking about the large man sleeping in her spare room. "Does he sing in the shower?" The question slipped out. Only because this was Gabi. And Marie was clearly spending too much time alone.

"How do I know?" Gabi laughed out loud. "His room is fifteen hundred square feet away from ours, and the bathroom is on the far side of that."

All of which Marie knew. She'd helped Gabi decorate the guest suite the month before.

Her friend called down numbers. Marie jotted in columns. And then held the ladder steady as Gabi climbed down.

"I'm losing it," she confessed, as soon as her friend was on solid ground. "Ever since Friday night...he's all I can think about. I mean, I thought of him a lot before that, too, but... I think you're right, Gabi. I'm falling for him. And it's nuts. I'm thirty-one, not sixteen. And I've only known him three months."

"I married Liam less than a month after I knew I had feelings for him."

"But you'd known him forever." They both had.

They stood there, both with their hands on the ladder, facing each other. "I just think that there are some things you can't quantify," Gabi said, her voice softer than Marie was used to hearing it. Gabi was the practical one of the three of them. The attorney who was always preparing for the worst. And counting every penny.

She dotted every i. Crossed every t. Marie tended to go more by the heart and forgot the i's and t's sometimes. While Liam just breezed by them, pushed them or found a way to get rid of them if they got in his way.

"And there are some things over which you have no control. No matter how hard you try." Gabi's eyes glistened. And Marie, nodding, reached out to brush a piece of her friend's short dark hair away from her face.

"Just let it happen," Gabi whispered, taking Marie's hand in hers. "Please, Marie. Just let go and let it happen. Elliott's a good guy."

"You really think so? Because it's not like I've got a great track record in that department."

"There's nothing wrong with your ability to choose a man," Gabi said, her voice getting stronger as she folded up the ladder and put it away. "You choose men who you know aren't going to tempt you to be in it for life. Men who are preoccupied by other things. Or who you aren't particularly attracted to."

"I do n…" Marie broke off as Gabi turned to give her the *look*. The one where she was challenging Marie to be completely honest.

"Freshman year," Gabi said. "He was more into his church than he was into you. To the point that you had to go to church with him to spend any real time together."

Maybe.

"And the doctor… He was in med school, Marie. And was going to be for some time. Years. He made it clear from the very beginning that his studies came first…"

"That still didn't give him the right to be unfaithful to me."

"Of course not!" Gabi was back. Right in front of her. "The guy was a schmuck as well as a med student. I'm just saying, you've never seriously dated anyone who didn't have something else that came first in his life."

"Then I'm doing it again," Marie said, her emotions settling down into some semblance of normal for the first time in what felt like months. "Because Elliott's career definitely comes first with him."

"Does it?" Gabi walked toward the door of the storeroom that led back into Marie's office. "Or is he just dedicated to his job? Maybe he wants a home and family just as much as you do but hasn't found the right woman yet."

In all of their talking, he'd never said much about his life. About his wants and needs. Marie needed to know about them. "Has he said something to you?"

"No. But if I were you, I'd be asking him the next time I had a chance."

"Yeah, right. Out of the blue I'm going to get all personal with him," she said. But she knew that the idea wasn't as far-fetched as she was making it out to be. While Elliott kept a professional distance, he'd also breached that line the other night when he told her he liked her. Too much.

She'd been going crazy ever since.

"So, you going to talk to him?" Gabi, with a handful of popcorn, sat down alone in the chair Liam had occupied with her the day before.

"You really think I should?"

"I think you want to, and if you don't, you'll regret it."

As usual, Gabi was right.

But Marie was still getting used to the idea of falling for someone. She wasn't ready to take that plunge yet.

CHAPTER TEN

ALMOST A WEEK PASSED. The Denver police had no leads on the man who'd hired a two-bit criminal mechanic to debilitate Liam's car. George Costas, the corporate attorney charged with fraud in conjunction with the Ponzi scheme that had been uncovered at Connelly Investments, still had no plea deal.

And Elliott Tanner was in real danger.

Marie Bustamante was not only a big part of his waking hours; she was appearing in his dreams now, too.

"What's up, Elliott? You look like I made your coffee too strong." The woman, dressed in black leggings, a cinched-in white top and her Arapahoe apron, slipped into the chair opposite him Thursday night. It was late. The shop was closed. Her last employee had left an hour before.

As had become their routine, she'd made him a cup of coffee—on the house—while he waited for her to tally up her day's income and make out the bank deposit that would be picked up the next morning by the free courier service provided by her bank. He'd then see her upstairs to her apartment before heading up to spend another long evening alone in his own room.

Liam and Gabrielle had invited him, every single night he'd been there, to join them. He'd politely excused himself.

He was working. And, until he'd met Marie Bustamante, he had always had very clear boundaries where his clients were concerned. The boundaries were blurred, but he was still determined to hold on to them.

"We should be getting upstairs," he said, picking up the napkin he'd dropped to the table when he carried his coffee over.

Her hand touched his. "Wait."

As carefully as he could, he extracted his hand. Picking up what was left of his coffee—cold now—and taking a sip.

"I…wanted to talk to you for a minute."

And her apartment wasn't the place to do it. He got where she was going with this. And relaxed. "What's up?"

Shuffling in her seat, she looked as though she wasn't sure what to do with her hands. Fold them together. Or leave them open on the table.

He voted for folded. In her lap.

They ended up on the table.

"I just…how much longer do you think this is going to go on? I mean, it's been almost a week and…nothing."

"If you remember, I told you last Saturday, in the office, that it's not all that unusual to have a period of inaction after an arrest. And this guy, while the frequency of his attacks might be escalating, doesn't seem to be in any hurry to let Liam off the hook. Either by hurting him or ending the harassment."

"So we could be living like this for months? Or longer? I got the impression last week that this was a very temporary arrangement."

"I expect it to be." Was she that eager to be rid of him?

Disgusted at the inane thought that he'd had it at all, and that there'd been real emotion attached to it, Elliott continued. "There was a surveillance camera at a shop across the street from the garage where our slasher was hired. I thought we'd get something from that." He hadn't told them before. Not while it had been part of the investigation.

"They didn't?"

"No." He'd just heard from the detective that evening. "But I believe, as do my contacts in the Denver Police Department, that once Costas pleads guilty, this guy's either going to back off completely, go after Costas or show himself again."

Marie nodded. Her brown eyes shadowed as she looked at him. Was she having trouble sleeping? Or was she just tired from a long day?

"Anyway," he said, feeling an uncharacteristic need to lighten the moment, "it's not like having me around is a death sentence or anything."

Was he actually asking for reassurance? From her?

Elliott sipped again. Things were getting out of hand. At least inside him they were.

"It's not like it used to be," Marie said, no hint of a smile on her face.

"What does that mean?" He'd only known her three months. Maybe if he reminded himself of that fact often enough, it would lessen the effect she had on him.

"We used to talk. All the time. You're the first man I've ever known, other than Liam, who I could talk to without measuring my words. I could just be myself with you…" Her voice faded and he wanted to know what she was thinking. Wanted to know everything that was in that fascinating and completely unpredictable mind of hers.

"I'm hard to talk to now?" Elliott groped

for ways to extricate himself. They weren't immediately obvious to him.

"I don't know, anytime I'm free, you're escorting me upstairs and are gone."

"I'm working." Completely true.

"Yeah, that's what I told myself. But the shop's closed now. The doors are locked. The blinds are shut. Liam and Gabi are safe upstairs."

He acknowledged the statements with a drop of his chin. "So talk." Her mother wanted him to keep her from getting hurt. If something was bothering her, he should know about it.

What if Threefold was having financial trouble?

There'd been no indication. And no indication, either, that Liam Connelly was foolish or frivolous with his money.

Or his father's company, either.

So what was bothering her?

"I just…you know how my mom sends me all those studies to read, and…" She broke off again. Shook her head. "This has nothing to do with any of my mom's studies. The truth is, I rarely read them anymore. Most of what I know is stuff she repeats to me ad nauseam when she calls."

"How often do you talk to her?" He'd wondered. Several times. He'd asked Barbara and she'd just said that she and Marie spoke regularly, in a way that let Elliott know that she didn't consider the information pertinent to the job he was doing.

"Used to be a couple of times a week. Lately it's more like every couple of weeks. Ever since the last time my father wanted to get back with her and I wouldn't get involved—maybe three or four months ago— she calls less and less."

Since Elliott had been on her payroll and had been giving her regular reports.

"Anyway, the thing is, you know so much about me...everything, really. You probably even know what kind of toilet paper I buy." Not that he accompanied her inside the store all the time, as he had the one time they went together. She and Gabi had gone to the grocery together that week, with Elliott waiting right outside.

"It's only for a little while, Marie," he said, leaning forward. "It's common for someone who's not used to being protected to get a bit of cabin fever. You're used to your freedom."

She shook her head. "It's not that. Though probably with Liam it is. But..."

He waited. Withstood the long look she gave him. And wasn't at all as prepared as he'd planned to be when she suddenly blurted, "What do you want out of life?"

"What?"

"What do you want? What are your goals? Do you ever want to get married? Have kids? You know everything about me, and I know nothing about you."

She could have whacked him over the head with a baseball bat and he'd have been happier. And better equipped to deal with her, too.

His immediate reaction was to shut her down with a single word. *No.*

But those big brown eyes bored into him. Trusting him to tell her the truth. He, who was bound by ethics to lie to her. "You know I have no siblings and that my parents were killed in a small plane crash when I was two."

He'd given her his life story late one night. Before he'd realized how dangerous sharing would be.

How the compassion she'd shown him, a grown man trained to protect, had touched him.

"And you have an aunt and cousin in California. Yes, I know. But that doesn't tell me a thing about you. About your life. Or your goals or..."

It shouldn't matter. He was a bodyguard. On the job.

"Why does it matter?"

She blinked. Sat back.

He was being paid not to hurt her…

And he knew that last thought was pure bunk. Justification for reaching out for her hand to hold her in her seat.

"I grew up on the outside looking in." He heard himself telling her something he'd never shared aloud before. "My aunt was great. She loved me and always made me welcome. But she was grieving, too. My mom was her older sister. Their parents divorced when they were little. Their dad remarried and their mom later died of heart failure. She, my aunt, looked at me and missed my mom. It was like I was always the cross on my mother's grave, never just a part of the family. Or even a full member of the family. I was the outsider—there because of a great tragedy."

When he started to feel like a sap, Elliott shut up.

"And later?" Marie asked, knocking him for a loop with the look in her eyes. No woman had ever looked at him quite like that. As though *she* could protect *him*.

And he couldn't pretend any longer that he didn't want her. All to himself.

"LATER I GREW UP."

Elliott answered Marie's question so long after she'd asked it, she had to think a minute about what he was saying and why.

"Of course you grew up," she said, recognizing that he was trying to wrap up their talk. But she wasn't done yet. Couldn't be until she had a clear understanding that there was nothing between them but her own imaginings, conjured up out of her own loneliness, the danger surrounding her friends and forced proximity to the bodyguard. She was driving herself nuts. "And when you grew up, did you ever think about having a family of your own?"

His gaze was piercing as he studied her. She had no idea why. And then he said, "Do you have any idea how it feels to be a foot taller than every other kid in school? To have to duck to enter your high school classroom?"

Marie was shorter than Gabi. Who was only five foot six. "Obviously not." But she remembered the stares he'd received, they'd received, when they'd been in the warehouse store together, and added, "You were on the outside looking in then, too, weren't you?"

She knew that kids weren't generally nice to anyone who was different.

He responded with that half nod of his.

"Surely you dated," Marie said next. "I mean, you're tall, probably the tallest man I've ever met, but you're gorgeous, Elliott. You're never going to convince me you didn't have girls falling all over you."

He grinned. And she heard what she'd said. She'd told him she thought he was gorgeous. Her face flamed. But…it wasn't as if it would be news to him. Presumably he looked in the mirror every morning. He was clean shaven, and that didn't usually happen all by itself.

"I like women," he finally said.

And it dawned on her what he was saying.

"You've dated a lot."

"Not until I was out of high school and had grown more comfortable with my size. But yes, I've had my fair share of women in my life."

"You dating anyone now?" She'd asked once before, the first month she'd known him, and the answer had been no. But that could have changed.

"No."

"Neither am I." He knew that. *Idiot.* She'd just been dumped by Burton—a guy who'd been too boring for words. "So, do you want a family?"

"Are you offering to be a part of it?"

Marie blinked. Held her breath. And then started to feel dizzy. Was he flirting with her?

"Sorry," Elliott said before she'd found her senses. "I just… That was inappropriate. We should be getting upstairs."

"What if I was offering?"

"Why all the sudden questions?"

"Because you said you like me too much." She'd made no conscious decision to put that right out there. She'd just been following Gabi's suggestion that she ask him what he wanted out of life. Because at the moment, she trusted her best friend's judgment more than she trusted her own.

"Yeah." He glanced down.

"Yeah."

He fiddled with his napkin.

"Because I think I might like you too much, too," she said. He looked up then. And his gaze told her what his words didn't.

She might be in deep.

But he was, too.

HE COULDN'T DO THIS. Couldn't let her confess feelings for him when he couldn't be honest with her about why he was there. He couldn't let her think that her feelings were unreturned, either.

"I think we should go on up," Elliott said

when the silence between him and Marie begged him to do something about it.

Like call Barbara Bustamante and quit this job.

"Liam has a sunrise breakfast, and we still need to go over last-minute protocol." Which he could do in the morning, but it was the best he could come up with…

Elliott saw the shadow a split second before he heard the sound of crashing glass. But it was enough time to dive for Marie and have her on the floor beneath him before things shattered around them. With his gun in his hand, he stayed over her, holding himself up enough not to crush her and waited.

Thirty long seconds.

Silent seconds.

Every instinct in his body screamed. Go after the guy before he got away. Never let Marie out of his sight again.

And he remembered the security guard out front. He'd be handling the situation outside. Unless he was hurt…

"Elliott?"

"You okay?"

"Yes."

He didn't want to move. And had to move quickly. Lifting himself away from her, Elliott shielded Marie while he took stock of her shop. The front window glass had a gaping hole. Glass shards stuck out all over. It was the kind of break that happened when someone threw something from a distance. Far enough that he could get away with it with a security guard manning the block. Not the kind you crawled through.

They were alone in the shop. He couldn't tell what was going on outside. But no one had tried the door.

With his cell phone at his ear, he waited for James Wilson, the Denver cop assigned to Liam's case, to pick up. "I don't think he knew we were in here," he told Marie. "The shop's been closed more than an hour, and the overhead lights are off. He's not looking to hurt you." That was his immediate professional assessment.

He hoped to God he was right.

CHAPTER ELEVEN

A COMMON FIREPLACE brick had been thrown through her front window. The guard out front had chased a hooded man he'd seen across the street right as soon as he'd seen the brick go through the window. He'd been several yards away from the shop's window and lost the guy before he got a good look at him. He'd called the cops next. And had been shocked to find out that Elliott and Marie had been inside.

There'd been a note attached to the brick—addressed to Liam on plain copy paper that could have come from any ink-jet printer in the city.

It asked one question.

Do you feel me yet?

If Elliott hadn't acted as swiftly as he had, Marie would most likely have been struck in the head.

She could have been killed.

But it was pretty obvious that the perpetrator hadn't meant to commit bodily harm.

Not yet, at least.

It was clear now, to the police and to Elliott, that someone was toying with Liam. Someone who wanted to make him squirm. See him hurt. Someone who probably was not going to stop until Liam had suffered.

As with any "game," the guy would continue to taunt Liam with proof that he could get to him. When issuing mere reminders of this fact failed to satisfy him, he would up his ante.

Everyone involved agreed on that point.

It was anyone's guess what upping the ante would mean to the guy.

But Elliott seemed to think that, based on the fact that every single act had been aimed at Liam—Marie's shop being the only public access the guy had to Liam—the escalated attempts would be aimed at him, as well.

While Marie didn't like any of this, she accepted the theory that she wasn't in immediate physical danger and so, when her mother called the next day, didn't mention the brick in her shopwindow. Her mother had always had an edge where Liam was concerned. No point in rocking that boat.

Elliott had had the window boarded up before the police left the night before. Between him and Gabi and Liam, her shop had been clean and ready for business before they all retired for the night. Liam had had a company there first thing that morning replacing the window. The full-time security that had been placed out front as well as in the back, not just when the shop was open, but twenty-four hours a day—at Liam's insistence and expense—was now of the gun-carrying variety.

There'd been no opportunity for her and Elliott to finish their personal conversation of the night before. Liam and Gabi had been with him when he checked her apartment as he'd dropped her off and then the three of them had gone on upstairs together.

He'd been downstairs that morning before she had, but before she could even greet him, Grace had walked off the elevator. Then he'd been busy reassuring the older woman—who'd seen the broken window—that everyone was safe.

Marie was open for business right on time, and life went on.

But he hadn't denied that he liked her too much. And now he knew she returned his feelings.

Barbara's call had come when Marie was upstairs, taking a break, just after lunch. She hadn't had much sleep. And had taken half an hour to sit on her couch alone with a glass of herbal tea.

"I have some news for you, sweetie." Barbara's voice practically bubbled over the line. But it was the hesitancy that also filtered through that had Marie opening her eyes and sitting up straight.

"What?" she asked. If her mother and father were reuniting for the third time, she couldn't pretend to be happy. Her mother was just going to be heartbroken again. And sooner or later, the woman would be unable to put herself back together.

Marie knew. She'd watched the decline over the years. She'd seen a strong confident woman lose all faith in herself until she'd become a paranoid fragile shadow of what she could have been.

"I'm getting married!"

She heard the excitement in her mother's voice. Knew Barbara wanted her to share in it. And she just couldn't.

Not again. She didn't say the words that sprang to mind first. Instead, she managed, "I just talked to Daddy last week and he didn't say anything…"

"He doesn't know yet." And there was the hesitancy again. "I thought it was best if you knew first because he's probably going to call you. I'm sorry, honey. You shouldn't have to deal with that, and I'll tell him to leave you out of it, but you know your father…"

Wait. Marie slumped back on the couch, her hand to her head. She shook her head. And sat up again. "You're getting married, but not to Daddy?"

"That's right."

Wow. But how… "Who are you marrying?" Had her mother gone completely mad?

"Bruce."

"I don't know a Bruce, do I? The only Bruce I've ever heard you mention is your therapist…"

"He's a psychiatrist, and yes, that's him. Dr. Bruce Mendholson. He's going to be here in a few minutes, but I told him I wanted to tell you about us myself."

"You're marrying your shrink?"

"Marie!" The sharpness of the tone surprised her. But made Marie feel good, too, in a little-girl kind of way. It was a remnant of the mother she'd known. The one who'd disciplined her. Set boundaries. And been an example to her.

"Don't be disrespectful, sweetie, please." Barbara's tone softened. "I know this is sudden. I knew you'd be shocked. Which was why I wanted to tell you first and by myself.

It's just… For so long I thought what I was feeling for Bruce was transference—it's not uncommon, you know, for clients to think they're falling for their therapists…"

Marie thought that was exactly what was happening.

"But after this last time with your father… I didn't hurt, Marie. I felt sorry for him. But I was fine. I realized I didn't need therapy anymore…"

"You quit therapy completely?"

"Yes."

"What about your medication?"

Barbara had been on one form or another of antianxiety and antidepressant medication since Marie was in high school.

"I've been off it for almost a year…"

"What?" Marie jumped up. Walked to the wide window in her living room, looking down at the street below. "You didn't tell me."

"I wanted to make certain I was ready, that I could make it without help, before I told you about it. My biggest regret is what my unstable relationship with your father did to you, Marie…"

"You've been medication free for almost a year." She had to get this straight. Barbara had been needy for so long…

Marie wasn't sure what to do with this new version of her mother.

"Anyway, after I quit therapy I realized that I hadn't needed it for a long time. What I needed—wanted—was Bruce. He makes me laugh. I make him laugh. He loves me in a way I've never been loved, Marie..."

She wasn't sure how much of this she needed to hear.

"Don't be angry, baby."

"I'm not." In the least. Shocked, yes. Doubtful, yeah, that, too.

"So... Bruce—he's, what, ten years older than you?" She'd met her mother's therapist once. When her mother had asked her to join them for a session. She and Gabi had been in town during summer break and Gabi had joined in, too. Because Marie had asked if she could. That must have been five years ago or so.

"Seven."

"And divorced?"

"He's never been married, Marie. I know it's hard to believe, but he said he just never met a woman he cared more about than his work. Until me."

Wow. It sounded like a fairy tale.

And a disaster waiting to happen?

"When's the date?"

"Next weekend. In Las Vegas. At our age, we just want to get the legalities out of the way and start living life. We're going on a nearly three-week Caribbean cruise for our honeymoon, and then, later in the year we want to take a trip to Italy."

A week and two days away. For once in her life Marie was speechless. Her mother was getting married—not to her father—in less than two weeks.

"I know I've shocked you, Marie. But please be happy for me, sweetie. Please?"

"I am happy for you." And she was also worried. "Even if the happiness in your voice only lasted a week, I'm thrilled to hear it, Mom. Truly. I'm just...as you say, shocked."

"Bruce and I... We were hoping that you'd be there. For the wedding."

Nancy and Eva could run the shop—especially with Grace there. And Sam would cover extra weekend hours, too, if she needed him.

"Of course I'll be there."

"And... Marie...bring Gabi with you, please? She's like a daughter to me. And I want her there for you, too..."

"Gabi's married, Mom, remember? You aren't all that fond of Liam. And I'm not asking her to leave her husband behind."

"I sent them a wedding present," Barbara reminded her. "And I'd expect her to bring him. He's part of the family now, too. Whether I'm fond of him or not."

There was no whininess in her mother's voice. Could Marie hope things really had changed?

She should have seen it before now. And maybe she would have if she hadn't been so caught up in her own drama.

She'd just been telling Elliott the night before that her mother's calls had been much less frequent for the past several months.

"I can't guarantee they can go on such short notice, but I'll ask them," Marie said. "I'll call you tonight and let you know my travel plans."

Barbara told her when she and Bruce would be arriving in a second city that never sleeps. Told her at which resort Bruce had already reserved rooms—for all of them. At his expense.

She told Marie, once again, how happy she was.

And then, just before she rang off, she said, "Do I have your blessing, sweetie? Do you think I'm making a mistake?"

The vulnerability that Marie's father had instilled in her mother wasn't gone. Maybe it never would be. And Marie didn't honestly know what to think. Except, "You should do what you've always told me to do, Mom. Listen to your heart."

"My heart tells me I need to do this. I *want* to marry Bruce. I can't wait. But your opinion is important to me, Marie. You really think I should go through with it?"

How the heck did she know? "I think a minute of pure joy is better than a lifetime of worry and unhappiness."

Which was all her mother had known in far too many years.

"Thank you, sweetie. I love you."

"I love you, too, Mom." Marie hung up the phone.

And burst into tears.

A NOTICE WENT out to all the Arapahoe residents, informing them of the recent coffee shop vandalism, listing the added security in the front of the building as well as the back, and assuring them that everything was in place to protect their physical safety. Marie, Gabi and Liam, with Elliott present on his insistence, held a meeting for any residents with questions or concerns after Marie's shop closed Friday evening.

Elliott didn't speak at the meeting. He stood

in a corner of the room, by the brand-new window, where he could see all the other windows, the locked front door and the hall leading back to the elevator, stairs and Marie's office, as well. He wasn't particularly concerned about imminent danger. He was just doing his job.

One he couldn't quit.

Whoever was after Liam Connelly was a threat, to be sure. One that was expected to escalate. At some point, if the police didn't catch this guy, violence was going to happen. But for now…

"We've not only doubled our live security coverage and have someone watching the building—both front and back—twenty-four/seven, but the police are also watching the area more closely. In addition, some of you may have noticed the crews working about the building this afternoon. We now have security cameras positioned strategically on every floor, in the elevator, in the front and back of the building, in the parking lot and in the laundry room." Liam, in jeans, and a shirt and tie, was addressing the mostly elderly tenants.

He fielded a couple of questions regarding his own personal safety from the tenants in the twenty or so apartments represented. The

Arapahoe had a total of thirty-eight apartments on eight floors.

Grace was there. And Elliott recognized the woman whose mother was a candy stealer, Janice. The mother, who was not present, was Clara. Dale and Susan Gruber had come down. Elliott heard Marie ask the woman if she'd enjoyed her trip to the theater. And was kind of touched by the way the woman's face lit up as she described the romantic date in great detail.

Matilda Schumann, wife of Ben, the smoker from Marie's floor, had come in alone.

He didn't see either Edith Larkin or her somewhat senile next-door neighbor, bathroom wanderer Gordon Brinley.

One of the two younger tenants was present. A man who wore black plastic-framed glasses and worked as a paralegal for a private law firm.

The other, a couple who'd been married within the past year, Elliott had only seen twice in the three months he'd been around the place.

Liam concluded the meeting and while Marie served coffee and cookies, Gabrielle answered a flurry of questions from the people who'd gathered around her. Elliott wanted to help. But he stood back.

Watching.

Because that was the job he was being paid to do.

"CAN I TALK to you all a minute?"

Elliott turned around at the door of Marie's apartment as she asked the question. Liam and Gabrielle had come in with him, as they had the night before, as he assured himself that nothing had been disturbed. He'd expected to be alone in his room within the next five minutes.

Needed some time alone. To assess. Plan.

To have a good long talk with himself. And pray that it worked as well as it used to do. Before he'd set eyes on Marie Bustamante.

"Something wrong?" Liam asked, placing his hand on Marie's shoulder. He was closest to her. And not for the first time, Elliott had to bite back a hint of irritation at the other man's perceived ownership of Marie. Gabrielle was his wife.

Of course, he knew the threesome had been best friends for more than a decade. Knew, too, that Liam would give up his life for Marie.

And knew that he had absolutely no business whatsoever feeling as though he was on the outside looking in. Or rather, being displeased with the feeling. Of course he was on the outside looking in. The Arapahoe belonged to the three of them. The friendship belonged to the three of them.

He was on a job.

Marie sat down and Gabrielle took a seat next to her, concern on her face. "I'm so sorry this is happening, Marie. You've had nothing to do with any of this and it's your shop that's taking the hit," Gabrielle said.

"What?" Marie looked at Gabrielle and then up at Liam. "Hey, we're in this together, you guys. I'm upset about the brick through the window because it means you're still in danger." She looked at Liam. "But I'm not upset with either of you."

"Then what..." Gabrielle's voice faded as Liam took a seat in the armchair perpendicular to them, leaving Elliott to remain where he was. By the door. An almost outsider.

He had a pretty good idea he knew what was coming. And wished it wasn't. Barbara Bustamante's call an hour ago had given him a headache that wasn't going to go away anytime soon.

"If you're worried about loss of business, I'll take care of it," Liam was saying, his elbows on his knees as he leaned toward the two women. "I've already spoken to one of

Connelly's top marketing people and will have something more solid for you by Monday…"

"No!" Elliott was a bit taken aback by the look of dismay on Marie's face as she replied to her friend's offer before he'd even had a chance to finish making it. "Business is booming and right now I can't afford to expand. We don't have the space, and I'm not prepared to hire and train more people. Besides, we promised that we'd keep Threefold and Connelly Investments separate entities."

She turned to Gabrielle. "Tell him, Gabi…"

Gabrielle smiled. "I already did. Before he made the call and afterward, too."

Marie stared at Liam, who looked prepared to stand his ground. Elliott had been right where Marie was. And was a bit curious to see if she'd get at least a compromise—which was all he'd ever been able to get out of the stubborn man.

Marie didn't blink. Neither did Connelly. Gabrielle looked from one to the other of them, her lips turned up in a slight smile.

No one said a word.

And Liam Connelly bowed his head in defeat.

Impressed, Elliott had to restrain himself from sporting his own grin. He'd wormed agreement out of Connelly several times—

but only by proving that Liam's physical safety and the safety of those he cared about was at risk.

"So, if this isn't about the brick, what's going on?" Liam asked. He glanced in Elliott's direction.

All hint of humor evaporating, Elliott kept his expression neutral. And hoped he was wrong about what was coming.

"My mother's getting married."

Nope, he wasn't wrong. Barbara had called him after she spoke to Marie. She wasn't thrilled about the way things had turned out in the conversation with her daughter—wasn't thrilled about the fact that now that Connelly and Gabi were married, she had to accept him as part of the wedding party. But she wasn't half as displeased as Elliott was. Or as she would be if she had any idea why Elliott wasn't pleased.

"You're kidding." Gabrielle's face held no pretense of a smile now. "Again? I really thought, this last time..."

"She's *not* going to do it again," Liam said, straight-faced, as well.

Marie shook her head, her eyes wide, and it looked as though she was trying to put on a happy face. "She's not marrying my father."

"What!" It was the first time Elliott had ever heard the prosaic attorney screech.

"Not your father?" Liam's tone changed, filled with more of his usual eagerness. "That's great, Marie! She finally let go and moved on."

"Who is he?" Gabrielle's question was sharp and shot right on top of her husband's congratulatory remarks.

"Bruce. Her shrink."

"We met him, didn't we?" Gabrielle asked Marie.

"Yeah, once."

"We liked him."

"Yeah."

Gabrielle nodded. "So maybe it's not so bad. I mean, I don't like the whole therapist/patient thing, but…"

"She's been out of therapy since that last round with Dad."

"That was right before we finalized Three-fold, right?" Liam asked. Elliott could have nodded right along with Gabrielle and Marie.

"Apparently she's been off her meds for almost a year, too."

"Wow." Gabrielle was smiling full-out now. "That's great news, Marie."

"I know." Marie nodded. Rubbed her hands together.

"So why aren't you happy?" Gabrielle asked next.

"Has your father called?" Liam asked. "He's not giving you a hard time, is he? You can get an order of harassment out on him, can't she, Gabi?" He looked to his wife.

And Elliott almost smiled. The man was a piece of work. A workhorse with a heart, who gave "make it happen" all new meaning. He was also irritating, frustrating and... kind of decent.

"No!" Marie said again. "No one needs to go after Daddy. Liam, I'm okay, really. You can relax."

"You don't seem okay," the other man offered with a shrug.

"Mom hasn't told Dad yet. And when she does, I'm sure he'll call. I can handle him. The problem is, the wedding is next weekend and Mom really wants you two to be there. I know it's short notice and there's probably no way you can leave..." She looked at Gabrielle first, then at Liam, and back to Gabrielle. "But I really want you there," she finished. "I don't want to do this one alone."

Marie's voice broke.

Elliott half turned away.

"Hey," Gabrielle said, and Elliott turned back in time to see her put her hand over Marie's. Elliott couldn't read Marie's expression now, but he saw her reach up a hand as though she was wiping away a tear. "I'm sorry," she said. "I'm being a selfish goon. It's just…first you and Liam. And then *Burton*. And now Mom…"

"We'll be there," Gabrielle said, shooting her husband a glance. "Liam's working a lot from home right now anyway. I can move my appointment schedule around. I don't have court Friday afternoon or Monday. And it'll be good for us all to get out of town for a few days. Away from this kook who's after Liam…"

Elliott wasn't a praying man, but he issued a silent request in the second that followed. One that would require Liam Connelly to say he couldn't possibly get away. Or even that he didn't want to.

"Of course we'll go," Liam said. And then added, "Are you sure the invitation included me?"

"Positive. I reminded her the two of you were married and she specifically said that you were part of the family now."

"Wow." Gabrielle knocked Liam on the knee with the back of her hand. "See what marrying me does for you? Gives you entry to the inner circles."

Liam was grinning. "I have to admit I never thought I'd see the day."

"Me, either." Marie and Gabi shared a grin as they both spoke at the same time.

Elliott knew that Barbara Bustamante didn't trust Liam. He hadn't realized how much the woman's disregard had affected the other man. Or the two women, either.

And that was when Liam turned to Elliott. He'd been expecting it to happen. Just wasn't sure what he was going to say. Or do.

Barbara expected him to show up in Las Vegas with them. She thought the trip would give Elliott time to observe the young financier in the city of sin. Specifically to see if he had his father's talent for, and addiction to, gambling.

Elliott doubted his ability to spend a weekend that would be emotional for Marie, in her company, without crossing professional boundaries.

"I guess you're going to Vegas," Liam said. Elliott had been hoping the other man would give him the weekend off. And had been trying to figure out a way to convince his number-one client, Barbara Bustamante, that he couldn't possibly leave Denver on such short notice.

He was trying to convince himself that he

could be just a friend to Marie, wanting to be there with her so she wouldn't be a third wheel everywhere they went.

Elliott felt compelled to tell Liam, "I don't expect you to be in any danger from this guy in Las Vegas." He couldn't ethically charge Liam for the hours in Vegas.

"Let's just say I'm getting kind of used to having you around," Liam said, sharing a glance with Gabrielle.

"That's not really necessary, is it?" Marie asked. Her voice was hesitant. And he was suddenly foolishly hoping that she was protesting his presence because she thought she should, not because she didn't want him there.

It would be for the best—her best—if she didn't want him there.

But he knew she did. Just as he knew he wanted to be there. With her.

"This guy's making me nervous," Liam said. And Elliott figured anyone would be hard-pressed to doubt the sincerity in the man's tone. "Who's to say he wouldn't follow us to Vegas?"

Everyone looked at Elliott. "There's an outside chance." One he couldn't completely discount.

"So, good," Gabrielle said. "It's decided. We're going to Vegas!" She made the announcement as if they'd just decided to vacation on a Greek isle.

Marie talked about the arrangements Bruce had made for their stay. Liam offered to have his secretary at Connelly book the flights.

And for the first time in his life Elliott wondered if he'd just taken on more than he could handle.

CHAPTER TWELVE

MARIE WAS TOO nervous to sleep. Too het up to
sit still. Had it only been a week since she was
in her bathroom with Gabrielle, getting ready
to go out to dinner on a pseudo-date with
her and Liam and Elliott? And now, in one
week's time, the four of them would be flying to Vegas to spend the weekend together?

She had her own room, of course.

As did Elliott.

But they'd be spending an entire weekend
together.

And her mother was getting married. On
hands and knees, scrubbing her bathroom
floor at ten o'clock Friday night, Marie
pressed harder on the ceramic tile that she
and Gabi had chosen as a replacement for
the ages-old cracked and yellowed linoleum
that had been in both bathrooms when they
first moved in.

If this relationship with Bruce was for real,
if he turned out to be good to her mother for
the rest of her days, then Marie was thrilled.

She was worried sick. After all, Barbara Bustamante had a poor track record when it came to her romantic choices—answering her father's calls, hoping, hanging on, remarrying him—all in the name of love. True love, she'd said.

And now she was suddenly over him? In love with someone else?

The floor was clean. Just needed to be wiped. Marie got an old toothbrush and worked at the grout around the baseboard. You could never be too careful about grout. And once it discolored, it was nearly impossible to get like new again.

Who looked at grout that closely?

Who cared?

Except a woman who was spending Friday night alone in her apartment. Because she chose to go out with men who would let her down. Men who had other priorities in their lives, according to Gabi.

Marie wasn't sure her friend was wrong.

But she'd seen what love did to her mother. How it took a strong, confident, smiling woman and slowly, year by year, chipped away at the smiles. At the confidence. And at the strength.

She wasn't going to be like Barbara.

Was that her cell phone? She stopped scrubbing, sitting back on her heels as she listened.

She'd left the phone on her nightstand. And yes, it was clearly ringing.

Dropping her toothbrush in the bucket of water she'd brought in with her, Marie ran. Someone was calling her.

A voice other than her own internal ones to pass time with.

Good Lord, she was losing it.

Had never expected to have such a tough time with Gabi getting married and moving upstairs.

Had never realized how much she'd jabbered to the other woman night after night after night...

"Hello?" She answered before she'd had a chance to read the caller ID.

"Hi, baby."

Marie's heart sank. Trekking slowly back to the bathroom, she said, "Hi, Dad," in her cheeriest voice.

"I just got off the phone with your mother."

At ten o'clock on Friday night? What had Barbara been thinking? Couldn't she have waited until morning? Until the light of day?

Barbara knew better than most how awful things looked, how much more difficult they were, in the dark of the night. Marie had certainly spent enough of those dark hours with her mother through her adolescence.

"She told you her news?" Marie asked. There was no point in prevaricating. Or pretending that her heart wasn't aching for him.

"Yeah, she told me. Bruce was there, too."

"You know him?"

"Of course. I went to several sessions with him over the years. Always at your mother's request."

"You don't sound bitter."

"I'm not. He's a good guy. And I'm not good for your mother."

Wow. This was going much better than she'd figured. "So...you're okay with them getting married?"

"No..." His voice broke. "No," he said again. It took Marie a few seconds to identify the sound she was hearing coming over the line. Sobs.

"Daddy?" she half whispered. In all the years...all the battles and hurt and back and forth...she'd never once known her father to cry.

"I blew it..." he said, clearly crying now. "I blew it..."

"Daddy."

He was in Phoenix. She was in Denver. What was she supposed to do? What could she do?

Except slide down to the floor, lean against the wall and talk to him.

Long into the night. About the past. And the future.

About wants and needs and about how, sometimes one person's own needs opposed another's.

And how a person can truly love someone and still, because of his own issues, hurt the ones he loves anyway.

Realizing, right along with him, that some things really were impossible and that some people just were not meant for marriage.

That some people were best spending their lives alone. Sometime in the wee hours of Saturday morning she hung up, scared to death that she, like her father, was going to be one of those people.

ELLIOTT DIDN'T HAVE a lot of opportunity to be alone with Marie that week. He arranged for her shopping trips to be in conjunction with Gabrielle's. But other than that, his schedule was out of his hands. Liam had two evening functions to attend on behalf of Connelly Investments—a charity art event and a dinner at a private men's club—and Elliott had to arrange for the front-door security guard to watch over Marie and escort her upstairs to her apartment.

She'd given the members of her staff who'd be covering for her that weekend fewer hours during the week, so she was short-staffed. And she was training Sam, the young man who worked full-time during the week, to cover Sunday's inventory and ordering.

But in deference to the fact that she'd let Elliott know his previous reticence had hurt her feelings, he made a point of stopping by at least once a day to say hello. To look her in the eye and ask how she was doing.

On Thursday, midafternoon, he found her alone in her office during a lull.

"You ready to fly out tomorrow?" he asked, standing in her doorway, hands in his pockets in an attempt to be nonchalant.

"I haven't even started packing."

He'd taken her and Gabrielle to a well-known women's dress shop earlier in the week. And while he'd waited out in his vehicle, they'd both purchased dresses for her mother's wedding.

Completely contrary to his normal ways, he'd wanted to ask what they looked like. But hadn't needed to as Marie chattered and Gabrielle responded all the way home. They were both going to wear short black shifts.

Gabrielle's was high necked but mostly back-less. Marie's was low cut in front, but high backed.

"How about you?" she asked when his mind had started to wander to what she might look like in that dress.

"Are you packed?" she tagged on.

"No."

He was taking the tuxedo he wore to formal events. And then his everyday blacks. Wardrobe wasn't much of an issue for him.

"Can you wear your gun in Las Vegas?"

"Yes. I'm licensed in most of the western states."

She was looking at him as though the sight of him in her doorway pleased her. And his attraction to her started to take over the more rational part of his mind.

He turned to go. Couldn't leave without saying goodbye.

Faced her again and said, "I've been wondering. You haven't mentioned your father, but Liam and Gabrielle both did. Have you heard from him?" He'd half wondered if the man could be a problem that weekend. Not for Liam. But for Marie. Or Barbara.

Jilted men, ex-husbands, were all too common as perps.

"Yeah," Marie said. "We've talked every day this week."

A man out of control?

"Is he coming to the wedding?"

"No, though Mom invited him." Marie stopped. Glanced at the forms on her desk and said, "She's trying to be friends with him."

"He's not open to it?"

"He wants to be."

Sounded like a man who could show up with some crazy idea that he wasn't going to let his wife, the mother of his child, marry another man. It happened. More than Elliott was comfortable with.

"So maybe he'll show up," he said.

Marie shook her head. "He's booked himself on a flight to Monte Carlo. He'll be in the air during the wedding. And drunk in a swanky hotel and casino for the rest of the weekend."

"He's a heavy drinker, then?"

"Nope. It's just the best plan we could come up with to keep him from doing something he'd regret."

"Like showing up to stop the wedding?"

"No." She frowned. "He really wants Mom to be happy. He knows he can't give her what she needs and thinks Bruce can."

It was Elliott's turn to frown. "He knows the man your mother is marrying?"

"He was invited to a few of her early counseling sessions."

Elliott nodded. Assessing. Looking for holes in what she was saying. For any sign that there could be a potential threat. For insight into the family in which Marie had grown up. The family that had helped make her the woman she was. For a key to her own emotional state.

Not because he saw a threat there. But because he'd promised her mother he'd protect her from hurt...

"So what would he do that he'd regret?"

"Get drunk here and call me or Mom instead of leaving her be to enjoy her day."

"Phones work from Monte Carlo."

"He's turning off international dialing on his cell. And hoping to meet some young Italian, French or Greek beauty who'll be bowled over by his good looks."

"Sounds like in some ways he's a pretty smart man," he said now. Thinking about Barbara. About what he'd heard of Marie's father.

And about the woman the two of them had created.

The woman who was looking up at him with a sheen of moisture covering those big brown eyes. "Yeah. In some ways. Just not smart enough to figure out how to be happy with only one woman. But that doesn't mean he isn't hurting. And it's hard."

She paused.

He nodded. He understood more than he'd like. Sometimes a man had to do hard things. Like lie to a woman who was quickly taking up the majority of his personal thoughts and starring in his dreams when he slept at night.

When he knew that her one vulnerability, the one thing that he could do to lose her forever, was to lie.

He'd called Barbara Bustamante the night before, after he'd returned Marie and Gabrielle to their respective apartments with their dresses—Marie first. He'd threatened to quit if the woman wouldn't let him come clean with her daughter about his place in her life.

Barbara had been adamantly opposed. She didn't want Marie to know that she didn't trust her to make her own choices. And most unrelentingly didn't want Marie to know that she'd lied to her by omission when Marie talked to her about Liam's bodyguard who would be joining them that week. The older woman had also been strong enough willed to remind him what was at stake if he quit on her.

Not only his own ruined reputation, but possibly danger to Marie as well because there was no way Barbara would be able to slide one over on her daughter again. And until Liam's stalker was caught, Marie's shop, if not her person, was in the line of fire...

"I worry about him," Marie was saying, still speaking of her father. "And worse, I feel so sorry for him..."

Elliott did, too.

"Anyway, sorry to go on like that," Marie said, standing. "It's time to get back to work." She approached him.

He was supposed to move from the doorway, but he didn't.

He stood toe-to-toe with her. Looking down over a foot into the eyes raised to his. And knew he had to protect her at all costs. From everything that hurt her. Even if one of those things was himself.

Lifting one hand, he pushed a strand of blond hair off the side of her face. There were always a few tendrils that had escaped from her ponytail by this time of day. "You don't have to apologize for talking to me, Marie. Not ever," he said.

Her gaze didn't waver. And she didn't step back. "I have a tendency to go on sometimes..."

"And I have an ear that enjoys listening to your voice." Some things didn't come with explanation. They just were.

"I'm glad you're going to be in Las Vegas," she said.

"Me, too."

Her lips were lifted toward his. He needed to kiss her. To claim her as his own.

And he needed to let her go. To send her away from him.

Before he could do either, she raised herself up on tiptoe and touched her lips to his. "Thank you," she whispered, and slid past him to hurry down the hall and back out to her shop.

CHAPTER THIRTEEN

THE WEDDING WAS scheduled for ten o'clock Saturday morning. To be followed by a catered brunch in the bridal suite.

On Friday night, while Elliott and Liam went with Bruce down to the card tables, Gabi and Marie spent the evening with Barbara, in her suite. They ordered shrimp and steak and lobster. The best champagne. And girly movies. Bruce had three cosmetologists sent up with portable whirlpool footbaths to give all three women manicures and pedicures with a full array of polish colors to choose from.

Barbara chose a light pink to match the pink gown with embossed white roses that she'd chosen to wear for her wedding. Gabi's nail color was a cross between red and orange. Pale, not bold.

Marie chose a deep maroon. With a hint of sparkle. For both her hands and her feet. By the end of the night all of them were wearing moderate-length gel-polished acrylic nails.

They ate and cried over *Fried Green Tomatoes*. And when Liam called saying the guys were on their way up, Gabi met him at the door and left. Marie was staying with her mother Friday night, while Bruce and Elliott both had rooms of their own.

The next day Marie would move into Bruce's room and he'd stay in the bridal suite with his new wife.

Bruce's older brother and his wife were also coming in the next day. Marie had never met them, but Barbara assured her the couple was lovely.

They were getting ready for bed. A king-size pillow-topped mattress on a platform.

Marie climbed beneath the covers on one side, feeling awkward. Strange. Sharing a room with her mom instead of Gabi.

The last time she'd seen her mom—when she and Gabi had taken a couple of days to go to Arizona between Christmas and New Year's—she and Gabi slept in twin beds in Barbara's guest room. They'd stayed up half the night talking. About being single. About the fact that Marie was never going to fall in love with Burton. They'd talked about Barbara and the way she seemed to have recovered from her ex-husband's most recent attempt to reconcile. They'd talked about the shop and Threefold. They'd been due to finalize paperwork on the LLC when they got back after the holiday.

They talked about Liam and the way he stood up to his father's abuse while still respecting the old man. About the woman he'd been engaged to...

And now, four months later, Gabi and Liam were married. Barbara was getting married to someone other than Marie's father. Burton was getting married.

And Marie was...

"You okay, sweetie?" Barbara's voice came from the other side of the bed. She didn't sound the least bit tired.

"Fine." Marie instilled her voice with a bit of the fatigue she'd been feeling. Not to be confused with sleepiness. No, her exhaustion was more emotional. But if her mother mistook it and left her in peace...

"You're not lying on your stomach. You always sleep on your stomach."

She'd been lying on her side. To stare out the fortieth-floor window at the scrolling and changing lighted billboards that lined the famous Las Vegas strip. Avoiding her mother, who was so close and yet so far away.

"You haven't seen me sleep in years," she said. They'd been sharing and talking all evening. She and Gabi and Barbara. She didn't want to share any more right now. "Things change."

"I saw you sleep when you were home for Christmas," Barbara said.

"You checked in on me?"

"Every night. Just like I've done since the day you were born."

Okay, that was weird. Or was it?

Would she ever know how a mother felt when she did that? She'd had her thirtieth birthday and…

No, now, that really was maudlin. She had lots of time before she had to start worrying about biology and her clocks.

"Tell me about this editor of Liam's," Barbara said next. Completely random. And yet Marie wasn't surprised her mother had picked up on the topic.

Gabi had mentioned that Liam had been texting with his editor before he left their room to go downstairs to play cards. Gabi had half thought Liam might be back upstairs early, to do some last-minute revisions. But had said she'd still stay for their girls' night together.

Marie rolled to her back. Staring at the mirror—she could see her mother, who was also lying on her back, without actually turning to face her in the bed. "What's to tell?" she said. "She's publishing a series he's writing on his father."

"You asked Gabi about her on three different occasions."

No. She'd just asked about her once. When Gabi had mentioned the text. And...no, wait, there'd been that second time. They'd been talking about Walter's affairs and Liam's taking over a lot of the responsibility of his father's company, and Marie had asked what June Fryberg, Liam's editor, had thought of the move in light of the story Liam had been writing.

Oh, and then there at the end, when Gabi had been leaving and Marie had wondered if Liam would be up late writing...

Okay, there had been no reason to bring up the editor again that last time, but...

"I'm just... I don't want Gabi hurt..." Marie's voice faded off. She didn't want Gabi hurt the way her mother had been hurt. Loving a man who might adore her but not be able to be faithful. A good man. Like Marie's father. One who would do almost anything for her.

And whose one weakness was enough to debilitate her.

"And you think Liam will hurt her? Something to do with this editor woman?"

"No!" Well. Maybe. "It's just… Liam has always had a bit of a roving eye where women are concerned. He used to talk to us about his girlfriends. And he told us how even when he was steady with someone…well, other women still attracted him."

"You've always told me Liam was the best man you'd ever known. You and Gabi, both. He's your best friend. You trust him with your lives. You went into business with him."

"He is! We do! I don't… I never expected the two of them to get married. I mean, I saw it happening, and I was happy for them. I *am* happy for them. I want them together. It's just that it was all so fast—going from best friends to…more than that. And I want them together forever. Not just for now."

She couldn't believe she was having this conversation. And knew that while she'd give her life for Gabi, it wasn't really just Gabi she was worried about. If she was going to believe that Gabi and Liam could make their marriage work, she had to open the door to the fact that a lot of marriages did work. That maybe Barbara and Bruce would live happily ever after, too. That maybe she'd been depriving herself of any chance to find out what that meant.

"More marriages work than fail, sweetie." Barbara's tone was soft. Somber.

Marie turned her head, looking at the woman who'd raised her, single-handedly when necessary. The woman who, no matter what she'd been going through, had always been there for her only child. "That's not what the most recent studies show," she said, though, as she'd told Elliott, she took the studies with a grain of salt.

Still, there was some truth to them. And Barbara had put a lot of stock in them.

"A psychiatrist, one of Bruce's colleagues from Harvard, actually, recently had an article published in a national journal of psychology. He says that some of those studies, the ones I used to take to heart and repeat to you, were not created by real statistics garnered from scientifically gathered information, but were results of skewed polls conducted by marketing companies who had been hired to promote companies that help others get over infidelity. Online relationship finders. That kind of thing."

"Places like the one where you read that seventy percent of men polled admitted to cheating on their wives?"

"Yes."

"But the US has national statistics. And those show that forty to fifty percent of first marriages end in divorce." She hated to admit it, but she'd looked. Three days ago.

"They also show that the divorce rate is declining. That ninety percent of the American public is married by age forty, and that women with college degrees who marry after the age of twenty-five are at the lowest risk of divorce."

Yeah, she'd read that, too. But…

"I made some mistakes, Marie." Barbara's tone was serious. "With you. I quoted statistics and figures, and maybe made some of the more bogus ones sound legitimate, because I was so afraid for you. You've always been so social. So open and loving. Ready to like everyone. You've got a huge heart. I was scared to death that as you got into your teens and early twenties, you'd be gooey-eyed like I was. And end up hurt. Like I was."

There were tears in Barbara's eyes. Choked up, Marie stared at her mother in the light coming through the window.

"I didn't want you to be like me. I didn't want you to follow in my footsteps," Barbara nearly whispered. "It was bad enough that my choices had ruined my life, but I felt so responsible for you, for the example I was setting. For the things you were learning at my hand…"

"I learned how to love at your hand," Marie said softly, trying to swallow the lump in her throat. And she'd learned how to protect herself by choosing men who didn't put her first.

"You were so trusting," Barbara said now. "It scared me to death. I was petrified some man was going to come along and take advantage of you. They say girls go for men like their fathers and…"

Marie wasn't trusting anymore. Not where men were concerned. If she'd ever been.

These days she was so lacking in an ability to trust a man that she was even doubting that her second-best friend in the world would be true to his wife. Her first best friend.

And she was alone.

Completely and totally alone.

"I'm just… I'm worried. I see what I've done to you, and I don't know how to fix it." Barbara started, stopped, and started again.

"You want me to suddenly open up and trust every man I meet?" Marie tried to lighten the moment. Life was what it was. People were, in part, what life made them. Experience had taught her that.

"No." Barbara didn't smile. "And that's the

worst part of it." she said. "I still worry that you'll be hurt. I want you to be discerning. I just don't want you to spend your life alone."

Marie didn't want to have this conversation. Didn't know what to say. Except "I'm glad for the things you taught me, Mom. I'm glad you love me so much. I love you, too."

It wasn't quite what she'd meant to say. So she tried again. "And I'm an adult now. I have my own mind and heart, my own accountability. It's up to me to learn from you and from everything else life has taught me."

"I know."

"I guess what I'm trying to say is that the choices I make aren't your responsibility. Or your fault, either."

That also didn't come out right.

"You're right, of course. But a mother never quits being a mother. She never quits worrying or looking out for her children no matter how old they get."

"I know."

So. Good. They'd reached an understanding. Marie was alone because alone was where her choices had led her.

And if she didn't like it, only she could change that.

But *not* being alone meant that someone else had to be involved. And she had no control over that someone's choices. Like Gabi choosing to marry Liam and move out.

Like what's-his-name choosing to move home to marry a girl from his church. And her med student choosing her coworker over her...

Like Burton choosing to go steady with the woman of his dreams. And her mother choosing to marry Bruce.

Like her father choosing to have girlfriends while he was married...

"I know you think my marriage to Bruce is too sudden." Barbara's voice once again broke the silence that had fallen. Only this time, Marie welcomed the sound.

Wished for a second there that she was young again. Young enough to roll over, snuggle up and be held within her mother's safe embrace

"I just don't want you to be hurt again," she said instead. The strong one. A role she'd taken on so many years ago she couldn't remember being without it.

And yet she had memories of the capable and confident woman her mother had once been.

"You know life gives us no guarantees of that. Tragedy could strike any of us tomorrow."

Yes, but...

"All the more reason to control the areas in our lives where we can prevent being hurt."

"So you think you hurt less alone than you would if you took a chance on loving completely?"

The question was curious, coming from her mother.

"You used to."

"No, sweetie, I didn't. Why do you think I took your father back? And kept letting him visit even though I was telling him we weren't ever going to get back together?"

"Because you loved him."

"Yes, but also because I loved having his companionship. Because he was my man, and I didn't want to be alone."

"So now you have a new man? You suddenly just stop loving Dad?"

When she said the words out loud, she sounded to herself like a disgruntled kid.

But that wasn't how she was feeling inside. At all.

"I'll probably always have warm feelings for your father. He's the father of my child," Barbara said. And then shook her head on the pillow. "But I haven't been in love with him, romantically, for years. He broke my heart, Marie. So many times. Until all that was left was scar tissue."

"You were still vulnerable to him."

"Yes. I still believed I needed him."

Turning to her side, Marie was inches from her mother, face-to-face, which was all that was showing of either woman, with covers up over their shoulders. "So how do you know you aren't just believing that you need or love Bruce?"

Barbara's smile grew slowly. And surprised Marie. It was an expression she didn't recognize on her mother's face. As if it held answers to life's mysteries or something.

Kind of like the Mona Lisa smile she and Gabi had made fun of during their freshman year art appreciation class.

Those days were so long ago. And seemed too close for comfort, too. As if she were still a kid hanging out with her best friend, rather than a grown woman with a successful business of her own and a slew of people who depended upon her.

"My past, my time with your father, was difficult. Painful," Barbara started slowly. "But it also served a purpose. A good purpose."

Marie wasn't following. And braced herself for whatever cockamamie thing her mother might come out with next.

"You know, they say that all things happen

for a reason. That sometimes the most painful journeys are the way to the greatest joys…"

She didn't want philosophy. She needed to know her mother was going to be okay.

"I knew the very first time I crossed the line from looking at Bruce as my doctor and started seeing him as a man, that my life had changed," Barbara said. She didn't look gooey-eyed. Nor did she sound it.

But she had to be suffering from the malady just the same. This was her mother. Not some twenty-year-old college girl who still believed in love at first sight.

"How long ago was that?" Marie asked. Curious. And trying to figure out what to say next. Did she try to discourage the wedding?

Or keep her worry to herself and give her mother the full support she so obviously wanted?

"Not quite six months."

"But you said…the whole transference thing. You thought you just had a thing for him, which is common between therapists and their patients. You said that had been going on for a long time." Or at least that was how Marie remembered it.

Something wasn't right here. It was up to her to figure this out. To be there for her mother.

"I'd had a crush on him, which I understood to be transference, for years. That's true."

"Did you talk to him about it?" Had the man taken advantage of Barbara?

"No. I knew enough to know what it was. That it wasn't unusual."

"I'm confused," Marie said, frowning. "So, when did you cross the line from therapist to man? What happened? Why did things suddenly change?"

Had the man come on to a lonely, vulnerable woman? Was her mother on the rebound?

"Nothing happened. I walked into his office one day to tell him that I didn't need therapy anymore, to tell him thank you and goodbye. He hadn't heard me come in. Didn't even know I was there. He was standing at the window, his shoulders were slightly slumped and he looked tired."

Marie waited, practically holding her breath. "So what happened?" she finally asked.

"That's it. I saw a man who was tired. Whose shoulders were heavy with the weight they bore. And long after I left his office, I kept seeing that man in my mind. Not the doctor. Not the medical professional who'd helped me. But the man."

The reply left Marie with more questions than answers. "So you said Dad's last effort to get back together was the catalyst. But you'd withstood his attempts in the past. What makes you think that this time is different? That you were really ready to be done with therapy?" She attacked the easiest confusion first.

"I'd been off medication for months. And your father had come to visit me."

Marie had known her father had tried, again, to get back with her mother. He'd tried to get her in the middle of it all. Neither of her parents had told her the attempt had included an in-person visit.

"At the house?"

"Yes."

Oh. Her stomach filled with dread. In-person visits always meant they shared a room. Maybe because they couldn't help it. Or just because they always had. Marie had never asked. But how could her mother have her father over and be suddenly in love with someone else? Marrying someone else?

Turning on her side, Barbara faced Marie, too. And sliding her hand out from under the covers, brushed a hand across Marie's face.

"He slept in the guest room, sweetie. Because I told him he could stay, but I had absolutely no desire to get back together. He brought flowers. Got on his knees and made promises. Big promises. Ones that should have won me over. He had this idea that he'd keep a tracking app on his phone, that I'd have all his accounts and passwords, he was putting a text app on his tablet and he'd leave that at home so I could see all his texts. He wanted us to have the same phone plan so I could see all numbers he communicated with if I needed to do so..."

Her father had told her about all his big promises. They'd been his attempt to keep himself in line. Because he wanted so badly to be a good husband to her mother. He'd need to have the measures in place that would ensure that he'd be caught *before* he cheated...

"I didn't want to live my life as a police warden," Barbara said, her eyes sad. "I couldn't face a life where I'd be constantly checking numbers and data and text messages to ensure that my husband was being faithful to me. I didn't want to even think about such things. And I didn't want to live life with your father anymore, either. I was saddened by the realization, but I wasn't heartbroken. I was well and truly over him. And that's why I went to tell Bruce that I wasn't going to be coming to counseling anymore."

"And then as soon as you told Bruce you were through, you started dating him?"

Marie had read the statistics, too. To appease her mother, she'd read far too much propaganda and professional opinion on infidelity and discourse on why men cheat. The ways they cheat. The probability of saving a marriage after cheating. How to save a marriage after cheating.

How to know when your husband was cheating. How to prevent him from cheating.

And one thing that had been clear in almost all the pieces she'd read was that women often turned to another man, another relationship, to give them something to lean on as they let go of an old one.

"We ran into each other," Barbara said. "I was at a shop I'd never been to before, getting new tires on my car, and he was there, too. He'd had a flat that morning, driven over a nail and was waiting for it to be fixed.

"I sat down next to him. He asked me how I was doing. And I saw those tired shoulders. I saw a man who had flat tires. And a life outside of counseling people. I asked him about himself. Somewhat to satisfy the curiosity that had been growing inside me ever since that day in his office. As it turned out, we'd just seen the same movie. We liked the same foods. The same kind of landscaping. He'd just had his redone. But mostly what struck me was the way he talked when he wasn't working. He has a sense of humor, a way of seeing the world, that delights me…"

Okay. Wow. Marie scrambled, looking for whatever had to be wrong in what her mother was saying.

"I knew, as I sat there in the greasy shop that smelled like rubber, that he was someone important to my life. As soon as I knew he felt the same, I was certain I'd finally found the right man."

"How can you be so certain, Mom? You remember the throes of first love. You told me about it often enough, when you warned me about how you'd fallen for Dad in the beginning."

"This is different, Marie. With your father there was always an element of…unrest. I don't know how else to describe it. There was excitement. And love. But there was…" Barbara shrugged, lifting the covers enough that a burst of cool air chilled Marie.

"With Bruce, there is peace. I know it sounds corny, but when you feel it, you'll know."

Peace. Gabi had said something similar the night before she'd married Liam. She'd said that it just felt right. That she wasn't worried. She saw all the dangers inherent in a relationship between longtime friends who knew more about each other than a lot of husbands and wives ever knew. Dangers inherent in people from two completely different social classes hooking up. Money mattered a heck of a lot more to Liam than it did to Gabi.

He was a fly-by-nighter. She was a planner.

If their marriage didn't work, Threefold would be in jeopardy, and the company currently held Gabi's entire life savings.

If their marriage didn't work, a lifelong friendship would end.

And Gabi had said marrying Liam still felt right.

"But..." Marie wasn't ready to give it up.

And didn't want to examine possible reasons for her to be holding so tightly to her need to believe that marriage was a business too risky to invest in.

"I need to marry him more than I fear being hurt," Barbara said. And then nodded, a smile breaking through on her face again. "That's how you know. When you need to marry him more than you fear being hurt, then he's the right one for you."

Maybe her mother's words wouldn't work for the general public, but to Marie, they made perfect sense.

They also calmed her enough to help her sleep.

Or at least to end the barrage of questions that had been attacking her mind.

Which was a good thing. She needed her rest.

Her mother was getting married in the morning.

CHAPTER FOURTEEN

ELLIOTT AVOIDED THE BRIDE. And her daughter. Dressed in the tuxedo he'd brought with him—one he owned for the occasions when he had to accompany clients to black-tie affairs—he trailed behind the bridal party as, all dressed in their finery, they made their way through the luxury resort to the small, discreet wedding chapel down a hallway on the second floor.

Until that point, he hadn't known there was anything small or discreet about Sin City. Nor had he known that the city famous for impromptu garish weddings officiated by Elvis impersonators also had on-the-spot facilities for more traditional unions.

He stood in the back of the chapel while final arrangements, including music and video choices, were made. The nondenominational pastor, Reverend Billings, introduced himself, gave a rundown of the proceedings, asked the bride and groom to choose their vows from the various ceremonies he had available and then directed the bridesmaids into a vestibule where they were to enter on cue. For the ceremony video that the bride and groom would have as a keepsake of their special day.

Barbara had chosen to walk up the aisle on her own. She'd be entering from the back of the chapel after her bridesmaids—Marie and Gabi—had taken their places from the side door. Bruce, Liam and Bruce's brother, Michael, were mingling up front, where, when they were told, they'd take their places at the altar.

Michael's wife, Erin—the token audience member—was already seated.

Elliott had it all down. He knew where every player was and where they would be when.

There'd been no one in the hallway as they approached the chapel. The outer vestibule had been vacant, as well.

Still, he was on the job. Prepared and focused.

"So?"

He turned when he heard the bride's voice. She was in the vacant vestibule. Talking in a pseudo-whisper so only Elliott could hear her. Because it would look odd for the bride to suddenly have reason to converse with Liam Connelly's bodyguard.

But as soon as she spoke, he knew what she wanted. Knew, too, that it was up to him to make himself available to her without raising suspicion.

She might be getting married. But her daughter's happiness was still on her mind.

Elliott texted Liam. Telling the other man to stay put. He was taking a very quick bathroom break.

And then he slipped into the vestibule.

"He played at a five-dollar table."

"And?"

"At the end of the night he was up a thousand."

"So he got lucky."

"No, he played smart." Elliott took some satisfaction in relaying this particular truth. Though he really had no reason to feel ownership of the outcome. Liam Connelly was just a job. "He took no big risks. And quit when he started to lose."

"Because Bruce was ready to come upstairs?" Most might have missed the hint of vulnerability in the woman's eyes. If he hadn't been trained to see such things, Elliott probably would have, too.

"Bruce spent twenty on penny slots, won thirty and then seemed to take great delight in cheering on Liam."

He wasn't being paid to spy on her intended. She'd never even hinted that he should.

But Marie had told him Barbara's history. She was Marie's mother.

And there he was, stepping out of bounds.

"He drank two beers. Liam had two, as well."

Barbara nodded. Looking a bit like a little girl, unsure.

"I had none," he added. Because the woman did that to him. Made him feel that he wasn't giving her enough.

"And women? Liam's a good-looking man. And there are women paid to please those with money to spend."

And Bruce had been at his bachelor party. A woman like Barbara, no matter how much she loved her soon-to-be husband and felt she was doing the right thing…had to have some doubts.

Not that it was his job to tend to that.

"Neither one of them did more than tip the waitress who brought them their beers." He'd have told her if either man had behaved differently. Because she was paying him.

And maybe…because he knew it would matter to Marie.

The woman he'd been hired to protect.

"One more thing." Barbara's eyes took on a steely glint.

He nodded.

"I need your word, here in this church, that you will never, not ever, tell my daughter that I hired you to watch over her." There was no vulnerability about the woman now.

She was pure businesswoman who knew her rights. With ethics on her side.

He knew his job. The answer was a given. And...

She held up her hand. "Do you think I'm stupid, young man? That I'm blind? Or that I don't know my own daughter?"

He blinked. Leaned back. Two minutes ago he'd been feeling sorry for the broad, and now...

"Marie has...issues. I'm to blame for a lot of them. If not all of them. And I'm telling you right now, she can't ever know that I hired you. You and I are the only two people who know. I haven't even told Bruce. As long as we agree never to say anything, she'll never have to know."

"I..."

"Please." She leaned forward, her tone no less adamant for being hushed. "We don't have much time. I've created the monster within Marie. It's up to me to do what I can to protect her from it. I know that I trusted you with my daughter's life…"

"Barbara?" Reverend Billings's voice came from inside the chapel. She wasn't standing in the opening as she'd been instructed to do. The music wouldn't start until she was in place.

So the video played smoothly afterward.

"Just a minute," she called.

Bruce was probably sweating bullets. Afraid she was going to change her mind. Two beers had loosened the psychiatrist's tongue the night before. He'd never met anyone like Barbara. Was having a hard time believing she really wanted to spend the rest of her life with a boring guy like him.

"If Marie ever knew that you're in her life because I'd hired you to be there…you think she'd ever speak to you again? And why else would you have called to ask me to let you tell her, unless you had some crazy idea that the two of you could hit it off?"

He was not going to answer to that. Not even to himself.

"She's too distrustful. The fact that you've gotten her to be friendly with you is a miracle I'm sure you can't fully comprehend. But I saw the difference in her the moment I saw her last night. And when you walked in behind her, when she looked at you, I knew you were the reason. And I'm warning you right now—it goes no further. Be her friend, if that's what you have to do to do your job, but in every other sense, stay away from my daughter."

"Ma'am, I—"

"She cried herself to sleep last night. She might like you, but she doesn't trust in relationships. And there will be other men for her to like. Men who haven't lied to her. Because, this I know, if she ever finds out that we've been duplicitous with her, not only would she shut herself off from you, but you'd probably be robbing her of ever finding someone else. If she's not already at that point."

And Barbara would lose the trust of the daughter she adored.

"Barbara?"

"Coming! I...pulled a thread..."

The woman was nothing if not clever. And determined.

"I know my daughter, Tanner," she said. "It would kill her to finally trust herself to a relationship and then find out that it was based on a lie. Leave her alone. And keep your mouth shut."

The woman didn't blink. "If you don't,

I'll sue you for everything you've got," she added.

Elliott was under pressure, unlike any he'd known before. A wedding party, a minister, was waiting.

He could only think of one thing to say. "I understand."

"I want your word on that. And you say nothing about our association."

He stood there, arms at his sides, feeling his gun beneath his forearm. Deflated. And hating this job more than ever before.

"Mom? Do you need help?" Marie's voice was coming closer.

"No! I'm coming! Get in place," she called. Waited to make certain her daughter wasn't going to appear and then turned back to him. "I need to know that you aren't going to sell me up the river to my daughter. Not for me, although that would definitely ruin my life, but for her. I'm the one person in this world, with the exception of Gabi, who she knows she can trust."

Maybe the woman should have thought of that before she'd hired a private investigator bodyguard to watch over her daughter.

"Tanner?"

The woman wasn't stupid. She had every base covered.

If he didn't agree to leave Marie alone, other than friendship, and to keep her secret, she'd do everything she could to ruin his career.

He couldn't fault her her motivation, though. She loved her daughter and was trying to protect her.

He just couldn't take the chance that Marie would never have anything more to do with him.

And really, she was only saying what he already knew himself. There was no future for him with Marie.

"You have my word."

PEOPLE WERE SUPPOSED to cry at weddings. People of the female persuasion, especially. Gabi didn't cry. But she had a tissue on hand to pass to Marie as Barbara looked into her intended's eyes and clearly and succinctly promised to love him until death did them part.

She promised to put him first. To be loyal. He promised the same. They each vowed to always protect the other.

And Marie could hardly endure all the emotions swarming inside. Happiness for her mother. Relief. Pure joy. Envy. Fear. And a loneliness that was threatening to smother the life out of her.

She didn't know what took her attention from the couple standing in front of the minister. Didn't know why she turned and looked to the back of the room where Elliott stood, in full wedding garb minus a boutonniere, his hands crossed at his midsection.

He overshadowed the room. Not because of his size. But because he was there. More than her mother or Gabi, more than Liam, she was glad Elliott was there.

Which made no sense.

And perfect sense.

He was there to guard Liam, but he was staring at Marie. She could feel him. As though he were holding her hand. Telling her that she was going to be fine.

That good things were in store for her, too.

The ache in her heart eased. Excitement filled the gaps.

He didn't smile.

Neither did she.

They just…looked. Giving and taking.

It wasn't until she heard the music start that she realized the minister had just told the groom he could kiss his bride.

The wedding was over.

And she'd spent the majority of it with Elliott.

CHAPTER FIFTEEN

HE'D BEEN TO Vegas before. But it had been a while. He'd forgotten the peculiar energy that buzzed up and down the Strip like a virus infecting everyone. Boundaries evaporated in Las Vegas. Partially because so did some laws. Many things that were illegal in other places were not only legal but openly accepted on the Las Vegas Strip.

The old saying about what happened in Vegas stayed in Vegas might not necessarily be true, but the perception that it was true clearly filled the veins of people who were probably straitlaced and responsible any other place on earth.

Not only did anything happen, but it happened twenty-four hours a day. Loudly. Boldly.

Las Vegas was one place where more people than he'd ever seen were capable of letting their hair down. It brought out the wildness in people—even those with only a tiny bit of wildness inside them. If it was there, Vegas would find it.

He had a wild side. Or he had had. It had been a long time since he checked in with it. Maybe he'd grown out of it. The point was, it didn't matter if it was there or not. It wasn't his to set free that weekend.

He had a job to do, and he was going to do it.

He accompanied the wedding party to the private brunch in the bridal suite, intending to stand back, to be the observer he was being paid to be—not a participant.

But when Liam insisted he come forward, and Barbara watched him without looking as though she was anything more than curious about him, he knew he was going to lose the battle.

Truth was, he'd been about to lose it anyway. He'd seen the chairs set around the square glass table in front of a wall of windows looking out over the mountains behind the strip. Eight chairs. The bride and groom sat together. Bruce's brother and his wife pulled out chairs that were side by side. Which left four chairs and Gabrielle, Liam and Marie.

Elliott couldn't let her sit alone. Even a guy who was just a friend wouldn't do that to her. Not on this day.

And the suite they were in was private. It wasn't as if he had to be on guard duty.

Seven people talked. About the wedding. The honeymoon. The food. Las Vegas. Their plans for the afternoon.

Elliott sat next to Marie. He ate. And when she smiled at him, he smiled back.

When she leaned over and asked him in a whisper if he liked his food, he nodded.

And when the meal was complete and everyone was having coffee, he leaned back, stretched his long body and was careful not to touch her as his hands fell to his lap.

Her rose scent had been filtering over to him the entire meal. And that dress…

He remembered the kiss Marie had given him back in Denver the day before they left.

Neither of them had so much as acknowledged it. But he was never going to forget the stupendous effect that chaste little peck had had on him.

As he sat there with her family, knowing that he was never going to have a real relationship with Marie, he thought about kissing her again. Really kissing her. For a moment he allowed himself to imagine that he and Marie were every bit as much a couple as everyone else sitting at that small private party.

And hoped to God that this time what happened in Vegas, even if only his mind, really stayed in Vegas.

MARIE HAD NEVER been to Las Vegas. By early afternoon on Saturday, she decided she loved the place. There was so much energy, so much to see and do. So much beauty.

There was filth, too, but she chose not to look at it. Not that day.

The luxurious resort in which they were staying was opulent. Beauty unimaginable and over-the-top, from life-size real floral art pieces that moved, mosaic art on ceilings and floors, live entertainment even that early in the day. Pretty clothes. Pretty shops. Pretty faces.

Her mother was married. She was laughing out loud. Something Marie hadn't even realized had been missing from their lives until she was pleasantly shocked by the sound.

Gabi and Liam were holding hands. Her new step-uncle, Michael, had just whispered something to Aunt Erin. And Elliott had sat next to her at brunch.

The party had broken up shortly after that as everyone went to change into jeans and sweaters for a day of adventure—except Elliott, of course, who stood out in his daily blacks. When she'd seen the length of the Strip, Marie was glad she and Gabi had packed tennis shoes.

She'd been alone in her hotel room while everyone changed.

But from the minute the party regrouped, Elliott had been by her side, staying by her side, as they made their way through the huge resort and out to the limo that was waiting to take them to the small airport that housed several helicopter pads. She was about to take a helicopter ride above the Hoover Dam, compliments of her new stepfather.

Elliott leaned in to ask her, "You scared?" He'd moved closer as the crowd grew thicker.

"Not in the least."

She couldn't wait.

For whatever Las Vegas might bring her that day.

As SOON AS Marie saw that the helicopter seats were in rows of two, the little dance going on inside her sped up. She and Elliott were going to be sitting together. As they had in the limo. She couldn't think of anything she wanted more in that moment than to experience her first helicopter ride, her first look at mountains and canyons she'd never seen before, with him.

"It looks like it's you and me again," he said as he buckled himself into the seat beside her in the back of the helicopter. Liam and Gabi were directly in front of them, with Michael and Erin directly behind the pilot. The bride and groom had their own helicopter.

"I don't mind if you don't." She was happy and didn't bother to hide that fact. They were in Vegas.

"Are you kidding?" He leaned over to speak so that only she could hear. "Of this whole group, you're the easiest one to be with."

Not the least bit romantic, but her heart soared anyway. She was grinning from ear to ear. As though she'd just received an avowal of everlasting love from the man of her dreams.

She was over-the-top. And didn't care. She was in Vegas.

And Elliott wasn't just another guy. He'd been different since the day she met him. Almost like what her mother had described feeling the first day she'd seen Bruce as a man rather than a therapist.

The pilot came on. Asked them all if they were comfortable. Checked their seat belts. Went over safety measures. Gave them a rundown of what they were in for. And told them it would be another couple of minutes before they were ready to take off.

Gabi turned around to ask, "You ready for this?"

"Yep!" Marie smiled at her. Gabi looked at Elliott and smiled back.

"Anyone want to go skydiving next?" Liam asked.

At which time Gabi elbowed him in the ribs. Whispered something to him. And he laughed. Marie had always loved Liam's laugh. It was full-bodied. Boisterous. Free.

But she didn't love it nearly as much as Gabi did. Liam and Gabi together...it made sense. Gabi had always been the one whom Liam had listened to most. When the girls had disagreed on ways he should handle things, he'd followed Gabi's advice most often.

Her friends were happy. Which only added to Marie's buoyancy.

The pilot was back. Rumbles filled the air. Marie felt ready to take off without an engine. Her hands clenched into fists on her thighs. She was ready for anything life had to offer.

And scared, too.

Nothing was as it had been.

Elliott moved. His shoulder touched hers, and she wanted to lean into him. And not just for the moment.

She, Marie Bustamante, who hadn't allowed herself to lean on a man since the first time her father walked out on them, wanted to lay her head on that shoulder.

She stared down. Bracing for takeoff. Knowing that helicopters weren't the safest vehicles.

Elliott's hand came into view. So much larger than hers. Strong and capable. It covered her fist, his fingers unfolding hers. And then intertwining with them. He was holding her hand. Elliott Tanner and she were holding hands.

Like a couple.

She was flying.

And they hadn't even left the ground.

THE FLIGHT WAS MAGNIFICENT. They had to yell to be heard, so no one said much. Marie saw such indescribable natural beauty that after a while she couldn't take it all in. Even the pristine blue of the sky became too much.

So she concentrated on Elliott instead. On the way he leaned over to see out. The expressions that crossed his face. Thoughtful. Assessing at every turn. And a weird kind of peaceful, too. His face softened in a way she'd never seen before.

Natural wonder? Because he wasn't working? Or because of her?

He didn't let go of her hand.

She didn't let go of his, either.

And she knew that holding hands with him wasn't going to be enough.

Not by a long shot.

THE TWO OLDER couples went their own ways after the helicopter ride. Michael and Erin had a flight that evening back to California. And Bruce and Barbara were spending the night in their suite before leaving in the morning for Florida where they were going to board their cruise. The flight back to Denver left a couple of hours before theirs so they said their goodbyes as soon as they all arrived back at the hotel.

Liam suggested that the four of them, he and Gabrielle, Marie and Elliott, hit the Strip. Elliott had the thought that he should call off on an evening of partying with Marie. But knew by the look on Liam's face that he'd be playing a losing hand if he tried to get the other man to stay in. Or to agree to go out without his bodyguard present.

Employer number one had just warned him off, and yet the second he'd seen the fear on Marie's face when they were ready to take off in the helicopter, he'd reached for her hand. Because he'd known she'd enjoy the ride if he did.

He'd be lying if he tried to convince himself he hadn't enjoyed it, too. It was becoming more and more obvious that Marie thought of him as more than a friend. He could no longer deny that he was falling for her.

But he'd given his word. Would lose everything, including her, if he pursued the relationship they both seemed to want and the truth ever came out.

Which it would. Somehow. Eventually. It almost always did.

As he was trying to come up with a good reason to leave the threesome to enjoy the rest of their day, Liam, employer number two, insisted that he wanted his bodyguard along with him as he perused the wonders that Las Vegas had to offer. Just as Elliott had known he would.

They were all three looking at him, and he knew it would draw more attention if he suddenly decided Liam was in no possible danger at all.

In spite of what his instincts were telling him in terms of staying away from Marie, he had to do as he was told.

THEY GAMBLED A little bit. Penny slots only. They ate. They had one beer apiece because in the casinos they were free, and they were in Vegas. What happened in Vegas stayed in Vegas.

Or so they kept telling each other as they walked from resort to resort with thousands of other people. On every corner men and women flicked cards at passersby. From what Marie could see, the cards depicted women posing with little or no clothing. Neither Liam nor Elliott seemed to notice. Gabi shook her head. Marie grinned and hooked her arm with Elliott's.

They were in Vegas.

By TEN O'CLOCK that night, Marie didn't feel like anyone she'd ever known. Her skin was alive. Buzzing. She wasn't the least bit tired. And couldn't wait to find out what was going to happen next. The city never slept. That meant the day never had to end.

Tomorrow would come. She would enter it when it did.

Gabi, of all people, suggested they go to the salsa nightclub they'd seen advertised in their resort. It had live entertainment. A dance floor. The three of them had learned some salsa in college. They weren't dressed for a nightclub.

And Liam had them on their way before

either Marie or Elliott had had a chance to disagree.

He also had Elliott on the dance floor soon after they got there, though it was obvious that Elliott had had no intention of dancing. Period. But when Liam wanted to dance with Gabi, and Gabi said no because Marie was the one who loved to dance and she couldn't do salsa the way she liked to without a partner, Elliott had given in to the demands Liam had made of him.

Marie wanted to feel badly for him, but she wasn't sorry. Most particularly not when she was on the dance floor with Elliott. As big as he was, she hadn't expected the natural rhythm with which he'd moved.

"You've done this before," she said as they stood, face-to-face, for a brief moment. He swung her out. Pulled her back into him.

"When I started getting so tall…"

With his hand holding hers, she twirled. And rested against him for a beat. "My aunt suggested that I take a dance class to offset the awkwardness."

Marie missed a step.

And fell head over heels in love.

AT MIDNIGHT, WHEN the band took a break, Liam suggested that the four of them head back to the casino to see how the tables were doing.

And Elliott was working again. Barbara was paying him to watch over the man. Walter Connelly had a gambling problem. Barbara wanted to know if Liam did, as well.

"I don't know how to play, but I'd love to watch," Marie said.

"I don't know how, either, but since you're so good at it, I'd like to know what it's all about," Gabrielle piped in. She and Marie were still in the jeans and sweaters they'd changed into after the wedding. Elliott followed them to the casino.

The dealer looked up as Liam slid onto a stool at a blackjack table with a ten-dollar minimum bid. He nodded. The other men and one woman at the table all nodded, as well. Making room.

They looked to Elliott. Who shook his head, taking a stance almost directly behind his number-two employer. If the dealer took him for what he was, Liam's bodyguard, so be it.

Anything and everything happened in Vegas.

HALF AN HOUR after they'd left the club, Gabi was sitting with Liam at the card table with a pile of her own chips in front of her. She wasn't betting high. She was just winning.

"She used to get so ticked off at Liam when he gambled," she said to Elliott. The two of them were in cushy armchairs in a lounge area just behind the card table, sipping diet sodas. A lounge with no live entertainment. Because it was still necessary to rest for a minute or two. Even in Vegas.

Marie had wanted a place to sit. Elliott had followed her. And was watching Liam as she spoke.

"Did he gamble a lot?" he asked. His tone of voice had changed. As though he was working again. Making note of things of which he had to be aware.

And Marie's heart softened even more. He wasn't just keeping Liam safe from bodily harm. He cared about his client.

And so she was quick to reassure him. "For a little bit, he did," she said. "During our first year of college. But it was only to get back at his father. Because he knew the old man would disapprove. I told him that was the wrong reason to do anything. But I understood. Gabi was just so disappointed in him for risking so much money—no matter the reason."

"He played high stakes?"

"Only after he won. Which he did a lot."

"And since then?"

"I'm pretty sure this is the first time Liam's gambled since his freshman year. He grew up hearing about what gambling did to his father. Knew how hard Walter had to fight to beat his addiction. Saw him build an empire from nothing. And then, as you know, he finds out a couple of months ago that his father had made himself vulnerable to blackmail because he'd returned to gambling and had used company funds to cover his debts."

Money that Walter had paid back before it was ever discovered missing. Money that was, technically, his to use as it had been a hardship fund that he'd financed with his own money and could terminate at any time.

But he'd left himself vulnerable. Making him ripe to cut a deal with his corporate attorney—who knew about the gambling—when Walter found out the other man had been running an illegal Ponzi scheme. In the end, Walter pleaded guilty to obstruction of justice in exchange for his testimony against George Costas.

A small roar came from the high-top table in front of them, and Marie grinned as Gabi turned around and gave her a thumbs-up.

"I can't believe that's Gabi up there," Marie said. Smiling. "You should have seen her even six months ago. Always so serious. Like her responsibilities didn't leave any time for fun."

Which in some ways was exactly as it had been. With a low-income single mother and two younger brothers at home, Gabi had been sending money even from college. She'd worked full-time, and still kept up a class load that allowed her to finish her undergraduate degree in the four years that her scholarship had lasted.

Her family, mother and both brothers, had moved down South a few years ago, but Gabi still sent them money.

"I saw her three months ago and she was that way," Elliott reminded her. "And I remember their wedding."

Marie and Elliott had been their witnesses at the courthouse for a five-minute ceremony. Because Liam had been adamant that there would be no press, and no Walter, trying to interfere. He was taking no chances on making Gabi his legal wife as soon as humanly possible.

Then they'd all gone out to lunch and then back to work.

"And you were at the shop when they got back from their honeymoon, too," Marie remembered. Liam had surprised Gabi with a three-day trip to Hawaii. As happy as Marie had been for her friends, she'd felt Gabi's sudden loss sharply.

"You saved me that weekend," she said to Elliott.

"Me?" His glance was completely personal again as he watched her. "I didn't do anything."

"You listened to me jabber."

"I told you before. I like listening to you. And you don't jabber. The things you say are interesting. Worth listening to."

He'd been hanging around the shop a lot back then. With the whole Connelly Investments thing going down. And anytime she'd been free, she'd sat with him. And after work, too, not wanting to go up to her apartment alone. She'd told him about meeting Gabi. And then Liam. About the years they'd all shared.

About the time she and Gabi had had car trouble in Denver and Liam had called his dad, who'd reluctantly rescued them. About the way Liam had always come to their rescue when guys were being jerks.

The table cheered again. This time it was Liam who turned around and grinned at her. Did it make her a bad person that she was envious of them? Her two best friends in the world?

"You should get married."

Had he read her mind? Marie stared at Elliott. Wished she had something stronger than diet soda. "That's not something I can make happen on my own."

Heart pounding, she watched people pass. A few were obviously drunk. Most were laughing. Having the times of their lives.

As she'd been doing all day long. With Elliott at her side. Pretending that he was really hers. That they were really a couple.

In some ways it had been the very best day of her life.

"There's a chapel right down the hall," he said to her, looking drunk, though she knew him to be completely sober. "I happen to know exactly how to get there and know, too, that they're open twenty-four hours a day."

She swallowed. Another roar of cheers came from somewhere. In the far-off distance. She'd been thrust into another vignette. Something that would never happen at home.

"I don't think they come with grooms," she said. Playing along with him. Her mouth was dry. Her palms sweaty. She picked up her soda. Held it with both hands.

"So I'll be your groom." He was joking. The grin on his face said so. Elliott wasn't a grinner.

"Okay."

His face sobered instantly. Completely. He sat forward, his elbows on his knees, hands crossed. And she prepared herself to accept his graceful letdown. To let him off easy.

To grin and pretend she'd been joking, too.

But just for the second, just one tiny second, she allowed herself to believe that the moment was for real. The sudden ache inside her was intense.

Consuming her.

The longing.

Not just for a marriage of her own. But for him. This man who'd walked into her life and been different from all the rest…

"I'm serious, Marie."

She dropped her glass.

CHAPTER SIXTEEN

"You have to know that I'm all for you and Marie hooking up, but this is a little crazy, man. Getting married at two o'clock in the morning?"

Back in their tuxes from the morning, albeit slightly wrinkled ones, the two men were standing in the chapel where they'd all begun their day—had it really been less than twenty-four hours ago?—waiting for the minister on call to show up.

Marie and Gabi were upstairs slipping back into their little black dresses.

It was crazy. He was crazy. But if he didn't do this now, he was going to lose her. Her mother had said Marie still didn't trust herself to a relationship. But all day long, Marie's actions had been telling him a different story.

She wanted him. As much as he wanted her. For the first time in his life, he had someone who wanted only him. Especially him.

Barbara be damned. She was wrong. And if he presented her with a done deal, if she saw how happy he'd made her daughter, surely she wouldn't cut his future out from beneath him. Because to do that would be akin to cutting her daughter's future, too.

"Our flight leaves in the morning," he said, as though that was explanation enough for his rush.

The real reason—because he'd never wanted anything in his life as much as he wanted Marie Bustamante as his wife—didn't sound rational even to his own ears. Or the other part—that he somehow knew that if he didn't do this now, he wasn't going to get another chance.

Back in Denver, with Barbara's paychecks and warnings pecking at him, he'd be too sensible. To conscientious. Marie would think he'd lost interest in her. And be hurt.

She'd shut him out…

And his word to Barbara? Was that worth nothing?

For most of his life, the only thing he'd had to stand on, to count on being there for him, was his integrity.

At the moment, in Las Vegas where anything was possible and people did things they didn't normally do, where they were happier than they normally were, he didn't care. He'd spent his entire life standing on his word from the outside looking in. Marie welcomed him in. She had since day one.

Liam looked around them. The lighting that morning, when combined with the sun shining in the windows, had seemed romantic. But now on its own was a bit garish. "Tanner, you do know there are other places to get married."

"I know."

"It's not like Marie's going anywhere…"

"You saying you don't approve?" He wasn't sure even that would make much difference at the moment. It was as if he were drunk, on some insane collision course, and couldn't stop himself. Whatever was driving him was stronger than anything trying to stop him.

Liam shook his head. "I've been watching out for Marie for well over a decade. I wasn't sure I'd ever see the day when a man walked into her life and had the power to break through the walls around her heart." He shrugged. "Marie needs you."

Now he was confused. "But you don't want her to marry me tonight." He wasn't the best catch. Marie could have children who grew up to tower over her.

Thoughts of children stopped him cold. And had his heart racing at Mach speed.

"I don't want you divorcing her," Liam

said. "This is pretty sudden. You sure you're in it for the long haul?"

"I knew a month after I met her that I wanted her to be my wife."

"I'd feel better if I'd been aware of that."

"You're my employer, Connelly. She's your friend." He hated the subterfuge and gave what he could of the truth. "But this is not your call."

"I'm still your employer."

True. But… "You going to deny that you set me up with her a week ago Friday night? That that dinner out after the shooting episode at the elementary school wasn't your weak attempt at matchmaking?"

Liam's ready grin finally surfaced as he cocked his head and said, "Must not be that bad at it if a week and a day later you're taking her to the altar. Maybe I'm in the wrong business…"

Elliott might have been subjected to more of Liam's cockiness if the minister hadn't come in through a secret door behind the altar, his hair somewhat mussed, in full robed garb.

"Who's getting married?" he asked.

"He is."

"I am."

Elliott and Liam spoke simultaneously.

"Who has the ring?"

Elliott looked at Liam. Who was looking at him.

"Where's the closest jeweler that would be open all night?" Liam spoke first.

"Right here," the minister said. "We have a decent selection of rings. If you'd like to follow me?"

Elliott was in over his head. He knew it. And he still didn't care. He was a man who'd learned long ago to live by his instincts. And they were telling him that marrying Marie was the right thing to do.

He turned to Liam.

"I'll wait here for the girls," the financier said. "And, by the way, Marie likes white gold."

Good to know.

Elliott nodded. And followed the minister out of the room.

"YOU THINK I'M CRAZY, don't you?" Marie moved closer to Gabi as they exited the elevator they'd been riding on alone, making room for the group of people who'd been waiting on the main floor to go upstairs to their rooms.

In their black dresses, the two stepped onto the carpeted hallway that led to the casino floor and throughout the resort.

Gabi took her hand, squeezed it, while the two moved as quickly as they could in their high-heeled shoes. "Believe it or not, I think that you're doing absolutely the right thing." She ran a finger through Marie's hair. It was curled a bit at the ends from the updo she'd worn that morning. Gabi had been ready to pin it back up, but for once in her life, Marie wanted it down. Loose and free.

She stopped in the middle of an aisle to stare at Gabi now, though, completely frozen with fear. Even at just past two in the morning, machines rang out bonuses as players sat pushing buttons again and again.

"Elliott might very well be the only guy who will ever slip past that iron gate you've got around your heart," Gabi said, pulling Marie closer to her and out of the way as a couple—obviously a little worse for the alcohol they'd consumed—teetered past them. "And I know you, Marie. If you don't do this quickly, you'll talk yourself out of it. I think you know that, too, which is why you're doing what you have to do. You're pulling one over on yourself."

"You make me sound crazy."

"I think you're careful. And paranoid where men are concerned. Not that that's your fault. But you love Elliott, don't you?"

"I haven't told him so." And she should, shouldn't she? Before she told someone else? Before she married him?

"And he loves you."

"He hasn't said so, either."

"Then I guess we have some business to take care of, don't we?" Always the practical one, Gabi led them around a corner, down another hall, up an escalator and to the second-floor chapel where their day had begun.

Marie stopped her just before she pulled open the door to head inside. Where Elliott would be waiting. She couldn't do it. She was in Vegas, but would be going home in the morning. And if she got married, what happened in Vegas definitely would not just stay in Vegas.

"Just…let it happen, okay?" Gabi whispered.

"What if I can't trust him, Gabi?" Marie asked, stilling Gabi's reach for the door handle.

"You don't trust Elliott? Has he done something to make you doubt him?"

"No." She shook her head. Feeling the little curls around her temples bounce. "I feel like I trust him completely. But that's kind of weird for me to say, isn't it? I mean, I've never trusted men. What if, after we're married, I can't trust him? Not because he isn't trustworthy, but because of me? Because I can't? What if I ruin things?"

"You need to tell him about your issues with men. And why you have them."

"He knows."

Gabi's eyes widened. "You told him about… everything?"

"And everyone." Marie was completely serious now. Needing her friend to show her the parts of herself that she couldn't find on her own.

"Wow." Gabi smiled. "I was beginning to fear there'd never be an Elliott Tanner in your life…"

"Yeah, I think I was, too. But…"

Gabi's finger touched her lips. "No buts. He knows how hard it is for you to trust and still wants to marry you. He knows what he's getting into. Now trust him to be up to the challenge."

Tears sprang to Marie's eyes. They were going to ruin her makeup. "Thank you."

Nodding, Gabi squeezed her hand again. And said, "You're absolutely sure this is what you want to do?"

Pausing, Marie made herself slow down. It wasn't as if there was another wedding pressing down upon them. She could take all night if she wanted to.

Or not get married at all.

Thoughts of Elliott's arms around her at the salsa club sprang to mind. Swinging her around. Pulling her in. Throwing her out. Bringing her back against his warm body. Catching her. Always catching her. She hadn't been afraid, even for a second.

"I'll be your groom."

"Okay."

"I'm serious."

"I am, too," she'd said. Or something like that. Maybe she'd just said *okay* again. The next thing she knew they'd been standing, holding hands and going to tell Liam and Gabi that they had to break up their card game for a wedding.

"Marie?" Gabi's voice was soft. Serious. And not the least bit threatening. She was there for her. Her support. No matter what she decided.

It had always been that way.

Always would be that way.

She wasn't alone. No matter how she'd been feeling over the past weeks, she wasn't ever going to be alone. Liam and Gabi and her...they'd been three misfits in college. Liam with his screwed-up dad. Gabi with her family who leaned on her but didn't understand the world she lived in, and her, with parents who didn't know how to love each other or to let each other go. Somehow three eighteen-year-old kids who'd needed family had found each other.

And formed a family of their own.

"I love you," she said to Gabi now.

"I love you, too. You want me to go tell them the wedding's off?" Gabi didn't seem disappointed in her. Or happy, either.

"No," Marie felt like the Mona Lisa when she smiled. As though she now knew the secrets. "Mom told me last night that when he's the right man, you'll need to marry him more than you fear being hurt. And…well… I need to marry him."

Gabi's silent smile, her tight hug, said everything else Marie needed to hear.

The door to the chapel burst open—and would have hit them if they hadn't both jumped back. "Oh, there you are," Liam said, sounding as though he'd just gotten out of bed and hadn't been up close to twenty-four hours. "I'm going to walk you down the aisle," he said to Marie. "I believe it's fitting that I give you away."

Marie laughed out loud. And nodded.

"But first, I must escort this lovely lady

to the altar, so she is there, standing by you. Now and always," he said softly, offering his arm to his wife.

And revealing the flowers he'd been holding behind his back in the process. "Oh," he said. "Here are your flowers." He handed a small bouquet of white roses to Gabi.

"And yours." Marie got an identical, but much larger, bouquet.

"Are we ready?" he asked, looking at the two of them.

"Yes," Marie said, but stepped forward when he offered Gabi his arm a second time. She was on his left. Marie hooked her arm through his right one. "We're ready," she said.

Together, at three o'clock that Saturday morning, the members of Threefold walked up the chapel aisle.

And with Liam and Gabi holding hands beside her, Marie Bustamante agreed to be Elliott Tanner's wife.

CHAPTER SEVENTEEN

THE PRACTICAL THING would have been to take a nap.

He noticed Marie looking at the shiny new ring on her finger as she walked beside him, holding his hand—the hand with the shiny new ring. He wasn't a jewelry kind of guy.

They were on their way to a wedding breakfast before going up to their rooms to change, pack and head to the airport. If there was time, they were going to stop at a jeweler's and buy Marie a diamond to go with her new band.

His wedding gift to his wife.

His wife.

He was married. Had the signed and witnessed certificate in the inside pocket of his jacket. His mind wasn't wrapping around the idea. But he was happy.

Maybe stupidly so. Because now that he'd come down off his high, he knew that his happiness was built on sinking ground. He'd married Marie under false pretenses. She had his heart, but she didn't know his truth.

He'd just sentenced himself to a life of hiding. And of constantly being aware that at any moment his happiness—and Marie's—could be snatched from them. If she ever found out that her mother had hired him…

Liam and Gabrielle walked a few feet in front of them. Breakfast was their treat, and Liam was looking for a place he considered worthy of the occasion.

Because, in Vegas, there were choices, even at three in the morning.

Elliott was more interested in setting up a home with Marie. Making a concrete life before the sand shifted.

"I don't mean to be presumptuous, but I'm assuming that you'll want to stay at the Arapahoe," he said when what he should have been doing was telling Marie how happy she'd just made him.

Marie stumbled. Her head bumping him halfway between his shoulder and his elbow. And he was reminded of how small she was. How easily she could be hurt.

He was reminded that he'd just promised to protect her for the rest of his life.

The thought of anything happening to her

scared him in a way he hadn't been scared since he'd been a little kid.

Elementally. To the bone.

And if she found out he'd lied to her about who he was? Even if only by omission? If she ever found out that her mother had hired him to watch over her, he'd lose her.

"I'd like to stay there," she said now. "I mean, if you want to move, I'll still be able to be there every day. I've got my shop. But…"

"I live in a one-bedroom apartment that's less than nine hundred square feet," he said.

"I have a three-bedroom apartment that is slightly more vacant than it was because my roommate just got married and moved out." She was grinning up at him.

"Good."

"It is good, isn't it?" Marie's big brown eyes seemed to see right to his heart, and it was as though they were in Denver. In her shop. Alone in the world.

"Everything with you and me, it just clicks," she said when Elliott couldn't find the right words to tell her all the things he was thinking. "You showing up right when I needed to find you. Us being in Vegas at the time that we're both finally acknowledging that we've found the person we want to spend the rest of our lives with. Our living arrangements gelling at just the right time..."

They'd left the hotel carpet for marble floor—were walking down a wide hallway filled with high-end shops on each side. The ceiling above looked like blue sky with clouds.

A sky that promised either sunshine or rain. Or neither.

She hadn't said she loved him.

They were married and he hadn't told her he loved her, either.

She thought they'd found each other by a quirk of fate. That they were simpatico. He wanted her to keep thinking that forever.

"I love you, Marie," he said as he walked by her side down that long hallway. "No matter what happens in our lives, I want you to know how much I love you."

She turned, looked up at him, and the smile she'd been wearing all day and throughout the night slid away. "That sounds ominous."

He stopped walking. Held both of her arms as he looked her right in the eye. "It's not." He swore it wouldn't be. Ever. Not because of him. Not if he had the power to prevent it. "I'm just that serious about this. I'm not declaring some note of passion in a moment of anything goes. I'm telling you, no matter where we are, no matter what we're doing, I love you."

Her eyes filled with tears. And she stood on tiptoe to bring her lips to his. "I love you, too, Elliott Tanner. So much." She kissed him then. It was the third time her lips had touched his. The brief caress outside her office. The more thorough but completely unsatisfying kiss with the minister and Liam and Gabrielle cheering them on. And now.

Elliott took her lips with his, sealing them together, a silent vow that nothing would ever split them apart.

And knew, even as he did so, that his word was worth nothing unless he told her the truth.

MARIE'S FIRST DAY married wasn't anything like she'd ever imagined it might be. There was another threat waiting for them when they got back to the Arapahoe. Of sorts. A package had come in the mail. It contained a bottle of the sports drink Liam drank. On the label in stick-on letters it read How Does It Feel?

She'd thought that was the threat. The idea that whoever was stalking him knew what kind of sports drink he preferred. As if he was being watched that closely.

Elliott told all three of them differently. He'd noticed that the cap wasn't sealed on the bottle and had immediately grabbed a towel, taken the bottle from Liam, placed it back in the box and backed up.

They'd been home less than an hour. Marie had been downstairs in her office, taking care of the weekend's receipts and deposits while Eva and Sam ran the shop, when Elliott called, asking her to come up.

No one knew they were married yet. Other than Liam and Gabi, of course. They'd all been up more than twenty-four hours. And she'd wanted a night to get used to the idea of actually being part of a couple before the residents, and her staff, converged upon her.

"No one touch that box," Elliott said. He'd already called the police. Before calling Marie upstairs.

"What do you think is in there?"

He was frowning. Moving around the apartment. "I have no idea. There's no liquid explosive I know of that would detonate by itself, but it could be laced with something. Cyanide, maybe."

Gabi's intake of breath filled the room. "He's trying to kill Liam?"

"I doubt that he expected Liam to drink it. He would have noticed the broken seal. And it bore a threatening note. I think this is more warning. Playing with him. Letting him know how easy it would be to hurt him. And showing, at the same time, that whoever is doing this means business."

"You think he's going to hurt him?" Marie asked. Life was as they'd left it. Someone was out there threatening Liam. And Elliott was working. It was as though the marriage that had happened in Vegas had stayed in Vegas.

Except that she had a shiny new wedding ring in her pocket. Matching the one Elliott had slid in his own. At her request. Just until they'd had some rest—and a night to get used to the magnanimous change that had just taken place.

"I have no idea what he's going to do," Elliott said. "But I know that only a mentally disturbed person continues on like this for months. And there's no telling what a mentally disturbed person is capable of doing."

Before he could say more, the police arrived. They asked their usual questions. Wanted assurances that nothing had been disturbed in Liam's apartment while they were gone. Elliott checked Marie's, as well. They talked to the security guards. And to Sam and Eva downstairs in the shop. No one noticed anything out of the ordinary.

When they were done, they took their notes, the box that had come in the mail and left. All Marie wanted to do was crawl into bed and sleep for a week.

It wasn't even six o'clock yet.

Elliott looked from her to Liam and Gabi. "I guess I'll get my things," he said.

And Marie felt that peculiar piece of joy start to unfurl inside her again.

She might be home again. Back to work.

But she was married.

To the man she loved.

And he was moving in.

THE FIRST WEEK of marriage turned out to be less...all encompassing...than Elliott had thought it would be. Sharing his nights with Marie was fantastic. Better than fantastic. When he was in her arms, he was willing to die there.

And when he woke up every morning, the sick feeling hit his gut. Toward the end of the first week, he could hardly stand to look at himself in the mirror of their bathroom as he shaved. On Thursday, still in her robe after a shower, she came up behind him just as he'd smeared his face with cream, slid her arms around his towel-wrapped middle and hugged him tight.

He wanted to turn in her arms and lose himself in everything good about her.

"I wish we could get out of the party tonight," she said. "I've always loved having people around, having parties, but now..."

Her body slid upward against his—standing on tiptoe—and she kissed him. "I don't want to share you," she said. "And I don't want to give up our alone time."

Other than work, they hadn't left the apartment all week. Had turned down two invitations to dinner with Liam and Gabrielle.

But everyone at the Arapahoe knew they were married and wanted to celebrate. After the first day, Marie hadn't been able to bear being without her ring. And Grace, with Gabrielle's help, had organized a reception for them.

Similar to one Marie had thrown for Gabrielle and Liam six weeks ago.

"Anticipation adds to enjoyment," he said, avoiding the mirror that was going to show him a picture of him and Marie together. "Maybe I should move to the other bathroom," he blurted before he'd even thought about what he was saying.

He didn't want to move. He wanted to stay right where he was. Sharing a bathroom, a life, with his wife.

The wife he'd married with a lie between them. Barbara Bustamante would be coming back from her honeymoon soon.

That reminder did not sit well with him, either. He'd lied to her, too.

"Am I bothering you?" Marie's hands dropped away from him.

She'd backed to the doorway leading into their bedroom. The room that had been hers alone for the past eight or nine years.

"Of course you aren't bothering me," he said. "I thought I was in your way. You've had this room to yourself for so long and…" He pointed to all his stuff on the counter. She'd said she was going to move some of the things that she didn't use every day into the cupboard in the spare bathroom to make room for him and hadn't done so yet. But stuff on the counter wasn't the problem.

The man in the mirror was.

The hurt he'd seen flash in her eyes quickly dissipated and Elliott breathed a sigh of relief.

"Whose fault is it that I haven't had time to move?" she asked him, grinning.

"Yours." He smiled at her. Might have tried to kiss her, uncaring of the shaving cream on his face, if she hadn't suddenly seen the clock on the counter.

"Oh, my gosh. The shop's going to open in

fifteen minutes and I'm not down there." She was in their bedroom, throwing on clothes, leaving him to concentrate on shaving.

He'd visited his apartment on Monday, long enough to grab everything he could fit into his two biggest suitcases, had emptied his bathroom drawers and vanity into a duffel. They were planning to spend Sunday over there together, going through the rest of his things. Deciding what to keep. What to donate or sell.

She'd be in his place. Going through his things. He'd show her the pictures of his mother. At some point he was going to have to call his aunt. Tell her he was married. Take Marie to meet her...

"I'm heading down." She was back. Fully dressed. Putting her hair in the ponytail he'd learned he loved to take out. He wiped the rest of the cream off his face and met her lips in a kiss that reminded him they were joined.

One.

Never to be separated.

"I'll be in as soon as I get Liam and Gabrielle to work."

"You can start calling her Gabi anytime," she said. "She's your sister-in-law now. Or as close to one as you're going to get. She's family."

He nodded. If it made Marie happy, he'd call her friend Queen Elizabeth.

"I love you," she called as she raced for the door.

"I love you, too."

The words came so naturally. And the stab that followed was just as potent. Marie was going to be in his place on Sunday. Going through his things.

He had records of deposits from Barbara Bustamante's checks there. Paperwork that she'd signed. She was in his list of business contacts...

If he hadn't remembered, didn't get over there to hide everything, Marie could have walked right in on the file folder on his desk.

And what if she ever did find evidence that he'd worked for her mother?

What about his computer? Barbara had emailed. The paperwork he generated for every client was there...

He added cleaning out his computer files to his list of to-dos.

Slid into black pants, a black button-up shirt and black shoes. Black. Fitting for a man who suddenly had a dark cloud of guilt, of fear, hanging over him. One he couldn't seem to shake.

And it wasn't just fear, he had to acknowledge to himself. It was shame. He was a man of integrity who wasn't being honest with his own wife.

He should have told Marie the truth. Being sued be damned. He'd had no idea loving Marie, holding her at night, needing to protect her from hurt, would instill into him such a sense of responsibility to be the best man he could be because everything he did reflected on her, as well.

He'd promised Barbara, outside a chapel, that he wouldn't betray her to her daughter. The woman, who was still on her cruise for another week or more, wasn't even around to defend or explain herself. But he'd also promised Marie's mother that he wouldn't pursue a personal relationship with her daughter.

Truth was, he'd acted selfishly. He'd married Marie because he loved her too much to let her go, knowing that she loved him, too. He couldn't walk away from her when he knew she didn't want him to do so.

But she wouldn't ever have wanted to be lied to...

He couldn't expect her to love him when he was beginning to not even like himself.

He couldn't put any faith in a union that had a gauntlet hanging over its head.

Waiting to fall. To take her away from him.

Keys in hand, he pushed the button for the elevator that would take him upstairs to collect Gabrielle and Liam.

He had to tell her the truth…

She was happy. In love.

A miracle. As Gabrielle and Liam had said every single day that week when he'd driven them to work. Neither of them could believe the change in her. The glow about her.

It was a miracle, all right.

One that was as fragile as Marie's newfound ability to trust.

If she found out he'd lied, before he told her himself, believing that he'd never planned to tell her, the damage would be worse. At least if he came clean, told her why he'd kept his secret, surely she'd give him a chance.

If she loved him as much as she said she did.

She'd know he'd never wanted to deceive her. She'd know he'd married because he had needed so desperately for her to be his wife.

Their love would see them through. After all, love was stronger than any of the evil forces that opposed it. Or so he'd been told.

All a man had to do was live with integrity and happiness would be his. Right?

He was going to stop borrowing trouble. Stop worrying. He'd tell Marie the truth and trust that everything would be just fine.

CHAPTER EIGHTEEN

"DADDY? IT'S ME." Marie turned her back to the closed door of her office Friday morning, leaning forward in her seat. "I have something to tell you."

"What's up, baby?"

She opened her mouth. Stared at the boring black walking shoes on her feet—shoes designed for those who stood all day.

"How was your flight?" He'd texted her when he arrived back in the States late the night before.

"Fine. Long. Same as always."

"And Monte Carlo? Did you win?"

"I did." Could mean monetarily. Might not. "Now, what do you have to tell me? Is it about your mother? Is she...okay?"

Translation: Did she go through with it?

"She's married, Dad." Her mother's business was her own. Barbara had given Marie's father enough of her life. But... "And I really think she's going to be happy. Bruce considers himself a very lucky man."

"He is one." Her father was not. The unfinished part of the sentence hung between them.

There wasn't a lot she could say to it. Her father had blown it. Many times. And now wasn't the time to lay anything else on him.

Or look to him for reassurance.

Her mother was on her honeymoon on the ocean or some island. And...

"Okay, well, I just wanted to hear about your trip," she said, changing her mind about the phone call.

She'd say goodbye and go make the best coffee drinks she'd ever made.

Elliott would be back soon. He had a meeting with a Denver detective and the FBI agent in charge of the Connelly case, Gwen Menard, later that morning. Apparently the report had come back on the boxed sports drink bottle.

"Wait! You said you had something to tell me."

She'd called in a moment of weakness. Of doubt. Afraid she'd let loneliness, her mother getting married, Gabi's marriage, all the change convince her that she was a marrying type of person. But what if she wasn't? What if she was her father?

Not in the cheating sense, but in the not-being-able-to-be-a-good-spouse sense.

She loved Elliott to distraction. But when he'd said he had the meeting with Gwen Menard, she'd had a doubt. For a second there.

Okay, for more than a second. She was still, that very minute, doubting.

"It's okay, Dad. We can talk about it another time…"

"Tell, me, baby. Whatever it is. I've been a good dad to you. The issues with your mother aside. You've always been able to come to me…"

"I… I don't really know how to tell you this…"

And didn't want to talk about the rest of it. Not anymore. She'd deal with her doubts. Beat them down until they didn't dare surface again.

"Just say it right out. Whatever it is. You're scaring me. Are you sick? What's wrong?"

"I… I'm married, Daddy."

Silence hung on the line. Total silence. For a second she thought they'd been disconnected.

But then she heard him take a deep breath.

"I knew I should have waited to tell you." First her mother. Now her.

"No! You should have told me sooner," he said. And Marie felt like an idiot.

"Oh, Daddy. It's not what you're thinking. I didn't deliberately cut you out. It wasn't planned! It was crazy, really. I'd been falling for this guy for a while, but wouldn't let myself admit it. Remember before when I called you late that night and you asked me if I was in love? Well, I guess I was and just wouldn't let myself see it. And then there we were in Vegas and it was the middle of the night and…it just happened."

"Does he consider himself a lucky man?"

Like Bruce did. Did he love her that much? She got the question.

"There's no doubt that he loves me as much as I love him," she said. And wished that the world were perfect enough for that much love to be enough. To guarantee happiness regardless of life's challenges. And people's issues.

"You really love him?"

"Oh, yes. There's no doubt in my mind about that."

Another pause. "So, what are the doubts in your mind?"

"Love wasn't enough for you."

"That's me. That's not him."

"It's not him I'm worried about."

"You think you'll be a cheater?" He couldn't

have sounded more astonished. She had to hold the phone away from her ear.

"No! I really and honestly don't think that," Marie said. "I'm not even worried about it. I'm worried about my ability to trust. What if I screw up and get all paranoid on him?" *What if I'm like you, Daddy, and love isn't enough to keep me healthy and happy in a relationship? What if it isn't enough to make me a good wife?*

She and Elliott should have talked about it before they'd married. About how her inability to trust, her paranoia, could affect their relationship. And now that it was too late, she wasn't sure how to bring it up to him.

They probably should have talked about plans for the future, too. Like where they'd been going to live. If either of them wanted a house in the suburbs someday.

Did he believe in starting college funds...?

Did he want kids?

"I suspect that if he gives you no cause to doubt him, he'll have nothing to worry about."

It was Marie's turn to hang on the line in total silence.

"A woman gives her whole heart to her man, baby. She's an emotional creature. More so than men a lot of times. It's in the genetic makeup. And in one sense, the instinct to bond and give all makes you vulnerable. To counteract that vulnerability, to protect her heart, a woman is given another emotion— an instinct that tells her that something isn't right. Sometimes she can hear it. Sometimes she listens to it. Sometimes she doesn't want to be bothered by it. But it's there for a reason. Be thankful for it. Trust it. And you'll be just fine."

By the time he finished, she had tears dripping off her chin.

"Thank you."

"Don't thank me yet, young lady." Her father took on a tone from the olden days. "I'm going to be flying to Denver as soon as I can get a ticket. I intend to meet this man."

"Can you wait at least a week or two?" she asked him. "We're still in the process of getting him moved in, and we'll want you to stay with us."

He harrumphed. And then said, "Can I at least have a name for this man who has become my new son-in-law? Can I know what he does for a living?"

"He's a licensed private investigator and bodyguard who runs his own private business. His name is Elliott. Elliott Tanner."

She was Marie Tanner. She still wasn't used

to that. And was struck anew with the oddity of life's changes.

She'd been talking to her father, and he hadn't even known her last name.

ON HIS WAY back to the Arapahoe after his meeting with law enforcement regarding his employer and now pseudo-brother-in-law, Liam Connelly, Elliott glanced at the digital screen on his dash as the phone rang.

Sailor Harcourt.

He had information to discuss with the members of Threefold, LLC. One of whom was his wife. He didn't need the hassles associated with a billionaire's spoiled daughter. However reformed.

Two more rings pealed. And a question was raised. Why was Sailor, Rod Harcourt's daughter, calling him? Why wasn't it Rod's ID popping up? Rod was his client. And had always been the one to make contact.

"Tanner here." He pushed the button on his steering wheel that activated the Bluetooth call pickup.

"Elliott, thank goodness. I was afraid I wasn't going to reach you, and I only have a few minutes to speak in private."

If Rod were hurt, or God forbid, deceased, his daughter wouldn't need to speak in private.

"I need your help, Elliott." He didn't like the sound of that. And had no intention of taking on any other jobs right then. Had no intention of being free to escort the stubborn and spoiled young woman ever again. He couldn't risk his reputation guarding someone who refused to follow his dictates regarding her safety. He'd dodged a bullet last time.

Few got that lucky twice.

"Are you in Denver?"

"Not yet, but I'm going to be."

There was time for her to find someone else. "I'm on a full-time job right now, Sailor," he said, watching his speed as he took the freeway back downtown. "I've got names I can give you…"

"It needs to be you, Elliott."

A bodyguard worth his salt was a bodyguard. He had names of associates worth their salt.

"The situation is…sensitive. It involves Terrence Metcalf."

The yacht designer. Elliott had let his charge ride with Metcalf to breakfast. He couldn't have forced her into his car. But he could have made himself known to the man. Put the fear of God in him if anything happened to Ms. Harcourt. He could have called her father, his employer at the time, and let him know that his daughter had refused to get in the car with him.

But he hadn't.

Because she'd been sober. And thought she'd met someone real. The guy had checked out. And Elliott had been dealing with an attraction of his own that he couldn't pursue.

He acted out of emotion. Commiseration.

His neck tensed.

"And I only need you for a few hours. Next Saturday night. A week from tomorrow. I land at five-thirty and fly out again at eleven."

His two-week anniversary. He'd planned on spending it at home with his wife. Still planned to. But…

"What's going on?"

"Turns out the guy's a bit of a stalker. Not anything I can press charges against. He just gives me the creeps. And won't give up. I've blocked his number, he found me on Twitter. I have to be on social media for the magazine. He also found me on Facebook, Pinterest, Tumbler and Instagram. I blocked him where I could. Then last week, he showed up at a charity dinner I was attending. He's got money, Elliott. He's a charmer, well-known and well liked. He can get whatever invitations he wants."

He got the picture. "I'm not really sure what I can do to help."

"Just hear me out a second, and I'll tell you," she said. He figured, considering the circumstances, that he owed her that much. He'd been preoccupied the last time Ms. Harcourt was in Denver. Hadn't done his best night's work.

He'd kept her safe. She'd never been out of his sight after she left the nightclub that night. But he'd let her get into a car that wasn't driven by him.

He passed beneath the sign that indicated his exit. Five miles ahead. He had a ways to go yet.

"I made some really stupid mistakes when I first became an adult. And earned a reputation I'm not proud of. This past year, with my work at the magazine, I've managed, slowly and in one small circle at a time, to gain some respect. There are those who probably won't ever forget little Sailor Harcourt and her drug use and antics, but I'm a different woman, Elliott. I can't afford another scandal."

Four miles until his exit.

"This guy, Metcalf, as soon as he found out who I really was, he figured I'd be up for a fun time. I've done all I can do to convince him I'm not that girl anymore. He's not taking me seriously."

He didn't like where this was going.

"I've asked around about him quietly. He's got a really good reputation. I don't think he goes around preying on helpless women. I think he got the wrong impression about me. I mean, I lied to him the first night I met him about who I was. He thinks he's all part of my game. He also thinks I was traveling without a bodyguard. That I've got this whole other life that he wants in on."

Three miles. And he really didn't like where this was going.

"I've been invited to a fund-raiser at the police commissioner's mansion in Denver," she said. "It's to benefit victims of domestic violence, which is the cause I've chosen to donate my energy and money to…"

He wondered why. Didn't ask. Didn't want to get that close.

"The commissioner knows my father, of course, and I know that's why I was invited. But Dad's not going to be there."

"Let me guess, Metcalf is."

"Yes. And so is everyone who is anyone in this fight. Political advocates, monetary support advocates and famous spokespeople, as well. They've invited me to be one of three speakers. I'm representing the magazine, explaining the different ways we are a benefit to the cause. I have to be there, Elliott, or look like I'm full of expensive air. I want to show everyone I can put my money where my mouth is."

One mile. And he knew what was coming.

"I don't want anyone, including my father, to know how stupid I was three months ago in Denver. And it was stupid, pretending to be someone I'm not. I just…"

"It's okay, Sailor. You stayed sober." A big reason why he'd given her the respect of choosing which car she rode in.

"I've been sober since that last time you escorted me in Denver two years ago. I can't remember much about that night, but I remembered how disgusted you looked when I sat in the back of your car, ready to get sick."

She was probably working him on that one. He didn't need this.

"You're the only one who knows about my night with Terrence the last time I was in Denver, other than him, and he's not going to tell anyone that he picked me up in that club thinking I was a nobody. He might be decent, but he's not dumb. He has people to impress who look down their noses at such things. Right or not. And you've seen him.

You'll be able to pick him out instantly just by his build."

She knew him well.

"But I know a different side to him and I wouldn't put it past him to follow me around at the benefit, and then catch up with me afterward, refusing to take no for an answer. He seems convinced that he's going to have the same fun time with me that others have had. He thinks I was holding out on him, that I owe him or something...

"I need you to go with me next week, Elliott. As my bodyguard, but posing as my boyfriend. Terrence never saw you that night. From what I hear, he has a definite code. Maybe just to keep his reputation sterling, or maybe because he's not a horrible guy. But from what I hear, if he thinks I'm taken, he'll leave me alone. Hopefully after that Metcalf will have gotten the message and leave me alone, period. If not I'll figure out something else when I get home. Right now I'm just going crazy about next week's gig. It's a private affair. No press, so it's not like your face would be plastered on a tabloid or anything. Please, Elliott. Help me out here. I already promised my father I'd call you or he was going to do so himself. Just like he always does when I'm in Denver. I just don't want him to know about Terrence..."

He got the picture. Problem was, he understood. And felt as though he owed her.

He also felt as though he owed her father. Whether Rod knew what was going on or not. He'd hired Elliott to keep his daughter safe that night a few weeks ago.

Clearly he hadn't done the job well enough.

And could now fix that.

"And I'm paying you because I pay my own way these days."

He took his exit.

"I'll pick you up at the airport," he said. "I'm assuming you're flying in on your father's jet?"

"Yes. But only because he's feeling hurt that I'm not letting him do more for me."

She didn't have to convince him anymore. He got it.

Just as he knew that he'd helped get her into this.

And was going to help her get out.

CHAPTER NINETEEN

SO THE NEWS wasn't good.

"The sports drink was spiked with cyanide," Elliott said. He'd been the one to suggest Chinese takeout after picking up Liam and Gabi from work. But none of them were eating very much.

Sitting at her own table, instead of Liam's, while her husband told her and Liam and Gabi what he'd found out that day, Marie said, "So, if he drank it, it would have made him sick?"

"It would have killed him." Gabi's cheeks were white. She'd set her fork down.

"He knew I wouldn't drink it," Liam piped in, shoving food in his mouth, but chewing a lot more slowly than normal. "The seal was broken. If he'd wanted me to drink it, he'd have found a way to inject the stuff into the bottle without breaking the seal. He also wouldn't have left the note on the label, clearly warning me that something was amiss."

Elliott nodded. He wasn't eating much, either. Which was really unusual. Danger was his business. And he'd been protecting Liam from this creep for months without losing his appetite.

"So he's upped his tactics because it wouldn't be any fun if Liam grew bored and started to ignore him." It made sense to her.

"Possibly." Elliott nudged her arm with his elbow. And when she looked at him, he leaned over and kissed her.

A reminder. That he was there. That they were going to be fine.

Or maybe just because he loved her and wanted to kiss her.

Then, his face serious, he looked back at Liam and Gabi. "There were no usable fingerprints on the box. And none on the bottle or the letter stickers. The guy's wearing gloves. Probably some kind of medical glove, based on the powder they found on both the bottle and the Bubble Wrap inside the box."

"They sent the Bubble Wrap to the lab?" Gabi's question was more indication that the situation they were dealing with was more serious than anyone had first believed.

"With the other various warnings that have been arriving over the past couple of months. Things are clearly escalating and because

Connelly Investments is involved they're giving this a lot of attention."

"And?" The question was Liam's.

"The same type of powder was on all of the letters that have come."

"We've got one stalker." Marie didn't want dinner.

"Who's either in the medical field—which would explain his access to cyanide—or knows someone who is." Gabi closed up the half-filled cartons in the middle of the table.

"He could have purchased the gloves at any medical supply place."

"But he can't just go buy cyanide, can he?" Liam sat back, his hands on his thighs as he addressed Elliott.

"No. But there are all kinds of ways to get it. Legally and not. They're following up on all legitimate ways they can, but it'll be a sheer stroke of luck if we get this guy that way."

"It's possible, though, right?" Marie cleared away the paper plates, some with food still on them, and dumped them in the trash.

"If he made a mistake, yes. And everyone does, eventually."

"And until then?" Gabi, who'd put the cartons of leftover food in the refrigerator, was back, standing at the corner of the table she and Marie had picked out together several years before.

"We continue as we are," Elliott said. "With the addition of the Denver police keeping someone nearby on every shift. We've got armed security on both the front and back doors. I'll be checking the mail every day. And none of the three of you go anywhere without an escort."

"Meaning you," Marie said.

He shrugged. Looked at Liam. "That's your call," he said. "There's no way, as Marie's husband, I can be considered impartial. If you want me to stay on the job I will. But there'll be no hurt feelings if you need to hire someone else."

"Anyone else would drive me crazy," Liam said. And then grinned. "Half the time you drive me crazy and I like you."

"We're going to be fine," Marie said. Life would throw them some curveballs. There would be challenges. But she knew that between the four of them, they'd handle whatever came their way.

As long as they stuck together.

She wasn't going to worry.

Or let fear run her life.

She was going to let herself have her happily ever after.

ELLIOTT WAITED UNTIL after the rush Sunday morning to head downstairs to the coffee shop. He'd taken some time, first, to look around and figure out where the possessions he wanted to bring with him might fit in. How he could complement Marie's décor, while having a piece of himself at the same time. As soon as the first rush was done, he and Marie were heading over to his place. To pack up the rest of his things.

Overall, he thought the prospects of his stuff fitting in with hers were good. As long as she was agreeable to his antique gun cabinet in the room that used to be Gabrielle's. They'd already discussed the fact that his bed would fit in there nicely. To have when her mother and Bruce came to stay. Or if his aunt ever did. He still hadn't called to tell her he was married. He had to tell Marie the truth before he could accept congratulations from the woman who'd raised him.

Hopefully Marie wouldn't have too much of a problem switching out the nightstand on his side of the bed with the locking one he had next to the bed in his apartment. It was where he kept his ammunition.

And there was no reason to think she'd have a problem. The wood actually matched what she had in her room. Just the style was a little different.

He was walking around, frantically cataloging his possessions in his mind—looking for a place for himself to fit in, to make Marie's apartment as much his home as it was hers—because he didn't want to think about their life together disintegrating around them.

Couldn't think about losing her.

And had to face the very real possibility that he might. He should have been honest with her from the beginning. And had waited far too long to tell her the truth once they got home.

But with the threats against Liam hitting them the second they'd walked in the door, and then being so exhausted by the time they'd finally been alone that first night... The next morning, waking up beside her, he couldn't even think about taking the happiness from her gaze.

He'd screwed up. Bad.

Yet, each time he'd missed his opportunity to tell her the truth, he'd done so for the same reason. Because they loved each other so much. How did you knowingly hurt the one you loved?

He still didn't know how.

But before he moved his things into her home, he had to tell her the truth.

MARIE CLIMBED THE flight of stairs up to Elliott's apartment with anticipation. She'd never been there before. Hard to believe, considering that she was married to him. But her work, her family, her life, were at the Arapahoe. He'd become a part of that life.

Which made it easy to forget that he'd had an entire life separate from her such a short time before she'd so impetuously and rashly married him. Elliott was a man used to being his own boss.

Answering to no one.

Used to dealing with women—alone—and sometimes in dangerous situations. Guarding them, even.

If she was still worried about what might have or have not been said or done at his meeting with Gwen Menard—apart from the obvious Liam information that she'd passed along—how was she ever going to deal with the rest of what she didn't, and sometimes couldn't, know?

"Funny how all this time, you've only lived a few miles away…" she said to him. "You've been here in town what, four years?"

He'd told her once, back when they were

chat mates in her coffee shop. "In this apartment, yes."

The glance he gave her was swift. Minus a smile. He'd been searching for the key on his ring. And yet...for the first time since she'd known Elliott Tanner, Marie knew a moment of fear. Real fear. Not imagined.

Not of him. At all. But of...something.

The intuition her father had spoken about?

"I warned you, I've only done a little packing up," he was saying as he pushed open the door. He'd slipped over a couple of times during the past week. In preparation for this Sunday move. Boxes were stacked along one wall. Packing paper and tape were there, too.

And Liam and Gabi, along with a small rented moving van, were on call for later that afternoon. The hope was that by evening Elliott would be able to turn over his keys and permanently vacate the apartment.

In Marie's mind, that would be when their marriage would really begin. When the only home either of them had was the one they shared.

"You don't even have your computer unhooked." She blurted the first thing that came to mind. Pushing aside uncomfortable feelings—a surge of them from the strange look she was pretty sure she'd seen on Elliott's face just before they'd come in the door—she focused on the task at hand. Getting the man she loved moved out of his old place and into his new one. With her.

"I hate dealing with the cords," he said. "Besides, with my laptop at your place, I wanted something hooked up here in case something urgent came up while I was here this week."

He was never without multiple forms of access to information. She knew that about him. He smiled at her. Kind of sheepishly. "I'm sorry I left so much undone," he said.

Maybe that was why he'd looked strange just before entering the door. He'd been feeling guilty about how much work there was ahead of them.

Shaking her head, Marie chuckled. And let the insidious doubts that plagued her slide away. "I expected to work hard today," she said. "We talked about going through things together to decide what to keep and what to donate. Or—" she walked over to peek into his bedroom "—we could check out the mattress first and see if we want to put it in the spare bedroom, or switch it with the one in ours."

His was bigger. And Marie liked the idea of going to bed every night in her apartment on the mattress Elliott had occupied before he'd met her. Melding their lives until the two became one.

EVERYTHING THAT COULD fit in a box was packed and stacked along the appropriate wall. The far end of the living area was for the things that were going to charity. The bigger pile, closer to the door, would soon be going on a truck bound for the Arapahoe. They had the truck already.

And were just waiting for a member of the Arapahoe security detail to drive Liam and Gabrielle over to help them.

His time was up. He'd told himself he'd tell her before he moved out of his apartment into hers. He'd been putting off the inevitable ever since.

All afternoon, as they'd packed box after box, he kept telling himself he still had time.

In less than half an hour Liam and Gabrielle would be joining them. The moving out would begin.

He had no more time.

Marie looked exhausted, but exhilarated, too, as she surveyed the less than nine hundred square feet of space that had been home to Elliott for four years—and to them for the past six hours—as though she couldn't wait to get home and officially settled in to their new life.

For a second there he talked himself into not saying anything. The time wasn't right. And what did it hurt, really, if he told her before he moved in, or afterward?

When the thought occurred to him that it would be better to wait because it would be harder for her to kick him out of her life if he didn't have anyplace else to go, if his things were already comingled with hers, he knew that he had to get off the slippery slope.

He was on the verge of crossing the line into manipulation.

There was no justification for that. Except selfishness.

He had two choices. Protect his client. His career. And hope that Marie would never find out the truth and his marriage would be saved. Hope that he could learn to live with the man he'd become, knowing that his integrity was a farce. Knowing, every time he saw his mother-in-law, that she'd know it, too.

Or he could tell Marie the truth and risk losing everything anyway.

"What's wrong?" Marie had finished taping the last box and was looking at him.

He opened his mouth. Tried to fill his lungs

with air. To find believable deniability. To tell her nothing was wrong.

"I have something to tell you."

The blood drained from her face, leaving her pale, as she slid down to sit on the box of books she'd just packed.

"It's Gwen, isn't it?" she asked. And it took him a second to figure out she was referring to the FBI agent.

"No! I haven't heard anything else about Liam's case, if that's what you mean. I need to talk to you about something else."

He sat on the floor in front of the box. Wanting to take her hand, but afraid the act would be a purely selfish one.

"I'm not going to like it, am I?" Her gaze was direct, which was why he could feel her fear all the way through him. He shook his head.

And all the words he'd rehearsed over the past week flew out of his mind as he said, "I knew your mother before you introduced us in Las Vegas last week."

She frowned, clearly just confused at first. "You'd met her before? Why didn't you say so? For that matter why didn't she? Are you telling me she didn't remember you?" Her voice had started to raise.

This was not going to be easy. Or go over

well. He knew that. Just as he knew there was no going back.

Part of him hoped Gabi would get there soon. Marie was going to need her.

"I hadn't actually met her," he said, inanely. As though that detail mattered.

"How?" Marie stood her ground, even sitting. Smudged T-shirt and all. "How did you know her?"

He straightened his shoulders when he wanted to drop his head to her lap. "She hired me." The words were killing him. He felt their blow.

He could feel the room deflate. Like a tire losing all its air. There was no anticipation, no energy or sense of family there. At least not that included him.

His gaze settled on his wife, on the emptiness in those brown eyes, and he lost every ounce of energy he had.

He'd known it was wrong. All of it. Marrying her. But way before then, too. Since he'd first started to fall in love with his client's daughter. He should have gotten out then.

Or been strong enough to fight the attraction.

Instead, he'd made one bad decision after another. For good reason, possibly, but he wasn't even sure about that anymore.

Maybe he'd just convinced himself the reasons were good. Because he'd met Marie and her friends, been taken in by the closeness they enjoyed, three nonbiologically related family members. He'd met Marie. And felt things he'd never felt before in his life. Hope. He'd started to see a future he'd given up without even realizing he'd done so until it was suddenly there, in front of him. For once in his life he'd refused to settle for being on the outside looking in.

"What did she hire you for?" The question was a good full minute in coming. Her voice sounded...cold. Something he'd never heard before. Not even with an irate customer.

Liam and Gabi would be there soon, and Elliott didn't doubt for a second that they'd both spring to action, too, just as soon as they knew what Marie needed them to do.

"To investigate Liam and watch over you," he said to her. He could leave it at that. But didn't. "Originally she was concerned because of the three of you forming a company and buying the Arapahoe. You'd told her you were sinking your life's savings into the deal and she was afraid Liam had talked you into something. It was supposed to be a quick job. Simple investigating, a written report and out."

Barbara's mistrust of Liam hadn't ever been a secret. But then, she mistrusted most men.

"She thought I had a thing for him," Marie said. Her calmness was off-putting. So unlike her. And he hadn't realized she'd known that about her mother. "She knew I wasn't in love with him, but thought that was because I wouldn't let myself fall in love with anybody."

She fell silent then. Saying nothing about his duplicity. Or her mother's.

So he continued. He wanted it all out. No more secrets. No matter what happened, being himself again, honest, a man of integrity, would, be a relief. "Shortly after I accepted the job, news of the Connelly trouble broke and there was even bigger cause for concern. The threats started coming against Liam, and Barbara wanted me to stay on in a bodyguard capacity to make certain you weren't in any physical danger. But she had one caveat. You were not to know, under any circumstances, that she'd hired me."

"That's how you came to be at Liam's car in the back parking lot that night…"

He bowed his head. In some ways the worst was yet to come.

"I'd met Jeb Williams, his father's bodyguard, during my initial investigation of Liam.

We exchanged professional courtesies and that was all. When I figured out that someone was after Liam, and that that also potentially put you in danger, I determined that the best way to protect you was to protect him."

"So you concocted the story about Williams's sending you…"

Elliott focused on truth now, telling himself it hurt less. But he was aware of Marie, every breath she took as she sat there on that box. "I mentioned Williams, hoping that the association would give me enough credibility to convince Liam to give me a shot. He assumed Williams sent me on behalf of his father. The assumption was a godsend and I used it."

There. It was all out now. Every last bit of it.

He was through. Done. He'd very probably ruined a client's relationship with her daughter. He'd lost a wife. A career. And lost any thought he might have harbored that he and Liam and Gabrielle would ever be close friends. But worse than any of it was knowing that he'd hurt Marie.

The one thing he'd pledged never to do.

"How did my mother find you?" She sat there, staring at him, her hands folded in her lap.

"A private investigators' directory I'm registered on. She chose me, initially, because I lived so close to the Arapahoe. She wanted someone who was familiar with the area."

"Had you ever been to my shop before she sent you?" He took a minute to answer. Actually considered lying to her. If he'd met her before her mother had called, if he'd taken the job because he'd already felt a connection to her...

"No." The word was in answer to her question, but also an admonition to himself.

No more slippery slopes for him. If he was all he was ever going to have, then at least he'd be a man he could count on.

He needed to touch her. To know that her heart wasn't completely closed off to him. To everyone. Had to know the extent of the damage he'd inflicted. And scrambled for a way to make it all right. To fix what he'd done.

"I'm sorry, Marie," he said. "So, so sorry."

Her silence was telling. She was shutting him out. Or shutting herself in.

Gabi and Liam would be there soon and he was glad. She'd have her best friends to lean on. To take her home. To tend to her.

He'd be left alone. Again. Knowing he deserved it this time didn't help. And he panicked a little. For just a second. Before he started thinking about her again.

And scrambled for a way to ease her pain.

"I love you so much. I expect that's hard for you to believe right now…"

"No." She looked him in the eye. "No, it isn't. My dad always loved my mom…"

The reference to her father was not good.

"I would never be unfaithful to you, Marie. You have to know that."

"And lying to me—okay, by omission—but lying…you don't think that was unfaithful?" Her tone was soft. Broken more than accusing. But he heard accusation. Each word pierced him anew.

"I can't deny that I married you knowing that you believed our meeting was chance," he said, thinking only of her right then. "But please know that I chose the route that I thought was most faithful to you."

She looked at him then and he tried to hold on while she seemed to study his soul—praying that she didn't see the weak part of him that had married her because he was scared to death he was going to lose her.

Huge bodyguard, protector of all, scared of a little five-foot-two woman…

"Believe me, I've been struggling since the second I suggested being your groom in the bar that night. My bottom line has been that I know, in my heart, that working for your mother had absolutely nothing to do with my feelings for you. She was the means by which we met, period. But if I told you who I was, how I came to be at the Arapahoe, there was a better than average chance that your trust issues would kick in and you'd run scared and never give happiness, give us, a chance...

"And I was under professional obligation to keep her secret. I could lose my license if I did not do so..." He refrained from telling her about her mother's threat to sue him. Because it wouldn't help Marie to know that. "And without a job, how was I going to provide for you? For our family? I have no other education. I don't know any other field..."

Her eyes filled with tears and Elliott figured he'd never seen anything so beautiful in his life. Because they told him her heart was softening. He couldn't stand back and watch. Going against every grain of instinct he had he said, "Please, Marie, don't throw me away because of this. I love you. I won't let you down again."

"You will," she said. "Because no one is perfect. Including me. The truth is, Elliott, I've been regretting our hasty marriage for reasons of my own."

His chest constricted so tightly he couldn't breathe. A sensation Elliott had never experienced before. It was like being outside himself, looking down. He had the bizarre thought he was having a heart attack.

"I do have trust issues. And this whole thing, you not trusting me with the truth because you were afraid that I wouldn't stick around, is exactly what's been bothering me. I don't think I'm good relationship material. I'm damaged goods. A combination of my mother's paranoia and my father's inability to be a good spouse—though for different reasons. I love you so much…too much to do to you what my father did to my mother…"

"You'll never be unfaithful to me, Marie. You don't have it in you."

"Not with another man, no. But isn't it unfaithful not to trust your spouse? Not to be able to believe in him?"

He didn't like where this was going. She was giving him a problem a gun couldn't possibly solve. He couldn't brute-force the danger away.

"And this whole situation with my mother just shows me another aspect of the problem," she said, her expression compassionate more than accusatory. He was beginning to think accusation would have been the preferable treatment to hope for. "You were under obligation to keep her secret. Like you will be with all your clients. Your whole life, outside of our home, will be unknown to me. I, a woman with trust issues, married a man with a secret life. It's a recipe for disaster."

He thought of Sailor Harcourt, the assignment he'd agreed to take on the following weekend, and knew she was right. Still, he couldn't just let go. Not this time.

"So we're aware of the issues, sweetie," he said in his most gentle voice. "We're way ahead of a lot of newlyweds. A lot of old married folks, too. As long as we talk about things, as long as we're honest with each other, we can do this. Everyone has issues. No one is perfect. But not everyone has love."

Having lived a lifetime without, he knew the value of what they shared.

Her lips quivering, she leaned forward to kiss him and he clung to her lips with his mouth, certain she was telling him goodbye.

"You win."

He thought he'd made the words up in his head, to get him through the moment, until he saw the pained look in her gaze.

"But only for now," she said. "If I can't handle this, if I see myself doubting you beyond what's healthy for either one of us, if

I start to see myself acting or feeling like a crazy woman, I'm out. I love you too much to ruin your life."

"The only way you're going to ruin my life is to leave it," he said. And wanted to be completely right about that. Love had to be enough. He'd waited too long to find it to have it not be. But he was trained to see danger. And when he listened to the truth she was telling him, he couldn't deny that there was huge potential for failure staring straight at them.

"I have one more condition…"

Anything. She was going to let him move in. Move home. He'd do anything.

"You tell Liam and Gabrielle the truth."

He'd already planned to do so. Agreeing to her stipulation was a piece of cake.

Earning her trust, being patient while she learned how to trust, might be the impossibility.

CHAPTER TWENTY

COMPLETELY TRUE TO his word, Elliott told Liam and Gabi about her mother's hiring of him, about the way he'd insinuated himself into Liam's situation, sparing himself nothing, before any of them loaded one thing into the moving truck.

Her friends had looked to her for her reaction to the news, and she'd done what a wife does. She'd supported her husband.

Inside, she'd been quaking. If she hadn't known Elliott was lying to her about her mother, how would she know how to discern any other time? Her father had said that a woman had a certain instinct about such things, but Marie hadn't had a clue.

Not until Elliott had been about to tell her the truth. That day when he'd been opening the door to his old life.

Her mother's hiring him, while it made her angry, didn't really surprise her. She'd been living with, and being at the brunt of, Barbara's paranoia for most of her life. Ultimately, while she didn't like it, she understood it.

And hadn't yet determined how she was going to handle that situation. Elliott was her husband. She wasn't going to run to her mother with the fact that he'd betrayed a professional trust. At the same time, she didn't feel comfortable keeping the truth from her mother. It was what her father had done. And she couldn't be her father.

Not unless she wanted to end up alone and lonely...

Figuring she and Elliott were going to have to figure out together what to do—and determining that they had time before they had to cross that bridge, she tried, instead, to focus on him. Loving him. Seeing him with her heart.

And just to be safe, she put off her father's visit for a bit.

THE WEEK WAS everything a second week of marriage should be. And yet it wasn't. Elliott's days were filled with a new anticipation, a greater capacity to enjoy everything, from the taste of his food to the blue skies above him. And he lay in bed every night, after his wife had fallen asleep, and wondered what he could do to hold them together.

His upcoming job with Sailor loomed over him as much as telling Marie the truth about their meeting had done.

If it wasn't Sailor, it would be another job.

How could he help Marie trust him? How could he trust her to trust him? Because that was what it came down to.

She was right. As a husband, he didn't just need to be loved, he needed to be trusted. He wasn't going to be able to live with constant mistrust at the core of his relationship.

He couldn't live his life concerned about telling his wife the truth for fear of her not believing him.

And he'd already fed that mistrust by marrying her under false pretenses.

She knew all about his job and what it entailed. Had known since the first night they met—in her coffee shop the night after Liam and Gabi had found Liam's car vandalized in the park.

But she'd known Liam for a dozen or more years, had gone into business with him and had still freaked when Liam had had dinner with his editor.

Elliott sat in her shop Saturday morning, the night with Sailor looming to the point of being dangerous. He was still working for Liam and had to be alert, not worrying about what his wife would think if she knew what the evening's assignment entailed.

She hadn't trusted Liam to go to dinner with his editor and her husband of two weeks was going to be posing as Sailor Harcourt's escort for the evening?

Time was closing in on him. Again. He had to tell her.

With dread in his gut, he waited until he saw her heading down the hall to her office and then followed her. He couldn't live a lifetime like this.

But he'd promised to give her time.

And knew, in his heart of hearts, he couldn't just walk away from her, either. Not while happiness still lurked in their midst.

"I've been thinking," he said as she greeted him with a kiss in the middle of the hall between the back elevator and the shop. "I should learn how to run all your machines. How to do whatever needs to be done behind the counter."

What the…? He hadn't been thinking any such thing. Not right then, at any rate.

He'd never been behind the counter of her shop.

"Really?" Her grin made him glad he'd had the thought at some point. And that it had come to rescue him.

He'd tell her he was working that night. She knew he worked on call. He'd taken other spur of the moment jobs since she'd known him.

And that was all he had to tell her. Pretty much all he could tell her. No point in letting her know he was posing as someone's escort.

Or even that he was protecting a young woman that night.

Sailor had assured him there'd be no press.

He'd been making too much out of nothing. Not doing his part in trusting her to keep her word to him to come to him if she started to doubt him.

"You're my wife. I should know what to do if you ever need help," he said, feeling somewhat better.

If he ignored the rock in his gut.

Her face serious beneath that ponytail that now only tempted him to take it down, Marie cocked her head and looked at him. "Okay," she said. "You want to start now?"

Eva was busy speaking with a customer. Another was in line. The shop was half-full. "Can we have the first lesson be when you're closed?" he asked. He wasn't sure how nimble his big fingers were going to be pushing buttons, or how much room he'd take up bending over the small refrigerators...

"Of course. Tonight?"

He should have seen that one coming. Might have if the entire conversation hadn't just come off the cuff.

Before he could answer, Eva called out an order and as Marie went back to work, Elliott went out to speak with the guard at the front of the shop. He'd just come on at eleven. They were working twelve-hour shifts. Meant the guy would be there almost until Elliott got home that night.

He wanted to make certain the man knew that Elliott would be out. That he was to make absolutely certain Marie was safe.

Pulling Marie aside only long enough to tell her he'd had a call and had to go to work for a few hours, he went up to visit with Liam and Gabrielle. Told them he had to go out for a few hours that night. A job guarding a long-standing visiting client. They were both planning to be in for the day—working from home. They offered to invite Marie up for dinner. And a movie. Told him to be safe out there.

It wasn't "out there" he was worried about.

IT WASN'T SO bad being alone on her side of the table at Gabi and Liam's that night. The pasta was good—great. Warm French bread, fresh salad and a small glass of wine were nice, too. Knowing that the seat next to her, while vacant, was also taken, was the best part of all.

"If you ladies don't mind, I really need to get some more words done on the next installment of Dad's piece," Liam said as the three of them were finishing up. "I'll get the dishes, though, if you want to head into the living room and relax."

Marie wasn't fooled. And didn't think Gabi was, either. He was giving them time alone. Girl-talk time. Liam was Gabi's husband now, but he knew them. And was their best friend. Still.

"So, tell me how you're doing. Really doing." Gabi didn't even wait until they were seated on the couch before starting in. Picking up the remote, she clicked on the TV.

They'd already decided what movie they wanted to watch. *Grease*, starring Olivia Newton John and John Travolta. It was before their time. But they'd seen it with Barbara one summer and loved it. When they'd passed a *Grease*-themed slot machine in Vegas, they'd looked at each other, said simultaneously that they needed to see the movie again and laughed.

"I'm really doing great," Marie said. And then added, "Mostly." She nodded. "Yeah, mostly great." If you didn't count that she worried about getting worried. Was afraid she'd start to fear that her husband could be unfaithful to her. Look how she'd freaked out when Liam had dinner with his editor. The residuals of watching her father rip her mother's heart out. Again and again. And being unable to do anything about it. A product of knowing that sometimes love wasn't enough. She'd chosen them because they'd had first priorities other than her.

Elliott didn't.

He was good at his job. But he loved her.

"Mostly?" Of course Gabi would pick up on that. "Do you regret getting married like you did?"

"Absolutely not." Elliott had been right about that part. She was glad he'd waited to tell her about his duplicity in their original meeting because if he hadn't, she might have done just as he'd said and bolted—robbing them of at least a chance of finding heaven together.

Except that his having done so had shown her she couldn't tell when he was lying to her. "I am so in love with that man. I… No." She shook her head. "Mom getting married in Vegas, Elliott needing to be there with Liam…it was meant to be."

Gabi watched her. "So why, mostly?"

"Do you ever worry about Liam? When he's out with his editor, for instance?"

"No."

Chin jutted out, Marie nodded. "And there's no reason to. But I do. You know?" The way Liam used to talk…about wanting other women when he was in an exclusive relationship. He'd been a kid then. And he'd never acted on the temptation. But it had been there. He'd talked to them about it.

"You don't trust Liam? Our Liam?"

"Of course I trust him! I just…"

"Oh, sweetie." Gabi moved scooted over. Gathered her close for one of the rare hugs she'd instigated over the years. "You worry, but you know why you do it. You realize it's unfounded. So while it's there, you don't give in to it. It's like someone who doesn't see well without glasses. She knows that, and she deals with it by putting on glasses. You took the big step. You let yourself love and get married. We'll keep the other in line. You aren't alone, you know."

Marie wallowed in Gabi's caring for a minute more, thanking the universe for the life, the friendships and love she'd been given. Until Liam coughed. "You guys want some tea to go with that sugar?"

He was grinning at them.

Gabi threw a pillow at him.

And Marie grabbed the remote. Definitely time to start the movie…

Facing the screen, her hand on the play button, she froze. And peripherally realized that Liam had come farther into the room. Gabi was completely still.

"And tonight, gathering at the…" Marie stared, the news announcer's voice fading out and back in, like a cell phone losing reception. "…and with all the domestic violence issues suffered by the NFL this past year, some of the NFL's biggest stars are in attendance…"

She shook her head. Knew when Liam sat down on the arm of the couch beside her.

"It's a no-press-allowed affair, but a local shelter, who helped plan the affair, passed along a couple of pictures…"

Still photos. That were plastered on the screen.

A woman standing at a podium, obviously one of the speakers. A gorgeous, rich, smiling woman. And her name on the caption. Along with the name of her escort for the evening.

Marie dropped the remote.

CHAPTER TWENTY-ONE

ELLIOTT HAD JUST dropped Sailor off at the airport with her sincere thanks for a successful evening, on all counts, when his phone rang.

Seeing Liam's name come up on the dash screen, he pressed the answer button on his steering wheel immediately.

"Tanner." He said the one word clearly and quickly. His mind geared to process just as rapidly. Something had happened. He shouldn't have left...

"You'd mentioned earlier about dropping your client off at the airport for an eleven o'clock flight. Are you alone?" The man's tone was different.

"Yes." He pulled onto the main thoroughfare that would take him to the downtown area where the historic Arapahoe stood among other stately homes—most of them housing boutique businesses now.

"So you're free to talk." The streets were dimly lit. Traffic was light.

"Yes. Is something happening there? Are

you all okay?" He'd ascertained no hint of alarm in the other man's voice, but Liam's usual congenial conversational approach was most definitely missing.

"We're fine. The girls are in on the couch. Marie was going to go downstairs to wait for you, but Gabi insisted that she stay up with us."

All things Liam—or Marie—could have told him when he got home.

"Soooo…" Liam paused. "You were working tonight?"

His neck tensed. "Yes."

"I don't suppose you can tell me what you were doing. Or with who."

Dread filled his gut. "You know I can't."

"But you *were* working."

"Absolutely."

"Good. I guess I'll see you when you get here, then."

Whoa. That was it?

Sitting back in his seat, one hand on the steering wheel, Elliott said, "Hold on a minute. You mind telling me what's going on here?"

"Caught a glimpse of the news this evening. A piece about a high-end fund-raiser attended by some pretty impressive people. A domestic violence benefit. Not a cause Connelly has ever supported—though I don't know why not and I think we should—so I didn't know about it until tonight."

Elliott swore silently. Twice.

The week of foreboding. He'd *known*. Or he'd brought this on himself by focusing on it so much. "It was a no-press-allowed event." He knew, as soon as the words were out of his mouth, that he was only making himself look worse.

"Someone from a local shelter took some photos. Shared them with a local news station."

He'd been *working*. But the only way he could prove that would be to break his client's confidence.

Elliott swore again. Not as silently. "Marie saw."

"Yep."

He couldn't believe it. Just couldn't…what the…? He'd been working. And couldn't live his life feeling he had to apologize for that fact. Or explain himself.

And needing to explain to Marie meant explaining to the other two triplets.

"She's the daughter of a long-standing respected client of mine. At his request I protect her anytime she's in town."

"I understand."

Did he?

"But she doesn't."

"That's between you and your wife."

Right.

"So why the phone call?"

"I felt it was my duty."

"You think I'm cheating on my wife?"

"Just checking."

Elliott didn't like it. But it was probably fair. "I wasn't. And I won't."

"I know."

He turned a corner and then made another quick turn. Onto the back lot. Pulled into his parking spot and stopped the car.

Was he understanding this correctly? Could Liam be calling for *his* benefit? "You want to give me a heads-up what I'm walking into?"

"I think I already did that."

Right. Okay.

Pocketing his keys, Elliott nodded at the guard by the back door and, once inside, decided to take the stairs.

Two at a time.

HE WAS A MAN used to going home alone at the end of the day. Answering to no one when he was off the clock.

Elliott kissed Marie hello, as though he'd done nothing wrong.

Because he hadn't.

She kissed him back the same way.

A trap?

"How was your evening?" she asked as they took the elevator down to their floor.

He shrugged. Told the truth. "Uneventful. Which makes it good."

A quick twinge showed on her upper lip. In the right corner. Once.

"Mostly you wait out in the car when you're on the job. Unless someone needs extra security, or there's no security where they're going to be."

Swearing silently again, he knew exactly where this was going.

"Mostly."

The elevator door opened. Key ready, Elliott let them in.

And waited.

What did he do now? Heading off to the bedroom, which was all he really wanted to do, probably wasn't good.

Her arms slid around his middle. "I love you."

Elliott held on tight. He was not a stupid man. "I love you."

Chin at his chest, she looked up at him. "You ready for bed, or you need to unwind first?"

Was there a right answer here? He'd give her whatever she needed. He just really needed to know what that was.

"I'd like to go to bed," he said. "But not until you're ready."

"I'm ready."

She took his hand. Started to lead him down the hall. Elliott pulled her back.

Held her to him and pinned her with a look he hoped reached her soul. "I was working tonight."

Her gaze didn't falter and he had a feeling she was struggling. She didn't believe him. He could tell by the way she was looking at him. She was trying. And she was failing.

"I know," she said. Lying to him. Tears filled her eyes.

He had to be honest with her. "Liam called me. About the photo on the news." There would always be things he couldn't tell her. Things she'd find out only if his clients happened to make the news. People who needed bodyguards were often newsworthy. And bodyguards were often in the background when they were photographed out in public.

The news could report. He couldn't. And so he had to have complete honesty when he could. Even if it wasn't easy.

Even if he could get away with less.

"I didn't know he'd called, but I'm not surprised. He's been slaying dragons that he thought might hurt my heart since I was eighteen."

They were talking. Just as they'd said they would.

"I work for her father. For the whole family. Anytime any one of them is in town." He could tell her that much. Harcourt didn't hide the fact that he had a bodyguard. Only Sailor had done that. The last time she was in town.

"The caption said you were her escort." Her doubts were there. Loud and clear.

"It was part of tonight's job."

She studied him. "I threw up when I saw you."

His stomach knotted.

"My head is telling me that you were working, Elliott. But my heart... It knows you were out with a beautiful woman at a fancy event—my heart knows that men get tempted all the time while they're working."

His heart sank.

CHAPTER TWENTY-TWO

IT HAD BEEN Elliott's suggestion that he pack a bag and stay elsewhere until they had time to sort through what was going on. To determine if their rushed, impromptu wedding had been a mistake. Not Saturday night. He'd stayed with her then. But they'd slept far apart, each hugging their own side of the bed.

He'd tried to get close. She'd pulled away when he reached for her.

Early Sunday morning after she and Grace had finished labeling the day's baked goods and before the shop opened, Marie had gone up to tell Liam and Gabi that she and Elliott needed some time apart. *She* needed time apart, she'd told them.

Because of the unsolved threats against Liam and the heightened security they were still under, Liam had suggested Elliott bunk in their spare room. He'd agreed.

In spite of her friends' protests, Marie went right back downstairs to work. She stopped in the office first, to put the wedding ring she'd removed in the safe. And then she spent the next several hours losing herself in coffee. In closing up alone, having let her overworked weekend staff go home early. Eva was too thrilled with unexpected time off to notice that Marie wasn't her usual cheery self. She was smiling. Eva would have had to look more closely to know that the expression only went skin deep.

Did he kiss her good-night?

The questions started to seep in.

Since when does a bodyguard pose as an escort?

Never.

Unless there was some reasonable explanation that she didn't know. Because Elliott was not at liberty to tell her.

She tried to shut down the doubts. She was screwing up the best thing that had ever happened to her.

She filled out orders. Counted receipts. Made out a deposit. Studied her budget to determine how many more employee hours she could afford, while still making a decent profit, and then made up a sign for the front door, seeking part-time weekend help. She'd put it up in the morning. Take it down every night. Until the position was filled.

In the early days...all the conversations.

The way he'd listened. I thought he was different. That we had something. And all the while, I was just a job to him. He was listening, asking questions, because he was being paid to do so. At least in the beginning.

Would you please just shut up?

She swept all the floors, moving tables as she went. Followed herself with a mop.

She didn't call anyone. Not even Gabi, who'd been texting her nonstop since they got home.

And when she was done with all she could do in the shop, she notified the security guard out front that she was going upstairs. She didn't tell him that Elliott wouldn't be at the elevator, waiting for her. She could get herself upstairs.

Once there, she drew a hot bath. Poured in two capfuls of rose-scented bubble bath. She lit a candle. Put in a CD she'd found years ago in an artsy bookshop. *Voice of the Feminine Spirit.* She had no idea who it was by. Didn't care.

With all the lights out, she slid out of her clothes and into her bath.

From there, by candlelight, she could see Elliott's cologne on the counter. He hadn't taken it with him.

His extra shaving cream and razors would be in the chest, too.

Marie turned around in the tub.

She closed her eyes. And thought about her mother. Did Barbara have so little faith in her that she'd felt the need to hire someone to babysit her?

She could let herself think so. If she wanted to wallow in self-pity. Marie didn't need pity. Nor did she need to go looking for reasons to hurt. The pain that she was barely holding at bay, one that was threatening to attack her so acutely she doubted her ability to cope if it broke free, had little to do with her mother.

Barbara's hiring of Elliott had very little to do with Marie. She knew that. It had to do with Barbara. With her own paranoia. Her need to reassure herself.

She'd hired Elliott because she loved her daughter that much. Not because she trusted her that little.

Still, it rankled. And she told herself again that she was going to talk to Barbara about all this.

At some point.

When the rawness wore off the wound.

And this wasn't about Elliott's lie to her. Not really. She'd be having the same exact reaction if he'd been exactly who he'd said he was, and she'd married him and then seen him sitting at a fancy dinner with another woman.

As tears threatened, she closed her eyes against them. Squeezing tightly. Holding them in. And imagined that young woman staring up at Elliott. *Marie's* husband. Her eyes flew open.

Towels were hanging on the rack. His and hers. Both hers. One had just been used by him.

Was Elliott sitting in the living room upstairs with Liam and Gabi? Or was he alone in his room?

What was he doing?

Had he had dinner?

Had Barbara paid him to marry her?

She sat up, sloshing water on the floor as she reached for her towel. Her robe was next, and then she was in the living room, grabbing her phone out of her purse.

He picked up on the first ring. "Hello?" He never said that. He always answered with his name.

This wasn't Elliott's issue. It was hers. Even her father wouldn't have been so crass as to step out in the first two weeks of marriage. And for what? To attend a governor's function?

Elliott wasn't anything like her father. And did not deserve to pay for his sins.

"Marie? You still there?" His voice wasn't as commanding as usual.

"Yes."

"Me, too. I'm still here."

Obviously.

So. She'd called him for a reason.

"Did my mother pay you to marry me?"

"Absolutely not."

"But she knew, didn't she? That you were… that we were…"

She remembered the conversation her mother had started in bed that night before her wedding. She'd talked about not being able to live her life as the warden. As she'd have had to do with Marie's father.

Barbara had been having a hard time with what she'd done—hiring Elliott behind Marie's back. She got that now.

"I think she suspected that you were falling for me."

"She gave her blessing?"

"To the contrary. She didn't want you to fall for me because of the duplicity between us."

"But she gave you the go-ahead, didn't she?" She was pushing. But she had to know.

"Why does it matter?"

"Because. If she didn't you never would have pursued me. You would have put the job first."

His silence gave her her answer. And still she said, "She gave you the go-ahead, didn't she?"

"No, Marie. She didn't."

"Then…you and me being married… She really is going to have your head for hiring you to watch out for me and then taking advantage…"

"I can assume so."

He'd sacrificed everything for her and she still felt sick to her stomach every time she thought about that picture. "I need to go."

"I understand." He didn't hang up.

She'd take care of her mother. Make certain that Elliott felt no backlash for any of this. Even if she had to play on Barbara's self-expressed vulnerabilities and remind her mother of her own culpability. She didn't want to. Would ordinarily not even consider doing so.

But to protect Elliott…she would if she had to. She didn't say so out loud.

They were married. Had to discuss that fact, too. Somehow.

"Your stuff is here."

"Yes."

"You're welcome to come in and out of the apartment as you need to."

"I appreciate that."

"We're still married."

"I know."

"I have to go."

"I understand."

Hang up, woman.

"Okay. So…goodbye, Elliott."

"Good night."

She hung up and, grabbing his robe off the back of her bathroom door, lay down on the couch and cried herself to sleep.

ELLIOTT DIDN'T TAKE any calls Monday morning. He'd had a couple from potential clients. He'd return those. He just needed some time to himself first.

Time to figure out how to move forward. Until he knew if there would be formal blemishes on his reputation—which he expected as soon as Barbara returned from her honeymoon, if not before—he was going to proceed with business as usual.

He would proceed with business afterward, too. He had to eat. He might not get any more gigs as a bodyguard, but the world was filled with shady PIs. And he was a darn good investigator. One of the best in the state, he'd been told more than once. Depending on any ethics complaints that came forth against him, if his private business slowed down, he could always look into police work. If nothing else he'd be able to support himself.

He'd reached that conclusion sometime around three that morning. And then he'd slept awhile. He didn't feel a whit better.

But he was at the table for coffee as he and Liam and Gabrielle had arranged when he came upstairs the night before.

Liam was at the table alone. Elliott chose an extra-strong coffee, brewed it and sat.

He could hear Gabrielle in the other room, moving around.

"You didn't date a lot, did you?" It was the first thing, other than "good morning" and "help yourself," that Liam had said to him since he appeared.

"No." Not that it was any of his business. But the answer didn't cost him anything, so he gave it. The way he looked at it, he owed the other guy. He'd taken his money under somewhat false pretenses. Though he'd also given Connelly the services he'd paid for. Was still paying for.

"Barbara can be a real pain."

"Understood."

"I have to know, Tanner, do you love her?"

"Completely."

"If you two were to stay married, you'd be faithful until the day you died."

"Unequivocally."

"You're a real pain in the...forget I said that."

Elliott hadn't expected anything could make him feel better. But he almost smiled as he said, "Forgotten."

Liam didn't say another word, and, when she finally appeared, neither did Gabrielle, other than to apologize for her lateness.

Neither asked any more questions. Or had any answers for him, either. Yet both had to have spoken with Marie.

He wanted to ask a few questions of his own. To hear someone else's words running through his mind for a moment or two. He wasn't about to talk about Marie behind her back. Or in any way risk putting any more shadows over his head.

Living with shadows was worse than being on the outside looking in.

CHAPTER TWENTY-THREE

MARIE WORKED UNTIL closing Monday night.
Gabi had texted several times. She'd even
come in the shop when she'd arrived home
from work. Marie had assured her she was
fine, and after promising to call as soon as
she came upstairs, her friend had reluctantly
agreed to let her handle things her own way
and had gone upstairs to have dinner with
her husband.

She did as promised. The minute she let
herself into her apartment, she phoned Gabi.

"I need you guys as much as you think I
do," she started in as soon as Gabi picked up.
"But for right now, I need some time to myself. I need to do what I'm good at. And then
have some time to process. All on my own."

"But—"

"Gabi." She cut her friend off. "I'm serious.
Right now this is between me and my own
mind. My own heart. Because it's my life."
She didn't want to be mean. Or in any way
offensive. "I feel like I'm fighting for my life

here," she told her best friend. Hoping that Gabi would somehow see the things she wasn't sure she understood herself.

"I'm fully aware that there are issues to be dealt with. A marriage that shouldn't have happened—at least not so quickly—for one. But right now, before I can talk to anyone, my mother included, I need some time to myself."

"Okay. I just wanted to—"

"I know." Marie cut her off again.

"Okay. Well…call me if you need me. Anytime. I don't care if it's four in the morning. You call me and I'll be downstairs in seconds."

"I know."

"And you will?"

"Yes."

"I love you."

"I love you, too."

"You're sure you're okay?"

"No. I'm not okay. But I'm sure I need some time to myself to get there."

"I don't like it."

"Neither do I."

"This sucks."

"Yeah."

"It wasn't wrong for him to take the job with your mom. And that woman, she was just a job. Her father hired him."

"My head knows that."

"He was doing his job."

"Yeah."

"He loves you."

"Yeah. I love him, too."

"It's a mess."

"I know."

"I'm sorry."

"Yeah, me, too."

Gabi wasn't going to hang up as long as Marie kept talking. Marie understood. So she told her best friend that she had to go. Agreed to have dinner upstairs the following night. And rang off.

SITTING OUT IN front of the Arapahoe, a burger wrapper and empty fries carton in a bag on the seat beside him, Elliott watched the darkened coffee shop. She'd drawn the blinds a couple of hours ago. He'd seen the guard out front respond to a call half an hour ago. That should have been Marie going upstairs for the night.

He'd done all he could. Time to call it a night.

So he got out of his car. Walked across the street. Around back. And in the private entrance.

Opting for the stairs, he climbed slowly. Not to the third floor.

He was ready to be in his room alone for the night. And wasn't about to sit out with Marie's friends as though he was one of them.

He had unfinished business with his wife.

Key in hand, he approached the door that had been home to him for the past couple of weeks. Put his keys back in his pocket, and knocked. Legally he might have the right to enter on his own. Ethically he did not.

"Gabi, I told you, I'm…" Her voice broke off and she stood there, openmouthed. And beautiful.

But…broken, too. As was usual for that time of night, tendrils of hair had fallen out of her ponytail and circled her face. If she'd had on makeup, not much of it had survived the day. Her T-shirt had what looked like a fresh stain on one shoulder. Her jeans were the faded ones he liked best.

And there was no light in her eyes.

"You obviously didn't check the peephole." He wasn't happy about that and didn't bother to hide it. Not because he was a bodyguard and she was a job. But because he loved her and needed to know that she was tending to her safety. "The police suspect the danger with Liam is escalating," he said. "It's been a week and two days since the last episode. And the time between episodes has shortened. Another could happen anytime. It's obvious to anyone watching—and let's be clear that this guy's been watching—that Liam is close to you. You're in business together, live in the same building. Several of the threats have been delivered via your shop. And you didn't check your peephole."

If he'd had any hope of reaching her soft side, he could probably kiss that goodbye. And it would be the only thing he'd be kissing anytime soon.

"Is that it, then?" she asked, standing there with bare feet in the doorway. "You just checking up on me?" She paused, but before he could figure out how to get through to her, she started in again. "Fine. I failed the test. And you're right. I should have looked. I'd just hung up with Gabi and I know she doesn't like that I'm down here alone. But as I told her, I'm fine. And from now on I'll check my peephole. I am well aware of the danger lurking right outside our door."

He could see the table to the right behind her. Part of it anyway. The big stainless-steel bowl she used to make salads was on the edge. As though she'd set it down on her way to answer the door.

She hadn't eaten yet.

"I didn't come to test your peephole compliance."

She stood back, leaving the door open for him to enter. She picked up the salad bowl and returned to the kitchen.

Was this it, then? Their marriage was over? There wasn't going to be a second chance? Or even a cooling-down period before they ended things?

He wasn't ready to collect his luggage, but accepted the invitation to enter her domain, closing the door behind him.

The only thing dirty in the kitchen was the cutting board and the knife still on the counter. No plates or silverware. As he'd thought, she hadn't eaten yet. But was reaching for the plastic wrap.

"I'd sure love some of that salad." The burger he'd eaten earlier was sitting like a rock in his stomach. But he wanted her to eat. Wanted to eat with her. Like the family they'd been for those few idyllic days.

Marie looked at him as if she couldn't believe what he was asking. Then she shrugged and took down two plates. She filled them both with Caesar salad, grabbed a couple of forks and carried it all to the table. Elliott fetched a couple of bottles of water and joined her.

Feeling…better. She was sharing her dinner with him. Life hadn't ended yet.

MARIE WAS HUNGRY, so she ate. It was nice, not being alone. Having another body in her space. But she couldn't talk to Elliott. She had some things to work out within herself first.

The salad was probably good. It filled her.

"Gabi tells me you're spending your time up there alone in your room."

"I am."

He'd cleaned his plate. But was reaching for more as he usually did.

"I just wanted you to know that I don't have a problem with you and them being friends. Not that I have any say one way or the other, but…"

He looked straight at her. "Of course you have a say. With me. And I'm certain with Liam and Gabi, too."

In fairness, he was right. If she went upstairs and told Liam that she couldn't handle having Elliott around, even if he kept out of her coffee shop, Liam would find another man to protect them.

"Anyway, it's fine."

He nodded. Carried his plate and hers to the kitchen. Towering over her sink, he rinsed the dishes and put them in the dishwasher.

In the same places she'd have put them. He moved with a grace that reached out to her and she remembered the feel of those capable hands holding her close.

He had to go. She didn't want him to leave. She needed to be alone. To figure out what she needed and was capable of giving.

Drying his hands, he turned to face her, leaning back against the cupboard. "I'm sorry."

Her throat tightened and she couldn't speak. She nodded.

"I was in Las Vegas, and I took a gamble. A bad one. But I need you to understand—I hope you can understand, for your sake as much as anything—that I'm not a bad guy. You didn't place your faith erroneously, Marie."

Was he trying to save himself? Or her? She was confused. And, leaning against the counter opposite him, she crossed her arms.

"Your mother and I talked, in the vestibule, right before she got married..."

"That's where she was? When she said she'd pulled a thread."

His forehead lined, he nodded. "I was seeking permission to tell you the truth. The way I was feeling...the way it was between us... I feared that something was going to happen between us in spite of my attempts to keep things platonic."

A trickle of warmth spread through her. A welcome respite to the cold. But not enough to begin a thaw. "You told her that?"

"Not in so many words, but she knew how badly I needed to be able to tell you."

"And she refused." It was a piece of the puzzle that she'd needed. As she tried to sort through everything. There were more.

"Yes."

Did that mean it wasn't until Vegas that he'd begun to feel the development between them? She gave herself a mental shake. There were bigger issues here. She just had to get everything in order and then see what she had.

She understood his job. She just didn't...

"You seemed to imply last night that I put the job before you. I don't. Your mother demanded that I stay away from you, and I married you instead. And the other night, it was... I was... Sometimes, for the safety of the client, it's better to appear to be part of the party, not a bodyguard. I was working, Marie. Nothing more. It's the first time I've had to pose as someone's escort. And if I can help it, it will be the last. I will never willingly accept such an assignment again."

He knew her well. And in the moment, that made her angry. Because she didn't know

him that well. She'd laid herself at his feet
for months, while he'd been holding back all
but a very few personal details about himself.

Because he'd been working?

He'd just told her about a job that was none
of her business. Put her before the job.

Marie stared at her toes. The polish she'd
had applied that night in her mother's hotel
room looked almost as good as new. No chips.
Funny...nail polish had seemed to have more
resilience than she did.

They had enough bad energy coming at
them from Liam's stalker. Didn't need it coming from the inside.

She'd worked that much out during the long
hours she'd put in at the shop.

Which was partially why she'd let him in
her door. And shared her salad with him. It
was how she'd justified giving in to her incredible longing to see him.

"I took a job, Marie. Like every other day
of my life. I get up. I go to work. So do you.
You make coffee. I watch over people and do
what I need to do to keep them safe from real
or perceived harm."

"I know."

"How was I to know that when I met you,
my whole life was going to change?"

He couldn't have known.

"And you were in real danger. You still are. What kind of man would I be to walk away from that? Through sheer dumb providence I'd walked into the 'in' with Liam. A way to protect you without you knowing that your mother was having you protected."

She nodded. "It's not really the fact that you married me without telling me that bothers me, Elliott. At least, that's not what bothers me the most. It's that I didn't know you were lying to me. How am I ever going to know? And knowing that I can't trust myself to know…"

She broke off.

He leaned toward her as he said, "I love you. Everything I did was to protect you. Not to deceive you. Trust me to help you with this, at least?"

She loved him. So much. "What about you, Elliott? Are you going to tell me that when Liam called to tell you I'd seen that picture of you on the news Saturday night you didn't die a thousand deaths? Because you knew you couldn't count on your wife to trust you?"

Elliott's silence told her all she had to know.

CHAPTER TWENTY-FOUR

ELLIOTT COULDN'T JUST stand there forever, raw, with his life a puddle at her feet. He'd trusted her heart to hear him. And she wasn't saying a word. "If I hadn't understood your issues regarding the trustworthiness of the men in your life, I would have told you who I was before I married you. By the time I knew you were far more than a job to me, I knew about your mistrust of my species. I was between a rock and a hard place. In the end, what it came down to was that if I told you, I lost you for sure. If I didn't, we had a chance at making it. That was the gamble I took. From my perspective, I didn't have a sure thing to bet on. So I took the choice that gave us the best chance at happiness. Your mother and I were the only two people who knew that I'd worked for her. I figured, at the time, which was when we were in Vegas, that the chance of you ever finding out, of being hurt, were minimal. Neither your mother nor I would ever hurt you that way. It wasn't until after we were married, and back home, that I couldn't live with myself, knowing there was a lie between us. I didn't have to tell you, Marie. I chose to. Because I understand your issues. I took them on. And I trust you to be accountable to them."

Starting right then. She needed to see that this was just her issue cropping up and let him come home.

Except that it wasn't just her issue. It was his, as well. He needed things, too. Like the security of knowing he wasn't going to come home some night to find the locks changed on his doors for some perceived wrong.

"I'm trying to tell you I married you knowing what I'm up against. I just need you to need this as badly as I do. To give us a chance."

But was he being completely fair to her? What he needed was a home of his own. A place to belong. And could he ever find that with her? If she couldn't trust him?

"I've realized, Gabi helped me see, that in my previous relationships, I always chose men who had other priorities in their lives. I don't ever date men who might actually be serious enough about me to form a lifetime bond. Or at least, not serious enough at that time in their lives…"

He had no idea where this was going. And

was still relieved. She was talking to him. Really talking.

"I think I did that, subconsciously, to protect myself from ever having to make the choice to commit to someone. I did it so I'd never be put in a position where I'd have to trust someone that completely..."

That sounded more accurate than her mother's version—that Marie just didn't make good choices where men were concerned.

"With you, it was different. It was like I didn't have a choice to trust you or not. I just...did."

They were the best words he'd ever heard. Until he realized that she'd been speaking in the past. And knew what he'd done by his bad gamble for good reasons. What he'd destroyed.

"That's what love does, Gabi said. But I already knew in my heart what she was telling me. I was in love with you. Trust grew naturally from that."

Past tense. Still past tense. He was waiting for the present to catch up with them.

"When I called my dad to tell him we were married, I told him that I was worried about the baggage I carried—the fear of being hurt like my mother was—by giving my ultimate trust and having it betrayed. He told me that women are gifted with this instinct to know when we're being lied to. On some level, we'll just know."

"I can tell you that in my business, I've seen more than one occasion when a woman's instinct has prevented danger. Or led authorities to a place they needed to be in an investigation."

He was so much taller than she was. Wanted to sit down. To meet her eye-to-eye.

To know that he could stay awhile.

"I told myself that I would be fine. That we would be fine."

So maybe this was going to be okay. Marie had to go around the block, to get all nuances in the telling. He was a guy who liked the full picture. Even if, in the moment, the waiting was excruciating.

"But then I found out that you'd lied to me, and I didn't have any instinct about it at all..."

He searched for something to say and came up blank.

"I've finally realized something." She met his gaze head-on, and that was when Elliott knew that the train was barreling down, coming straight at him. Full speed...

"I don't have the ability to discern whether or not someone is lying to me. I looked you in the eye. I opened my heart. I was certain I could feel your heart. And I had no idea, that night we got married, or anytime during the week afterward, that you were hiding something from me. You made a deliberate choice to do so—and I'm speaking from Vegas on—and I had absolutely no idea. Then Saturday night I see your name on the news as the escort of a beautiful woman—not her bodyguard, her escort—and the original lie plays through my mind and… The other guys I dated, I'm sure now that part of why I went out with them was because they felt safe to me in that they weren't going to ask me for more of a commitment than I felt safe giving. But still, when they lied to me… I had no idea. The rodeo guy was the only one I saw through, but only because Gabi and I talked and it was obvious that he was lying to us. Until then, I'd believed him.

"And even my own mother… She hid you from me, and I had no idea. Surely, if your mother is hiding something that intense from you, you'd have some inkling…"

In a way, Marie's speech comforted Elliott. She was trusting him with her real thoughts again. But he also knew it wasn't going to end well.

She stood away from the counter. So did he. Toe-to-toe with him, she said, "It's not just you I don't trust, Elliott. That's what I've been forced to see head-on. It's myself. And until I figure out how I live with that, without driving myself and everyone else crazy, I have nothing to give anyone."

He took it on the chin. At least on the outside.

"Would you agree to leave our marriage intact until you've had some time to think everything through?"

What he thought he might be buying himself, he didn't know. But time was better than nothing.

"I can't sleep in the same bed with you right now."

"I understand."

"You're asking me not to file for divorce."

"Correct."

She nodded. "Believe it or not, divorcing you is the last thing I want to do, Elliott."

Her gaze begged him to kiss her.

Fool that he was, he tried.

And got pushed away for his effort.

BARBARA CALLED WHEN she and Bruce were off the ship and back in Florida. Marie had spent three full days working, and then alone—other than a quick dinner on Tuesday night with Liam and Gabi while Elliott was out somewhere. She'd hired a new woman for weekend help. A divorcée with enough money to be comfortable, no children, a love of coffee and people and a need for something to do. Her name was Betty. Marie liked her.

She was no closer to understanding herself than before. But she liked Betty.

And had turned more profit that week than ever before.

There'd been no more word from or about Liam's stalker.

Elliott had warned them it was probably the calm before the storm. An attempt to lure him into safety.

There was no more word on a plea deal for George Costas. Walter was still in Florida, and the next installment in Liam's piece about his father was due to go to press with simultaneous internet publication.

Marie was no closer to finding any answers about herself. But she was calm.

And missing Elliott. He'd been around. She'd seen him coming and going. Seen him in his car across the street from the shop a time or two. And in the shop.

Doing his job for Liam.

And watching over her, too.

That wasn't all bad.

When Barbara's call came on Friday morning, Marie had just finished helping Grace bag and label cookies and was in the office getting Grace's check before heading out to open the shop.

"It's early" was the first thing she said to her mother when she recognized the number and picked up.

"So people can make plane connections," Barbara said back. And then, "I feel like I've been gone for months. How are you?"

"Fine. More important, how are you? How's Bruce? How was the cruise?" *Are you still as happy as you were three weeks ago? Is your life still intact?*

"Happy, happy and wonderful." There was almost a giggle in Barbara's voice. "We're in the rental car, on our way to a hotel on the beach…"

"Wait. I thought you were due home tonight."

"We were. But Bruce hasn't had a vacation in years. And we're having such a good time. He was able to rearrange his schedule. The doctor who's covering for him has agreed to do so for another week in exchange for Bruce's reciprocation in June. So we're spending the next week on the beach."

Marie smiled. And felt a stiffness in her face.

She had a tight rein on her self-control. Maybe a little too tight?

"So, tell me about you." Barbara's statement opened the door for Marie to have the conversation she'd been waiting to have.

But her mother was happy. On her honeymoon. Everything else could wait.

Except that she couldn't lie. Couldn't be upset with her mother for deceiving her and then practice deception herself.

"I know you hired him, Mom."

Dead silence hung on the line.

"I know why you did it. And I understand. You were tending to your own need to know, to your own worries, not checking up on me because you didn't trust me."

"You know me well."

"You're my mother. And we've been through some hard times together."

"Yes, we have."

"But it still hurts…you lying to me."

"I know." Barbara sniffed, and Marie knew her mother was crying. "And I'm sorrier than you'll ever know. It really only started out as one small investigation—just to make certain that Connelly wasn't somehow robbing you of your life savings. It wasn't you I didn't trust. It was him. And you've always known that. I liked him, by the way, last weekend. He's changed. Anyway, right after I hired Tanner to check into the Threefold deal for me, all that mess happened with Connelly Investments and you really were in danger, and by then I didn't know how to explain to you why I'd done what I'd done."

"You could have trusted me to understand."

"You're talking to a woman with trust issues…" Barbara's dry response made Marie smile again.

"But that wasn't the only reason, Marie. You're thirty-one. And still unattached. I wasn't just afraid that you'd think I didn't trust you, I was afraid I'd feed your own sense of not trusting yourself."

Marie had just figured that out this past week. That she didn't trust herself. "You knew that?"

"Of course. It's been clear since you left for college and called home for the first week to run every single decision and conversation by me. You weren't relying on your own judgment on anything."

"I was homesick, Mom. The calls stopped after the first week."

"Because you had Gabi. You were living with her. And relied on her judgment."

She sat back. Stunned.

Her problem was worse than she'd thought.

"For what it's worth, I came clean with Bruce this past week, talked to him about all this…"

"He didn't know Elliott was working for you when we were all in Vegas together?"

"No."

Her mother had married Bruce under the same pretenses that Elliott had married her?

The more she learned, the more confused she became. There was no doubt how loyal her mother was to Bruce.

"He wasn't pleased when I told him, but he understood, too. And he had an interesting take on things."

He was a psychiatrist. He would. "What was his take?"

"That you are very careful, obviously because of the horrendous relationship experience your father and I exposed you to during your formative years…"

Psychobabble…

"But that you have every reason to trust yourself."

Marie rolled her eyes. "Do I?"

"Yes."

"And how would he know that?" The man hardly knew her.

"You exhibit great trust in your judgment in that you find someone you know you can trust, and you stay there. And most important, you don't always agree with them. You aren't a follower. You stay strong in your belief. I can think of a lot of times that you've disagreed with me and told me so. And times when you disagreed with Gabi. And told her so, too. Not many people can do that, Marie. A lot of people with trust issues are more apt to agree with those they're closest to in fear that if they don't, they'll lose them. And they also tend to agree with whoever they're with while they're with them, and then change what they say to suit the next person. Also, trust issues and closed minds commonly go hand in hand. Because one who fears his own ability to assess, doesn't open himself up to that which would require him to assess."

"He said all that?"

"He's nodding right now. I got it right."

Wow. Maybe having Bruce for a stepfather was going to be better than she'd known. Though, as long as her mother was happy, she was thrilled to welcome him into the family.

"I did some things I'm not proud of, Marie. I knew I needed to tell you about them even before Bruce and I talked. Elliott Tanner, he practically begged me to let him tell you the truth about our association and I refused to let him."

"I know. And I need to talk to you about that…" Since she brought it up. "You can't go after Elliott for breaking his word to you, Mom. Because you'd put him in an unfair position—making him pose as my friend, and then telling him to lie to me about who he was. He's a man of integrity and…"

She heard her own words—not her inner critic—as if she were giving advice to someone else. The advice she would have given if she'd been able to step outside herself. She stopped.

"I'd already made that determination, too," Barbara said. "He was going to be my next phone call. So…you're not angry with me?"

"I told you I wasn't happy you lied to me. And if you ever do again, we're probably going to have some serious issues."

"I have to tell you something else."

Marie's heart made a rapid tattoo against her chest.

"I threatened him, Marie. The first time he came to me, asking to be let out of our agreement. And then in Vegas, too. I told him I'd sue him if he broke client privilege and confidentiality."

"The first time? I only know about one time. Right before your wedding."

"That was the third time he'd asked."

Feeling a little dizzy, Marie laid her head back and closed her eyes. "And you threatened his career."

"I told him I'd sue him," Barbara repeated, and the words hit Marie as strongly the first time as they had the second. "I also told him that I knew you, inferring that I knew you better than anyone, and that if he told you what I'd done, he'd be robbing you of your mother. Or some such hogwash. It's been eating me up ever since. Which is why I finally came clean with Bruce."

"He didn't tell me any of that." He'd kept more secrets.

To protect her mother. And her. When he could have sold her mother out for his own benefit. He had integrity. Was steeped in it.

"I have to tell you something, too, Mom." She took a deep breath. Scrambled for what to say. How much to say. "We got married. That night in Las Vegas. We went back to the same chapel…"

"You're married?!"

Marie had to pull the phone an arm's length away from her ear and could still hear her mother clearly. "You and Elliott Tanner? You actually… My baby girl is *married*?"

If she'd been afraid, even a little bit, that

her mother would be upset by the news, she'd wasted her energy.

"I can't believe it. We've got to have a celebration! We'll cut our week short in Florida and fly to Denver! Or you two can fly down here and we'll have a few days together in Florida. Our treat. A wedding present. And, heck, bring Liam and Gabi with you. It'll be..."

"Mom." Marie spoke firmly.

"Bruce just said absolutely, Marie. He's as happy as I am to welcome you all down—"

"Mom. Elliott and I...we're...not together."

"What?" The word was drawn out on a whine. "But you got married."

"I know. But it wasn't right. Marrying in haste. I just... You and Daddy. He loved you so much, Mom. But there was no trust between you. And... I can't live like that."

"You're hanging him out to dry for a promise I made him keep."

"He made his own choice, Mom. But no. I'm hanging myself out to dry because I'm afraid I won't trust him."

"But..."

"And I realized this week what you've apparently already known. I can't trust myself to discern when someone is lying to me. And knowing that, how do I trust anyone?"

"But… I just told you… Bruce said…"

"I know what you just told me. And I'm going to think about it. Which is what I'm doing full-time these days. Thinking. I told Elliott I needed some time to figure myself out before I can know what I can give to someone else."

"But, Marie…guys like Elliott, you don't always get second chances…"

"I know, Mom. And sometimes, even when you have loads of them, you still can't be the good spouse you want to be." Her father was proof of that.

"Can I just say one thing?"

"You can say whatever you want. I'll always listen. You know that." She just wasn't going to be swayed simply because her mother wanted or needed her to be.

And wasn't that what Bruce had called evidence that she could trust herself? Because she listened. And then, if she still knew what she knew, stood her ground.

"I just wonder if…maybe the reason you couldn't discern, as you call it, that Elliott was lying to you was that in terms of the things that matter to you, deeply matter, he wasn't lying?"

Exactly what Elliott had said to her.

She closed her eyes again. Laid her head

down on her desk. Was a search for clarity supposed to hurt this much?

Was there ever an end to the number of sides to this story?

She wanted one of Grace's chocolate-chip muffins. And a cup of dark roast Colombian. Straight.

"I have to go, Mom. I'll call you tomorrow."

"I love you, Marie."

"I know. I love you, too. Say hello to Bruce for me. And tell him thank you, too."

"Okay. Be safe, sweetie."

"Always." Marie hung up, feeling as if she were cutting her mother off at the ankles. Just as she'd cut Gabi off earlier in the week.

And wondered if maybe—just maybe—she was doing so because she somehow subconsciously knew that it was time for her, that she was ready, to take full responsibility for her own life.

She owed it to herself.

And maybe—just maybe—to Elliott, too.

Or maybe she was cutting everyone off because she was nothing but a coward. Afraid to take on life. So easy to sit on the sidelines and help everyone else win their games.

But when it came to her own?

Could she trust herself to play?

CHAPTER TWENTY-FIVE

ON FRIDAY AFTERNOON, in a closed settlement conference with his attorney, the district attorney and the judge, George Costas agreed to plead guilty to half the number of charges originally brought against him, avoiding a lengthy and costly trial for him and the taxpayers. He would serve no less than ten years, but could serve up to forty. Part of the leniency awarded him had to do with the fact that all restitution was being made. His sentencing date was set for June. Until then he was out on bail.

Elliott stopped in the shop to warn her to be extra vigilant in her safety awareness. And to let her know that he would be right upstairs, all night, if she needed him.

She thanked him.

Almost called him back to tell him that she was ready to be courageous. To give them a chance. But watched him walk out the front door with a lump in her throat.

SATURDAY WAS CRAZY busy in the shop. Liam and Gabi came down midmorning, to have coffee and show her Liam's article—a copy they'd printed off the internet as soon as it had been published that morning. She read the first paragraph, was impressed but had to put it down to wait on customers. Gabi told her to call if she needed help. She'd worked in the shop all through law school and made a great cup of coffee. Eva was on that morning and Nancy would be relieving her midafternoon. Betty would be training with Marie on Sunday. Maybe it was the weather, or the fact that the days were getting longer, but coffee drinkers were steady the entire day.

By early evening, she was beat. They were down to one customer—a woman in her thirties who was in law school and used their free Wi-Fi to study and who was known to sit awhile whenever she came in. By seven, after a lull that lasted half an hour, Marie, sent Nancy home. The cleaning up Nancy would normally have done was a welcome respite from going upstairs alone. While the hot bath she planned to take did call out to her, her skin could only soak so long before it started to prune, and it was far too early to go to bed.

Sulking was out of the question.

Television didn't hold her attention.

And she knew she had to talk to Elliott. If

she couldn't find the courage to call him, to try, to offer to do whatever it took to make their marriage work, then she didn't deserve him.

While her lone customer typed on her computer, headphones on, Marie stepped to the far end of the counter and dialed.

He picked up on the first ring. "You okay?"

"Fine," she was quick to assure him, reminding him that she had an armed security guard right outside her front door. "I don't trust myself, so I discern who I can trust and then I tell them everything, just to get a second opinion to my own thoughts before I make a decision." She was repeating what her mother had told her.

But only because the truth rang all the way to her core.

"Okay." He was clearly at a loss, and she didn't blame him.

"I…we need to talk, Elliott. If that's okay with you, that is…"

She had to tell him that she'd figured it out—the fact that she *did* trust him. Her mother had said how her whole life she'd relied on her—even calling from college—until she'd met Gabi and knew that she could trust her, too. And Liam. She only had two best friends, and a mother, but she'd placed her trust well. They'd all been standing by her for a very long time. And then she'd met Elliott. And within a week, she'd been telling him her secrets...

"Of course it's okay with me." He didn't hesitate on that one. "I'd rather not do it on the phone, though."

"I know." She glanced back at Law Girl. She'd never thrown anyone out before, but... "I'm still in the shop. I have a customer." Her heart started to race.

"I know. I drove the perimeter five minutes ago. I'm heading to get some dinner and have one thing to do for another client. I'll be back within the hour."

"Call me when you're back and we can talk here, in the shop."

"It's a date. And just to be clear, no matter what it comes to, I'll be here for you, Marie. Always." He said the words as if they were news to him. "No matter what happens. Whether I have a home or security with you or not. I love you and I am more certain than ever, after these past days of not having any home of my own at all, that I will always be here for you. My security is in myself. It came at an early age, and has formed, I think, in a way that is healthy for me. But you are my heart. I just want you to know that..."

He was rambling. And she started to grin. Thinking that maybe, just maybe, she'd have her husband in her bed again that night.

While she waited for her customer to leave, she scrubbed and shined everything behind the counter. She wanted her customers to feel welcome—always—not as though she was rushing them out. But she gave every hint she could that she was closing up.

She refilled canisters. Stocked condiments. When the door opened, she even smiled at the new customer who came in. A friendly guy who'd been in a few times. Technically it wasn't closing time yet.

"Latte, low-fat, low-foam with a wisp of nutmeg," she said, greeting him at the cash register. She loved her job. Loved having a business that became a neighborhood in and of itself. If that was all she ever had, she'd be at least somewhat happy. But if she could have it all? Was she really going to rob herself—or Elliott—of that chance?

"That's right," he said, pulling out his wallet. She probably remembered him so well because he was a cash customer. Credit card receipts made the books easy, but she didn't have to pay fees on cash.

Her heart was still thrumming at a brisk

pace as he took his coffee and turned, but peace was slowly descending, as well.

The guy walked toward her one other customer. Greeted her as though he knew her. Her smile and ready response indicated that she knew him, too. He'd be pulling out the other chair at her table any second now.

And Marie was about to offer to pay their way anyplace they wanted to go.

Latte Low-Fat Low-Foam Nutmeg Wisp leaned over, speaking in Law Girl's ear. Marie emptied the last pot of coffee. She closed in fifteen minutes. Officially.

Latte didn't sit down. He stood back. Law Girl was packing up.

They were hooking up without her help!

He followed her to the door.

Stan, the security guard on duty out front that night, said good-night as Law Girl exited first. Law Girl started to speak and Stan was taking a few steps with her. Toward a car parked at the curb. Latte hadn't left. And Marie forgot all about the people outside.

She heard the click of the lock on the front door—it was an old door with a dead bolt that turned with a knob from the inside and it squeaked...

With a flash, she remembered seeing Elliott's car pull away shortly before Latte had come in.

"Don't move." There was nothing friendly about the man approaching her. He had a gun. Held close to his arm so you'd have to look close to see it unless you were right in front of him. As she was. Staring down the barrel.

"I already made a bank deposit, but what's left of the day's take is in the drawer. I'll open it for you." She leaned toward the register. And he was over the counter, one arm around her throat, the other holding a gun pointed to her neck.

She could hear rattling at the door. And Stan yelling. Calling her name.

"Come in and she's dead," her captor hollered.

"You aren't going to get away with this." Cold with stark raving fear, Marie blabbered. Probably something she'd heard from TV. Tears filled her eyes. But when her captor pushed her forward, toward the hall leading back to her office, she didn't stumble.

And she didn't fight him.

"I don't intend to get away with it," the man spit in her ear as he spoke. "That's the beauty of my plan. I don't have to care about getting caught. And my plan is unfolding with perfect execution."

They were at the end of the hall already. He pushed her into the stairwell. It felt like a freezer.

"Where are we going?" *Stay calm. Keep him on the stairs. Residents use the elevator.*

"Just go."

She had no real choice, certain that if she tried to stop him, he'd just shoot her. The longer she kept herself alive, the longer someone had to get to her. Stan would have called 911. And the guard out back.

"Go," he said again, when her toe hit the tip of a stair and she hitched. The only heat in a cold world was his body pressed up against hers. Hip to hip. Thigh to thigh. Mouth to ear.

Gun barrel to neck.

They were on the landing, halfway up to the second floor. His body shoved hers and they turned. Climbed the next step. She wasn't going to leave the stairwell. On the second-floor landing, if he reached for the door she was going to shove with all her weight. Push him into the railing. It was old. And hopefully wouldn't hold. He could go over. If his gun went off in the process, if she died, she'd have spared everyone else in the building.

"Good. Keep going."

She was keeping him calm. And trying not to think about his intentions.

He knew he was going to get caught. Didn't care. He was willing to give up his life for what he was doing.

They reached the second-floor landing. He didn't move for the door. Instead, he forced her body around and to the next step.

And she knew.

Liam's stalker. Someone who felt he'd already lost everything. Or had nothing left to lose.

They were headed up to Liam's apartment. A vision of her and Gabi and Liam shot execution-style on that new floor flashed in front of her eyes. Accompanied by a loud bang. A gunshot.

She felt a thrust, a sudden push to her back and she was free. Not hurt. Spinning, she turned in time to see her attacker, feet planted firmly on the floor, pointing his gun back the way they'd come.

At Elliott. And she realized that the bullet that had fired had been from the gun he had aimed at the man who'd kidnapped her.

In that second another round of gunfire rang out. She saw Elliott's arm jerk as his gun went off. Saw him rear back as he was hit. Saw his gun go off again.

He couldn't die. She'd just figured out that she'd trusted him all along. That it was her head playing with her the other night—taking the easy way out by repeating over and over in her mind that picture of Elliott with that other woman.

Her father had been right. She had instincts—strong ones—about whom she could trust. Not on a case-by-case, statement-by-statement or promise-by-promise basis, but on a heart basis. A lifetime basis.

Elliott's right shoulder had been hit.

Latte fell right in front of her as his gun slid out of his grasp.

"Elliott!" Marie kicked the gun as she sped down the stairs. "Elliott! Please! Someone help! Elliott!" She was screaming like a banshee. Could hear herself.

She could also see Elliott, his shirt wet, but still on his feet. Coming up the stairs toward her. Stairwell doors flew open. She heard them hit the walls behind them with force. No door stoppers. Uniformed men filled the stairwell.

Shouts of "Clear!" Scurries. Voices in hallways.

But the only one in her world was Elliott.

"Are you okay?"

She heard the question. But couldn't answer. Arms gathered her close. Familiar arms. Encasing her in safety.

In love.

And Marie lost consciousness.

"I WANT MY WIFE."

Sitting on the side of the examining table in the emergency room where he was being stitched up, Elliott looked at his stained pants. He'd refused to lose them.

Refused to be more thoroughly examined. He was fine.

"She's been checked out, and is fine." The resident, who was irritating him no end with his voice filled with fake cheer, cut thread for the last time.

And Elliott slid to his feet, taking the shirt beside him on the gurney with him. He'd left the vest that had saved his life out in the waiting room with Liam and Gabrielle.

"Sir," the resident, and then a nurse, called back to him.

"I want my wife," Elliott repeated.

And they let him go.

Sometimes it paid to be an overly large man.

A COUPLE OF detectives were sitting with Liam and Gabi in the waiting room. Marie—who'd taken the advice of the doctor on duty in the ER and had a glass of juice once he'd pronounced her traumatized but healthy and had given her a list of emotional symptoms to watch out for—saw the detectives, before she recognized her friends.

Heart pounding, she pushed herself forward.

She'd listened to the doctor's warnings about psychological shock. But hadn't really heard him. If she started to have panic attacks, she'd call Bruce. She had a shrink for a stepfather.

"Where's Elliott?" she asked the group at large as she approached them.

"Over in ER getting stitched up. He refused to let anyone even look at him until you were taken care of."

He'd ridden to the hospital with her in the ambulance, she'd been told. She couldn't remember anything clearly after seeing the flash of gunfire until the gurney she was lying on was pulled out of the bus. There were sounds. Movement. Strong arms. More sounds. More movement.

Elliott's voice telling her that it was all over now.

More voices. More movement.

"Do you mind if I get a swab of your hand?" A woman in beige tweed pants and jacket approached her.

Marie held out her hand.

Gabi took the other one. Pulling Marie down into a chair and taking the one beside her.

"The guy who was after Liam, his name is Hank Chassen. After his father lost everything in the Connelly Ponzi scheme, he committed suicide. The money Walter was paying back was like salt in his wound. It didn't bring his father back. He's not stable, Marie. How you managed to keep him so calm...you were great." Her lips were trembling as she smiled.

Marie felt as though she might cry, too. But wasn't sure how at the moment. Everything was still so...distant. As if she were outside her body looking in.

She'd made such a huge mistake—thinking she didn't trust Elliott—convincing him that she couldn't be a good spouse to him. She had to see him. To tell him how very much she loved him. And knew that even a day of happiness with him was better than a lifetime of being safe.

"The woman who was in your shop, the law student, he told her that no one would get hurt as long as she packed up, walked calmly to the door and then pulled the security guard away long enough for him to get the door locked. He said she could call 911 as soon as she got to her car."

She remembered now. A swarm of people. Calls of "All clear."

"He told me didn't care if he got caught."

Liam was answering the male detective's questions. They were speaking softly, and she could only make out the rumbles of their voices. They were in a family trauma area of the hospital and were apparently the only family with trauma that night.

"He knew your routine," the female detective said. She might have introduced herself at some point. Marie couldn't remember. "And waited for Elliott to leave before making his move."

"But… Elliott was there…"

"He said something just hit him," Gabi said, pushing hair out of Marie's face. "He had a letter to hand-deliver for a client, but then wondered why in the heck he'd stop for dinner when you'd said you wanted to talk to him. He was coming in to wait in the shop until you were finished working when he heard Chassen tell you to keep going."

Marie frowned. "I was going to push him over the rail," she said, the memory clear and encased in fog at the same time. "It's old," she said, as if that explained everything.

And she had to know… "How bad is Elliott hurt?"

"He's fine."

At Gabi's words, tears filled her eyes and ran down her cheeks. She was listening but couldn't stop the tears. Gabi wiped at them as she spoke.

"He has one superficial wound. A bullet grazed his shoulder. Chassen didn't get so lucky. Elliott's first shot hit the ceiling. He'd used it to get Chassen to let you go and turn around. His second and third shots to Chassen's arm and thigh hit their marks perfectly."

"A hostage negotiation team was on the way," the woman, who'd taken a cotton swab with something cold to Marie's hand, said as she put her vial away.

"And if I'd waited for them to get there as requested, he could have killed her," Elliott said. "A life I'd been hired to protect was being threatened. I was within my boundaries to take action."

Marie swung around, her throat closing up again as she saw the man who'd just spoken coming up behind them. She didn't think about jumping up.

She just did it. And ran straight into his opened arms. He held her so tightly her ribs hurt and she didn't care.

"You can make me doubt myself for the rest of my life," she said, knowing she probably sounded crazy and didn't care. "I'd much rather have you worrying me than spend the rest of my life living without you."

The words poured out of her, not at all the way they were meant to. They'd have a long talk. She owed him that. But loving him, being his wife, couldn't wait.

Elliott's eyes glistened as he gazed at her.

The others were there, maybe talking, maybe gawking.

"I am going to spend the rest of my life protecting you from hurt, little one," he said. "Hopefully you'll make it easy on me and let it be from by your side. I do much better up close."

"You didn't do too shabby from down a flight of stairs." Liam had joined them, holding out his hand to Elliott. The detectives, obviously having all they needed for then, were back in the distance.

Gabi came up and Liam drew her to him with his free arm. "You saved our lives."

Marie missed the warmth of Elliott's arm when he let go just long enough to shake the hand Liam proffered. She didn't want to let go of him at all.

But wasn't going to let herself give up autonomy again. She was a new woman. Standing on her own two feet. Ready to love. And to let herself be loved.

"I trusted Elliott all along," she heard herself say inanely. "Like Mom. And Gabi. That's why I talked to him so much from the very beginning." She needed everyone to know. Right then. That minute. Because she'd almost lost her chance to ever say those words.

"We knew that," Gabi said, looking at Liam. "Just like we knew that this was something you were going to have to figure out on your own."

"Well, you could have clued me in," Elliott said, looking at the two of them. His eyes were boldly bright and Marie started to cry again.

Liam grabbed her and pulled her up against him. Gabi's arm came around her, completing a circle. "You, my girl, were going to die for us," Liam said, obviously choked up. "You're the best friend anyone could ever have, Marie."

"That's why I'm lucky she's my best friend." Gabi grinned, teary, too. She pulled back and looked at Marie. "You are the glue that keeps my pieces together, my friend. You always have been. I don't know what I'd have done if anything happened to you."

Something inside her loosened. Gabi needed

her just as she needed her friend. Even married, they needed each other. And that was as it should be. As it was meant to be.

People finding each other. Connecting. Giving and Taking. Trusting.

Elliott took a step forward, Marie felt his body touching hers. For one brief second she was reminded of another body behind her, forcing her forward to witness death—either her own or that of her friends. She shuddered. Elliott's hands caressed her shoulders. Liam and Gabi each still had an arm around her.

"We've got your back, Marie," Liam said. "The doctor warned that you're going to have some moments. Your job is to trust us with them."

"He came out and talked to you?"

"Of course. We're your family. The doctor always consults with the family after treating the patient."

He made life sound so simple.

And in some ways, it could be. If people—like her—weren't so busy making it so complicated.

"You all are pretty incredible," Elliott said. "You prove that true family doesn't have to be biological."

"I was just mentioning to Gabi last Sunday, before we headed out to your place, that she should look into modifying the LLC," Liam said.

He and Gabi exchanged glances. And then looked at Marie.

"I was thinking Fourfold would be a good name for us," Gabi said. Instead of Threefold.

Everyone was looking at her. Was she ready to take on the marriage she'd dared to start in Las Vegas? Ready to trust herself to have it all?

Marie's eyes filled with tears again. "I completely concur," she said.

"So it's settled." Liam dropped the arm around Marie to hold his hand out to Elliott a second time. "The board of directors has voted you in as our fourth director," he said.

Marie felt his one hand that was still touching her tremble. Elliott might be a professional, used to dealing with guns and violence. But he didn't shoot people on a normal basis. And he wasn't a rock.

"I think we should go," she said, taking his hand in hers. "It's been a long night."

"My car's just outside." Liam led the way, pulling Gabi with him.

Elliott looked at Marie. She looked up at him.

"What happened in Vegas came home," she said to him.

"It happened at the historic Arapahoe, my love. I walked in the front door of your shop, you smiled at me and for the first time since my mother died, I wasn't on the outside looking in."

"No one has ever been as far *in* as you are, Elliott. It's kind of scary, you know?"

He nodded. "Like almost losing you tonight?"

"Or almost losing you. So…we take each day, and if I get whacked or paranoid…"

He put a finger to her lips. "We all have faults. We all have bad days. The trick is to not shut each other out. You've got it down, Marie. Better than most. All you have to do is talk about it. Just don't ever stop talking to me…"

Lips trembling, she nodded.

"Hey, you two, you coming?" Liam was back. "I was going to suggest an all-nighter to celebrate, but I'm guessing the two of you would just gaze into each other's eyes all night…"

"Liam!" Gabi nudged him.

"Just kidding." He threw up his hands. "Can't a guy have a little fun around here?"

Marie laughed. And cried a little more. She held Elliott's hand as they left the hospital and knew, without a single doubt, that she was right where she belonged.

By his side.

* * * * *